THE CLUB

CULMINATION

1

JONAS

Sarah giggles. "*Jonas.*"

"What? I've got to partake of your crumpets as much as possible before they're off limits to me in a couple months."

"They're extra sensitive, baby. Be gentle."

"They're too delicious to resist."

I take her hard nipple into my mouth and give it a good, strong suck, and she shrieks.

"Go easy, Jonas. They're *sensitive*." But she can't suppress the bloom rising in her cheeks.

"Oh, you mean you want me to take it easy doing *this?*" I give my wife's other nipple an even harder suck and she shrieks again.

"Holy crap," she says, laughing. "I can't decide if I love it or hate it."

"You know you love it." I sit up and assess Sarah's naked body on the bed. Her newly massive tits. Her glorious baby bump that's grown as big as a basketball these days. "Damn, woman, just looking at you gives me an epic boner these days."

"These days?"

"Play along. I swear, my dick grew three inches just looking at you right now." My cock twitches. "Look at your tits!" I palm Sarah's enlarged breasts and marvel at the way they overflow from my hands.

Sarah looks down. "I've turned into the Latina Dolly Parton."

"You're a fucking Botticelli, baby—*The Birth of Venus*. Are you looking at yourself?"

"I'm looking. That's some serious boobage."

"You're Demeter, baby." I look down at my straining cock. "Have you ever seen a boner this big before?"

"Every day since I met you."

"No, baby, look again. This is no ordinary boner. It's a behemoth—a revelation. *The divine original form of boner-ness.*"

Sarah laughs. "I thought you weren't a boob-man."

"Whatever gave you that idea?"

"Gosh, I dunno. The various bite marks on my ass?"

"Hmm. Speaking of which . . ." I reach around and grab a fistful of my wife's right ass cheek and greedily sink my fingertips into the spot of her second tattoo—the one she got in Thailand on the juiciest part of her ass cheek as a gift to me. But when I tilt her body toward me, intending to chomp Sarah's ass like I always do before diving into eating her pussy, she gasps and winces sharply.

Instantly, I release my grip. "Did I hurt you?"

She brings her hand to her bulging belly and winces again.

I sit upright, my heart pounding in my ears. "Sarah?"

"I'm okay." But when she winces a third time, I leap up from the mattress. "I'm taking you to the hospital." I lean down to scoop her naked body into my arms when she opens her eyes, exhales with relief, and stops me with a raised palm.

"I'm okay, honey. Crazy Monkey was doing Zumba on a nerve, that's all." She shoots me a crooked smile. "He's shifted position now. I'm fine." She looks at me sympathetically. "Aw, you poor thing. You've broken out into a cold sweat."

"Are you sure you're okay?"

"I'm sure." She pats the bed. "Come back and tell me more about your transcendent boner to end all boners."

I remain frozen in place. "I think I should take you to the hospital, anyway. Just in case."

Sarah pats the bed again. "Sweetheart, it's jampacked in there, that's all. Four arms and legs and elbows and feet and two heads crammed into one belly gets a wee bit crowded." She pats the bed again. "Come back. There's nothing to worry about."

I flap my lips together and return to the bed—and a moment later, Sarah laughs, puts her hand to her belly, and declares, "Crazy Monkey is kicking the crap out of me!" She places my hand on her bulging belly. "Do you feel that?"

"Whoa! It feels like tiny karate-chops against my palm."

"Crazy-Monkey never stops moving. He's a chip off the ol' block."

I move my hand to the other side of Sarah's large bump, searching for signs of life over there, too. "What's Chillin' Like a Villain Monkey doing?"

"Don't worry. He's there, too. I'm sure he's rolling his eyes at his brother. Telling him to chill the fuck out." She contorts her features to look like my brother's when he's rolling his eyes at me and says, doing her best Josh impression, "Jesus, bro, you get so riled up sometimes.'"

"That was a spot-on impression," I say, moving my hands around her belly. "I think you should stop saying 'he' and 'brother' and keep things gender-neutral from now on. We don't want to get attached to any particular outcome."

"But I know in my bones we're having two boy monkeys. Call it mother's intuition."

I run my hands over her curves again, trying to stuff down the near-constant dread I've been feeling for months that something will go wrong, causing my heart and soul and very sanity to shatter into a million tiny pieces.

"It'd be a moot point if you'd let the doctor tell us the babies' genders," she mutters.

"There are too few surprises in life," I say. It's what I always say when Sarah suggests we find out the babies' genders. Not because I want to be surprised in the delivery room, as I keep suggesting, but because I self-ishly want to limit my emotional exposure to total and complete decimation.

Married life with my sexy Latina these past three years has exceeded my wildest dreams. Plus, Climb and Conquer has already smashed our most ambitious projections. Which means something's got to give. Prob-ably soon. And I'm scared to death that 'something' is going to be the two little monkeys growing inside Sarah's belly. But since no husband should ever tell his pregnant wife he's terrified heartbreak, rather than two bundles of joy, awaits them at the end of her third trimester, I haven't said a word to Sarah about my premonitions of disaster.

"So, husband," Sarah says, running her hand through my hair. "I don't know if you've noticed, but my hormones have been going crazy lately."

"I've noticed," I say with a smirk. It's an understatement. Sarah's sex drive has been through the roof during these last two trimesters. Plus, her emotions have been skin-deep.

"I know Dr. Johnston told us not to get too freaky-deaky during my third trimester, and I certainly wouldn't want you denting our poor babies' heads with your gargantuan hard-on."

I cringe. "*Sarah.*"

"But I think we could find ways to introduce some new kinds of freaky-deaky that won't create any kind of physical risk for me." She runs her fingertips through my hair. "Role play, maybe? Or maybe there's a position we haven't tried yet, we could—"

"I'll be happy to try any new thing you want, *after* the doctor has given the clear."

Sarah bites her lip. "Obviously, I don't want to do anything risky, either. But maybe we could pretend to be back in Thailand. We could pretend I'm a train wreck and you're pissed as hell at me?"

I stare at her, shocked she's invoking Thailand. I wasn't *pissed as hell* at Sarah that night, I was fucking *enraged*. Surely, I couldn't duplicate that state of mind, even if I tried. And even if I could, I certainly wouldn't fuck her like that in her current state.

"Okay, okay, I know we can't do Thailand *exactly*," Sarah says, backpedaling. "I meant that night was so delicious, so I'm thinking we could role-play something *like* that."

I sigh, well aware my wife wants me to tie her up

again, the way I did in Thailand. It's something I've only done that once, due to the highly unique circumstances of that night—and it was plain to see she absolutely loved it.

"We only need to play it safe a little while longer," I say. "When we get the all-clear after the babies are born, I promise I'll fuck you every bit as carelessly as you could possibly desire."

She bites her finger. "Okay, well, maybe we could do a safe version of Rio, then?"

"There is no safe version of Rio."

She flaps her lips together. "It just feels so frustrating to have all these hormones making me the horniest I've ever been, when we can't capitalize on them."

"Oh, you want *capitalization*, do you?" I tease.

She giggles. "Please and thank you."

I begin kissing her breasts. "Is someone looking for a loophole to doctor's orders?"

She grabs my hair and yanks on it roughly. "Definitely. Loophole me, baby." As I kiss my way down her torso, she arches her back and purrs, "Looooooophoooooooole me, Jonas."

I can't help chuckling. For some time now, my wife and I have been faux-turning each other on with words that sound dirty but aren't. "Damn, I love it when you talk dirty to me, baby." With that, I roll over to my computer on the nightstand, put on some music, and return to my horny wife. "Get ready, baby. I'm now going to bring new meaning to the term *motherfucker*."

As Sarah giggles at my joke, I crawl between her legs, lean in, and get to work. And soon, in record speed, her body is rippling with what feels like a forceful orgasm against my fingers, lips, and tongue.

"Beg me to fuck you, dirty girl," I say, panting.

"*Please*," Sarah whimpers, widening her legs.

My breathing shallow and ragged, I grab a bottle of lube from the nightstand, roll Sarah onto her side, and sink my cock inside her wetness and a lubed finger up her ass, all the while massaging her clit with my free hand. These days, since I can't fuck her hard, I try to overwhelm her senses, as best I can. And I must say, the strategy has been working for me like a charm.

"You're not allowed to come until I tell you to do it," I whisper into Sarah's ear, as her pleasure rises higher and higher.

"I can't stop myself," she chokes out.

"Yes, you can. And you will, until I give you permission."

She's clearly on the cusp now. Dangling by a pinky over the edge of the cliff as she awaits my command.

"That's a good girl," I coo into her ear. "You'll come when I tell you to, baby."

She pleads with me. Whimpers. Before making the sound that always comes right before The Sound. And I know she won't be able to hold off much longer. Not if I keep doing what I'm doing to her. Not to mention, I'm in serious danger of losing it myself.

"Now, baby," I grit out into her ear. "Come for me *now*."

With a loud groan, she surrenders to the pleasure she's been staving off, gifting me with glorious sensation of her pussy rippling around my cock, her ass clenching around my finger, and her clit fluttering underneath my fingertip. It's a DEFCON one-level orgasm that's so fucking hot—and so fucking elusive—I come along with her, so powerfully my eyes roll back into my head during my release.

When we've both quieted down, I kiss the tattoo stamped on Sarah's ass before lying alongside her, my face mere inches from hers. "Was that enough of a loophole for you?"

"Hell yeah. That was incredible." She giggles. "The monkeys thought so, too. When things were ramping up, they started going crazy. And the minute that hurricane of an orgasm hit, they stopped moving and said 'Aaaaaaah,' like they'd just slid into a warm Jacuzzi after a long, hard day of work."

"That's an interesting mix of metaphors. Do monkeys work? And if so, do they really get into a Jacuzzi after a long, hard day?"

"You funny," Sarah says, mimicking something our niece has recently made part of our lexicon. "Should I have said the monkeys stopped and said, 'Aah,' like they'd sat down in a big pile of bananas after a long, hard day of swinging through trees?"

"Better."

"Either way, my point is that you did a *'bang-up'* job, sir."

"Glad to hear it."

"You woman wizard, you," she whispers, her dark eyes sparkling.

My heart skips a beat at the way Sarah is looking at me—like I walk on water. Suddenly, I can't resist giving Sarah the gift I've been planning to give her months from now.

"Hang tight," I say. "I've got a little surprise for you."

As I leap out of bed and stride toward our walk-in closet, Sarah calls out to me, "Gimme a little shaky-shake of that hot ass!" So, of course, I grace her with an extra-enthusiastic ass shake before disappearing into the closet.

When I return to Sarah in the bed, I place a large box before her.

"What's this?" Sarah asks, sitting up.

"Open it and find out."

She opens the lid, peeks inside, and gasps. "How did you know?"

"Remember when your laptop went in for repairs and you used the computer in the office for a week? You left quite an interesting search history."

Sarah bursts out laughing and buries her face in her hands. "Oh my God."

"That was quite the trail of breadcrumbs you left for me. I assumed you did it on purpose."

"No, not at all." She shrugs. "Well, maybe subconsciously, who knows?" She begins pulling out the bulky contents of the box, and when everything is laid out on the bed, she looks it over, her brown eyes ablaze. "Holy Bondage, Batman," she says quietly. "I never thought I'd see the day. *Thank you*."

"You're very welcome." I take a steadying breath. What have I done? I thought I was ready to take this leap with Sarah, but now that she's opened the box, I'm not sure.

"You do understand I want *you* to cuff *me*. Not the other way around?"

"That's the only possible combination."

"You're seriously fine with this?"

We both know I've been hardwired since the age of seven to recoil from the mere thought of bondage, and The Lunacy in my teens certainly didn't help matters. But

I think what happened in Thailand proved I'm capable of enjoying bondage, now and again, if I'm the one who remains untethered. Or, shit, could it be the circumstances of that night were so fucking bizarre and impossible to duplicate, I'm biting off more than I can chew here?

"I'm fine with it," I manage to say, even though I'm suddenly not sure I'm telling the truth.

Sarah pulls one of the four Velcro cuffs from the box. "How does this work?"

I grab another soft cuff from the box and open it. "The sheet gets strapped onto the mattress and the cuffs attach to the sheet."

"That's a whole lot more efficient than a web of neckties tied to bedposts." She laughs. "Thank you so much for getting this. I'm amazed."

"Of course."

Sarah pulls a face. "Not 'of course.' This is a one hundred-eighty-degree turnaround from where we started. You were pretty damned clear on your application that any kind of bondage was a nonstarter for you."

I shrug. "I didn't know I was writing those words to the future mother of my twins. With the right woman to tie up, a man can overcome any kind of bullshit-hang-up."

"Hold up. I'm the future mother of your *twins*?" She looks down at her massive belly. "Oh, fuck. When did *that* happen?"

I chuckle.

"But seriously, baby, are you sure about this?" she says. "I don't want you to feel pressured."

"I don't. Think of this as a little dangling carrot to get you through the next few months."

The look of sheer euphoria on her face makes me want to give her the second box, too. If I can't get over all my childhood bullshit for the woman I love more than life itself—the woman who's willing to bear my children—then when am I ever gonna get past it? And isn't it my soul's mandate to at least *try* to get past it? I look down at the inside of my left forearm. *For a man to conquer himself is the first and noblest of all victories.* Why did I get that inked onto my skin if I wasn't going to commit to it as my life's mantra?

"But wait, there's *more*," I say, leaping back up. Fuck my past. Onward and upward, baby. Climb and conquer.

"*More?*" Sarah says behind my back. "Hey, gimme a shaky-shake, baby."

Once again, I shake my ass for my wife with gusto and she hoots at me.

In my closet, I grab a second, smaller box—this one from the farthest corner of the highest shelf—and bring it back to Sarah on the bed. "Happy Valentine's Day, baby. In April."

Sarah stares at the box with wide eyes. "What is it?"

"Do I really need to explain how presents work *again?*"

She eagerly dives into the box and pulls out a bag filled with assorted sex toys.

"Breadcrumbs," I explain. "You left me lots and lots of breadcrumbs."

Sarah blushes. "I hope you know I didn't google this stuff because I'm unsatisfied or bored in any way. I'd had a conversation with Kat about some of the crazy stuff she's been doing with Josh, and I got a little curious, that's all."

I must admit I was initially taken aback when I found

my wife's search history on my computer. But almost immediately, it made perfect sense to me. Sarah didn't take a job reading kinky sex club applications out of nowhere, after all, whether she realizes it or not. And, yeah, I'm not blind—I saw the way her eyes blazed in Thailand when I impulsively tied her wrists, not knowing how else to handle her. Back then, I told myself it was a one-time thing. But looking back, my actions that night clearly planted some kind of seed inside her. Or maybe it simply ignited a fuse that was already there.

"Jonas, I've known from day one this kind of stuff is off-limits with you," she says. "I was just browsing for the sheer entertainment value of it. I'm sure it's a simple case of being attracted to forbidden fruit. The doctor said we're not allowed to get too freaky-deaky, so . . ." Her cheeks flush. "So, of course, that's all I can think about doing. But it's okay. Obviously, you have very good reasons not to want to—"

"Fuck it, baby. Fuck my bullshit. Fuck the past." I practically spit out the words. "You're curious? You want to explore some kink and see if it gets you off? Fine by me. Don't let all my baggage make you think this stuff is somehow weird or shameful, because it's not. I want to fuck you however you wanna get fucked. Nothing's off-limits—just as soon as we get the all-clear from the doctor."

Her face aglow, Sarah picks up an unidentifiable sex toy, a glass dildo that looks more like a bong than a sex toy and scrutinizes it like it's an alien carcass. "Honestly, I don't know if I'm going to like any of this stuff or not."

"Doesn't matter. We'll have fun finding out."

Sarah drops the bag of toys and scoots closer to me on

the bed. "Jonas, you know I'm a thoroughly satisfied member of the Jonas Faraday Club, right?"

"Yes, I harbor no misunderstanding about how much you like getting fucked by me and my big ol' cock. And neither does anyone within a half-mile radius of our bedroom." I kiss her nose. "We're good, love. I'll plan to shock and awe you with a whole new brand of fuckery the minute we get the all-clear from the doctor." I touch her belly. "It'll be something to look forward to after our little monkeys arrive."

Fuck. As those words leave my mouth, that familiar tsunami of anxiety crashes down on me again—the one that's been slowly building inside me, ever since the doctor confirmed Sarah's pregnancy.

Sarah's face instantly flashes with concern. "What's wrong?"

"Nothing. I'm thinking about how I can't wait to tie you up and shove a dildo up your ass."

She's not amused. "Jonas, talk to me."

My stomach won't stop twisting. "I worry about you, that's all." I try to smile at her, though I'm sure I'm not successful.

She touches my cheek. "I can tell you've been struggling lately. Talk to me."

I glance at the clock. "I'm fine. It's time for you to get your massive tits and juicy ass in gear. The dumber half of the Faraday clan and his sassy wife will be here in thirty minutes."

2

SARAH

Jonas opens the door and Kat's one-and-a-half-year-old mini-me tears into our living room, squealing at the top of her lungs.

"Hello, beautiful," Jonas coos to his towheaded niece, kneeling down. When she leaps into his muscled arms, he adds, "Gimme my kisses, Gracie-cakes."

Immediately, Gracie complies, peppering her doting uncle's face with kisses the way he's trained her to do, as Josh stands over the pair, chuckling, and Kat saunters toward me, her petite baby bump leading the way.

"You missed a spot," Jonas says to his niece, tilting his chin. And, of course, little Gracie lays another wet one on him. "Aw, thank you," Jonas says. "That one was extra sweet."

As usual, watching Jonas dote on Gracie makes me swoon. I can only imagine how much I'm going to melt when I get to witness him doing the same thing with our own babies.

"Can I get some kisses, too?" I call to Gracie, and she

immediately barrels toward me like a bat out of hell, clomping maniacally in her pink, sparkly cowgirl boots.

"Careful of Aunt Sarah's belly," Jonas calls out, just before Gracie slams into my legs.

"She's fine," I assure Jonas, before sliding Gracie onto her bottom on the couch next to me. "Wow, look at those pretty sparkly boots! Who gave you those, I wonder?"

Gracie points at me and laughs.

"She wants to wear them twenty-four-seven," Kat says, taking a seat next to me on the couch. "Whenever I have to take them off for bath time or bedtime, she does this." Kat lets out a dinosaur-like shriek in mimicry of her strong-willed child, and then adds, "I'm convinced she's a pterodactyl in a toddler suit."

"And why shouldn't my darling niece wear whatever footwear she desires in the bath?" I tease. "Who wouldn't want to be fashionable and sparkly at all times?"

Kat rolls her eyes. "I'm going to say the same thing to you when your own darling children become headstrong little pterodactyls. Let's see how you like it."

I jokingly cover Gracie's ears. "Such slander." I bend down toward Gracie's angelic little face. "Can you say slander, Little G?"

"Shwandah."

"Yes! Oh my goodness, you're a genius. Can I have a kiss, you brilliant child?" When Gracie nods enthusiastically, I pucker, and she smashes her lips into mine. "Thank you so much! That was yummalicious."

"Yummaleesh," Gracie agrees, making Kat and me laugh. It's a new development. She doesn't normally repeat big words, spontaneously. It's usually only after being prompted.

I say, "That was amazeballs, Gracie! Can you say *amazeballs*?"

"Mayzbilz."

Kat and I laugh hysterically and praise Gracie to the moon and back again, which makes Gracie giggle and say, "You funny." It's her catchphrase these days. Something she says whenever anyone makes her laugh. So, of course, Kat and I laugh some more.

"What nefarious thing are you doing to make my daughter laugh like that, OAP Cruz?" Josh says. Having left their conversation at the front door, Josh and Jonas are now striding into the living room, taking armchairs next to Kat, Gracie, and me on the couch.

"Only the most important words in the English language," I reply. I exchange a look with Jonas regarding Josh calling me "OAP Cruz." Ever since that video of me in Thailand went viral, Josh has relished calling me that repeatedly. But for the life of me, I can't fathom what my brother-in-law thinks OAP stands for, since we've certainly never told him or anyone else.

"How's the double-incubation going?" Josh asks, indicating my swollen belly.

"Good, other than the fact that Crazy-Monkey here" —I put my fingertip on what's got to be Crazy Monkey's insistent elbow or foot—"has been stomping on my sciatic nerve lately and making it hard for Mommy to get a good night's sleep."

"Like father like monkey," Josh says with a wink to his brother.

"Are you still feeling certain they're both boys?" Kat asks.

"Absolutely," I reply. "I know it in my bones."

"But still no confirmation from the doctor?" Kat asks.

"Nope. Jonas wants to be surprised." I smile at Jonas and his half-hearted smile in return tightens my stomach. What the fuck has gotten into my husband? He's truly not himself these days.

Josh nudges Jonas' arm. "Hey, we should start a baby pool at work. Everyone can throw in ten bucks to bet on both babies' genders, their birth date, their—"

"No," Jonas says, his tone sharp. "I don't want to do that."

"It'll be fun," Josh assures him. "Everyone is so excited about the babies. Let them—"

"No, Josh," Jonas says. "Please. This isn't a game. Sarah's health is on the line here."

This time, I exchange a look with Kat. While it's true my pregnancy is high risk, simply because I'm carrying twins, I'm young and healthy, and the odds of something going wrong are still low. And yet, Jonas seems to be growing more and more anxious that something might happen to the babies or me. That's a guess on my part, though, since my stalwart husband won't talk to me about whatever is stressing him out so much.

"I was just trying to have a little fun," Josh mutters. Apparently trying to change the subject, he addresses his little girl on the couch. "Will you give Uncle Jo Jo a hug? I think he needs one."

Gracie slides onto Jonas' lap and rests her fat cheek against his chest and everyone oohs and aaahs.

"Thank you, love," Jonas says, patting Gracie's little back.

"That's so sweet of you," I say. "Will you tell Uncle Jo Jo everything is going to be okay?"

"Ebby ting ees okie, Unkie Jo Jo."

Once again, everyone oohs and aahs and compliments her on her kind heart.

"Can everyone stop coaching her to call me Uncle Jo Jo?" Jonas says.

Josh snickers. "You should be glad you're not something worse, like 'Uncle Peen' or 'Uncle Rum Cake.'" He's talking about the nicknames given to two of Kat's four brothers: Keane and Ryan Morgan. The Morgans are notoriously fond of nicknames—some of which are hilariously brutal. Josh continues, "I've actually been trying to teach Gracie to call you 'Uncle Jo Jo the Dancing Clown.' But so far, I can't get it to stick."

"Oh, we'll get her there," Kat says. "Practice makes perfect."

"Absolutely," Josh says.

I address Gracie on Jonas' lap. "Will you say 'Uncle Jo Jo the Dancing Clown' for me?"

"Unkie Jo-Jo-Dahn-Keehn," Gracie replies, and everyone except Jonas laughs.

"Traitor," Jonas mutters, and I shoot him an amused wink.

"Give that girl a cookie!" Josh says to Kat. "It's like training a dog. If we reward her every time she performs a trick, she'll start doing it like clockwork."

"Stop," Jonas mutters.

"Never," Josh teases.

Exhaling, Jonas stands and plops Gracie onto her daddy's lap. "Take your instrument of cruelty while I get us some drinks." He begins striding toward the kitchen, tossing over his shoulder, "Sparkling water, ladies?"

As Kat and I confirm that's our drink of choice, yet again, Gracie shouts, "Joos!" apparently thinking her uncle was addressing her.

"No, you don't need the sugar, honey," Kat says. She holds up a sippy cup. "I've got your water right here."

Gracie scowls. "*Joos.*"

"It's water or nothing."

Gracie leans forward, clearly intending to argue her case. But Kat cuts her off at the pass.

"Look, honey, I've got your farm animals bookie. You can read it while drinking your water."

Gracie's face lights up. Apparently, it's an offer she can't refuse. Babbling excitedly, she slides off her father's lap and toddles over to her mother's. And a moment later, she's reading and sipping and, at least for now, in no danger of releasing the pterodactyl inside her.

"I'll help Jonas with the drinks," Josh says. And off he goes.

When we're alone, Kat asks, "How are you really feeling, sis?"

I roll my eyes. "Like shit. Everything hurts."

"You poor thing. Thankfully, it's not too much longer now."

I rub my belly. "It's a small price to pay to get two for the price of one, right? How about you? Still feeling like a barf-o-matic twenty-four seven?"

"Yeah, pretty much."

"Crap. I was hoping that would have tapered off for you by now."

"It has. But not by much. Lately, I only feel like barfing about twenty hours a day. But that's okay." She rustles Gracie's platinum hair. "At least this time, I know for a fact it's all worth it in the end."

Jonas and Josh return from the kitchen with everyone's drinks, and Kat feigns offense. "You boys aren't drinking sparkling water in solidarity with your poor pregnant wives? The audacity."

"Actually, Jonas suggested we do exactly that," Josh says, taking a sip of whatever's in his tumbler. "But I told him to stop trying to make me look like a selfish bastard."

Kat laughs. "I was joking. There's no reason for everyone to suffer."

"See?" Josh says to Jonas. "That's what *I* said. Word for word." He bends down into his gorgeous wife's face. "You want a taste, Party Girl?"

"I thought you'd never ask, Playboy."

Rather than handing Kat his glass, like I'm expecting him to do, Josh takes a sip of his drink, leans in, and kisses Kat deeply.

"Mmm, gin and tonic," Kat coos. "Delicious."

I glance at my husband, eager to exchange a look about this latest grotesque example of PDA from the ever-touchy-feely Josh and Kat, but Jonas seems oblivious to his surroundings—too lost in his thoughts to have noticed Josh and Kat or anyone else.

Josh gets settled in his armchair and raises his glass. "Let's have a toast." Everyone raises their glasses, including Gracie—everyone except for Jonas, who's still distracted. Josh nudges his brother's thigh. "Jonas. *Hello*?"

Jonas blinks at his brother like he's been yanked from a trance, sees our raised glasses, and quickly follows suit.

Josh bellows, "To Gracie soon becoming an expert at saying 'Uncle Jo Jo the Dancing Clown!' To the Faradays —the ones who are here and the ones on the way! And to Uncle Jo Jo the Dancing Clown for always being such a festive, light-hearted, and easy-going host."

"Hear, hear!" everyone calls out, with Gracie mimicking the words.

As I sip my club soda, a torrent of joy floods me, the same way it always does when Josh makes one of his toasts. Even after three years of marriage to Jonas, I still can't believe my life has turned out this way. That I'm married to the man of my dreams and part of a family that now officially includes Kat, my best friend in the world, as my sister. The amazing way my life has turned out takes my breath away on a daily basis. Or wait . . . is it that weird, breathless feeling I'm having in this moment something physical?

Ouch.

What the hell is this weird pain?

I bend over, clutching my belly. "Ow."

Jonas leaps out of his chair and hovers over me. "Sarah? Talk to me."

I exhale and sit back up. "I'm okay. The pain is gone."

"What kind of pain was it?" he asks. "Was it Crazy Monkey doing Zumba again, or something else?"

I purse my lips as my brain tries to identify the weird, brief pain I felt. It didn't feel like Crazy Monkey doing Zumba this time, but I'm not entirely sure. "It felt like a weird tightness across my belly," I say. "A sharp squeeze. But only for a few seconds."

"Hmm," Kat says. "It could have been a contraction. Braxton Hicks. Did it *hurt* or was it an uncomfortable squeeze?"

"It was . . . I don't know, honestly. Everything hurts these days."

"We're going to the hospital," Jonas announces. "Come on, baby. Do you need help walking?"

"The pain is gone, honey," I say. "I'm fine."

"When's your next doctor's appointment?" Kat asks.

"Tuesday morning."

Jonas shifts his weight. "I think we should go to the hospital now."

"Honey, we can't keep rushing down to the hospital every time I have a cramp," I say. "They're going to start locking the windows and doors when they see us driving into the parking lot."

Jonas shakes his head. "Better safe than sorry."

"True. Yes. I agree. But my appointment is in two days, and the pain is gone. If it comes back, we'll go to the hospital. For now, though, please, let's relax. I'm sure it was nothing."

"Either way, let's see the doctor first thing tomorrow," Jonas says. "I don't want to wait until Tuesday."

"Aren't you and Josh supposed to go to Denver for the day tomorrow?" I ask.

"Not anymore. I'm going with you to the hospital."

"I don't need him to come with me to Denver," Josh says. "Jonas is nothing but the pretty face of Climb and Conquer, anyway. We both know I'm the brains behind the whole operation."

To my surprise, Jonas doesn't acknowledge his brother's joke with an eyeroll as he usually would. We all know Jonas is the mastermind behind Climb & Conquer, without a doubt. Instead, he paces the room, looking stressed.

After exchanging looks with Kat and me, Josh says, "Who's hungry? Should we start grilling the fish now?" When everyone says that sounds good, Josh scoops up his daughter, places her on Jonas' back, and says, "Come on, cowgirl! Say 'giddy up,' and ride Uncle Jo Jo the Dancing Horsie into the backyard!"

"Gid-ahp!" Gracie shouts happily.

And off the trio goes through the sliding glass door, taking my heart along with them.

"What's up with Jonas?" Kat asks when the sliding glass door has closed behind the rest of our group.

"My best guess is that he's freaking out about something going wrong with the babies and me. But who knows for sure, since he won't talk to me about whatever he's feeling." I rub my forehead. "It certainly doesn't help to calm him down when I buckle over with aches and pains."

Kat looks concerned. "Does it happen often?"

"It's always something. Two babies in one belly is a lot."

Kat twists her mouth. "Listen, honey. I know Jonas can be ultra-sensitive at times. But just because he's paranoid doesn't mean he's not right."

"I know that. Trust me, almost bleeding out on that bathroom floor taught me to respect Jonas' intuition. But, still, if we went to the hospital every time Jonas insisted, we'd live there. And that's not an exaggeration."

"Please, just promise me you'll err on the side of caution."

"Of course. The thing is, with Jonas so amped up and worried lately, it's becoming increasingly difficult for me to gauge where I should reasonably draw the line between caution and total hysteria."

"Well, at the very least, I agree with him you should see the doctor tomorrow. Better safe than sorry."

"I agree, too."

"Good. Let me know how it goes." As she says the words, she suddenly turns a distinctive shade of puke-green. "Oh, God," she mutters.

"Feeling sick?"

Nodding, she pulls a package of Saltines from her diaper bag and begins weakly nibbling on a cracker.

"You poor thing," I say. "Can I help somehow?"

She shakes her head. "Nothing and nobody can help me." She nibbles on several more crackers before adding, "Actually, yeah. Distract me from my misery. Tell me something fun or salacious that will take my mind off myself."

"Something salacious? Hmm." I twist my mouth. "Well, Jonas gave me a big box of sex toys as a gift this morning."

Kat's eyes saucer. "Holy shitballs. I wasn't expecting you to be able take my mind off my misery, but mission accomplished, girl. Tell me more, sis. What kinds of toys did Jonas give you, exactly?"

I can feel my cheeks burning. "A bunch of different things. He saw my search history on his computer and figured, correctly, that it was my wish list."

"Give that man a cookie."

I chuckle. "We've never used toys before, so I don't know what half the stuff is supposed to do, but I'm excited to find out."

Kat's eyebrows ride up. "You and Jonas have never used sex toys?"

I shake my head. "He's never been interested in that stuff. And sex with Jonas has always been so good, I've never felt the urge to switch things up."

"Your search history would suggest otherwise, my darling."

I chuckle. "Only recently. The doctor told us to be extra gentle and careful during the third trimester, and now, all my body wants to do is the extreme opposite of that."

Kat laughs. "I know the feeling. These days, all I want to do is get railed. Hard. Tied up and spanked."

"Oh my."

She pats her petite baby bump. "But this isn't a high-risk pregnancy, like yours. Ask your doctor tomorrow, but I'm thinking if toys are a new thing for you, the third trimester of a high-risk pregnancy isn't the time to start trying out new things."

I pout. "Yeah, you're probably right."

"If you want to show me the box," Kat says, "I'd be happy to tell you what everything does, so you can enjoy them to the fullest when the happy day finally arrives." She snickers. "You know how much I love my toys."

I blush. "Yes, I do. Honestly, I'd love a tutorial. But another time, when the guys and Gracie aren't here."

"You've got it." Kat giggles. "Oh, man. Just talking about sex toys is making me insanely horny. Damn these pregnancy hormones."

I laugh. As long as I've known her, my best friend—now, sister-in-law—has never been shy about how much she loves sex. And these days, about how horny she gets during pregnancy.

"If you want to pull Josh into one of the back guestrooms," I say, "I'd be happy to watch Gracie for you."

Kat gasps. "Seriously?"

"Absolutely. That is, if you think you can get plowed by your husband without barfing all over him."

"Oh my God, you're a saint! Being spontaneous is so

hard, once you've got a little one. You'll see. You've got to seize every opportunity." She flashes a demonic smile. "Honestly, I'm not sure I can get plowed by Josh without barfing all over him. But I'm very willing and grateful to be able to give it the ol' college try."

3
JONAS

"Jonas, what the fuck is going on with you?" my brother demands.

I flip the swordfish over on the grill and say nothing.

"Bubboos, Dada!" Gracie calls out from the lawn. She's been chasing a butterfly for the past few minutes. But now, she's clearly got a new activity in mind.

"I'll blow bubbles for you in a couple minutes," Josh replies to his toddler. "Can you twirl for Daddy and make your dress go *poof*? Good girl." As Gracie happily twirls on the grass, Josh returns his attention to me. "Are you stressed about our expansion?"

He's talking about the new gyms we're poised to acquire. It's a huge expansion for our business, but one I'm extremely excited about.

"I've got no qualms about the deal," I say.

"Good. Me, either."

"Daddaaa!" Gracie shouts. "Watch me twoooorl!"

"I'm watching, honey. Wow. That's awesome!" Josh

returns to me. "So, you're worried about Sarah and the babies, then? Is that it?"

I begin adding the veggies to the grill. "It's a high-risk pregnancy, Josh. And every day, she's got a new ache or pain."

"You're in the home stretch now, Jonas. Everything will be fine."

"But what if something goes wrong? I won't survive it, Josh." I look up from the grill. "I'm being literal. *I won't survive it.*"

Josh exhales. "Aw, Jonas. You think you're the first expectant father to feel like your happiness hangs in the balance? Well, you're not. And I've got news for you, that fear of losing the ones you love never goes away. It only gets worse, as you realize your every happiness is tied up in your family's health and happiness. But that's the price of admission to experiencing love at the deepest level."

I swallow hard, stuffing down a lump in my throat.

"You think I don't feel the same way you're describing?" Josh says. "I do. All the time. But if I let myself wallow in that fear, if I focus on it, then I'd become a slave to it. I'd be paralyzed by it. And worst of all, I wouldn't be able to feel any of the good stuff—the stuff that's the whole point of loving people in the first place."

I exhale with frustration. "I hear you. But not focusing on the fear is easier said than done."

"It might not be easy, but it's doable. All you have to do is consciously force yourself to be present. Make yourself think about the moment you're living, not some future moment that might never come to pass. Think about the good stuff, and how grateful you are for it, and soon, your inner dialogue about all the good stuff will crowd out your thoughts about 'what if.'"

I flash my brother a skeptical look. "That works for you?"

"It does."

I scoff. "Must be nice."

"Dada?" Gracie says, pulling on Josh's pant leg. "Bubboos?"

"Okay, baby. We'll do bubbles. I think Mommy has some in the diaper bag. Oh! I saw a bunny over there!"

"Bunny?" Gracie says, gasping and looking around.

"He hopped into those bushes over there!" Josh points, and, of course, Gracie toddles off to find the bunny.

"Look, Jonas," Josh says, returning to me. "I know your brain doesn't work like mine does. But all I know is, if you focus on what *might* happen, what you *might* lose, you'll miss out on everything you've actually got. And that would be a crying shame."

I ponder that for a moment, before nodding and whispering, "'There are two things a person should never be angry at—what they can help, and what they cannot.'"

"Plato?"

"Correct."

"Yet again, he's nailed it. Listen to your homie, man. He's right."

"And so are you. Thanks."

"You're welcome. Do you feel better?"

"I do."

"You know why, right?"

I can't help returning my brother's sly smile. "Because . . ."

We say it together: "Talking lets the feelings out."

Without warning, music starts blaring from our backyard speakers—"Love Cats" by The Cure, and a moment later, Sarah ambles through the sliding glass door, looking like the Latina goddess she is. As she approaches, Sarah calls out, "Hey, Joshua! This song isn't a coincidence. It's a coded message to you from your wife." When Josh looks perplexed, Sarah adds, "Your horny wife requests your presence in one of the back bedrooms. She wants you to '*love* Kat.' But replace *love* with another four-letter word."

Josh practically jumps for joy. "Gracie, stay here with Uncle Jo Jo and Auntie Sarah while Daddy goes inside to show Mommy some love."

"Bubboos!" Gracie shouts.

"Hey, Gracieeeee," Sarah coos. She's holding up a bottle of bubbles. "Look what your smart mommy gave me."

"Bubboooos!"

"Bless you, OAP Cruz!" Josh calls out, before turning on his heel and sprinting toward the house.

"Take your time, Joshie Woshie!" Sarah shouts to Josh's back. "*Love* can't be rushed!"

"No, it cannot!"

As Josh disappears into the house, Sarah leads Gracie to the middle of the lawn. "Time for bubbles, *cariña*."

Sarah begins blowing bubbles for Gracie to chase. I turn off the grill and watch the pair, feeling mesmerized by the joyful, easy way Sarah is interacting with our niece. *Damn, she's going to be an amazing mother . . . assuming everything works out as we're hoping and praying.*

"How are you feeling?" Sarah asks, before blowing another stream of bubbles for Gracie.

"Good."

"You seemed stressed earlier," she says. "Actually, you've seemed stressed for a while now."

I finish taking everything off the grill and wrapping it up in foil. "I've been letting my worries get the best of me," I admit. "I talked to Josh about it, though, and he helped calm me down."

Sarah blows another string of bubbles for Gracie. "What have you been stressed about? The babies?"

"And you. Naturally."

"What'd Josh say that helped you calm down?"

I tell her the gist and Sarah ponders that for a moment, until Gracie pulls on her skirt and asks for more bubbles.

"Oh, sorry, love." Sarah resumes blowing bubbles, sending Gracie running to chase them again. This time, as I watch the scene, I tell myself to enjoy this moment. I do what Josh said to do—I focus on the here and now and try to drown out my worry with positive affirmations and gratitude. And I'll be damned, it works. Sort of. In fact, I'm suddenly tingling with arousal as I watch Sarah and the natural mother she is. She's Mother Earth. Demeter. The sexiest woman alive. *And I'm the luckiest man on earth.*

"Watching you pucker to blow those bubbles is S-E-X-Y as F-U-C-K," I say, walking toward Sarah on the grass.

"*Jonas Faraday,*" Sarah whispers. She glances at our niece.

"She doesn't know how to spell," I remind her.

"Yeah, but she could repeat some of that to Kat, and then we'd be in big trouble."

I chuckle. "Kat's getting babysitting while she boinks my brother. I think that'd be a fair trade-off."

I reach Sarah in the middle of the lawn and take her

ass in my palms. "Oh, the things I'd do to this A-S-S, if this little bleep-blocker weren't here."

Sarah giggles. "Welcome to our future. Kat says life with little ones involves daily bleep-blocking. With twins, I'm sure we'll experience twice the bleep-blocking."

"We'll find a way. I'm going to make sure of it."

"Grassy bwow da bubboos!"

"Okay, I'll show you how," Sarah says. She crouches down, as best she can with her swollen belly, and holds the bubbles wand in front of Gracie's face. "Make your lips like this. See? Now, blow." But Gracie's attempt is hilariously inept. Laughing, Sarah says, "You know what? You can hold the wand and twirl around. That way, the wind blows the bubbles for you! Like this!"

Sarah shows Gracie what she means, and a moment later, Gracie experiences the thrill of victory, which prompts Sarah and me to cheer her on.

Soon, Gracie is absorbed in her task, which gives me a moment to take my wife into my arms and plant a passionate kiss on her luscious lips.

"Wow," Sarah says. "You seem happy."

"I am. You know why?" I smile. "Because you're the goddess and the muse, Sarah Cruz Faraday. And I'm the luckiest man in the world."

4
SARAH

Jonas comes out of the bathroom, a towel around his waist, his body as chiseled and ripped as ever. He rips off his towel and chucks it across the room, giving me the view of him that never gets old.

"Why, hello, sirs," I say, addressing both Jonas and his hard cock.

"Damn, I wanna fuck your brains out, woman." He leaps onto the bed and hovers over me, his muscles taut and his erection straining. "Oh, the things I want to do to you."

"Do 'em. I won't tell on you."

"Not till we get the all-clear." He kisses my nose and slides to the side of me. "But in the meantime, I promise to show you a safe and gentle good time."

My heart is dancing. Ever since Jonas' conversation with his brother this afternoon, he's become a new man. He's actually playful again, thank God. No longer looking like the weight of the world is crushing his spine. "Safe and gentle sounds good, as long as it's with you."

"Good. Because that's the only thing on the menu for now."

"That's a mighty big boner, sir," I say. "That sucker deserves its own zip code."

He kisses my neck. "What can I say? You do crazy things to me." He kisses his way up to my ear. "How are you feeling?"

"Good."

"You promise?"

"I do. I'm as big as a house, so I'm uncomfortable. But I promise I'm a very happy house."

"You're not as big as a house." He touches my swollen belly. "You're as big as a condo."

I giggle. "Now that's a Valentine's Day card, if I've ever heard one."

"You know how much I love dazzling you with Valentine's Day bullshit."

I open my mouth to reply . . . and a huge yawn escapes me.

"Tell me how you really feel," Jonas jokes.

"Sorry. Gracie wore me out today. I can't even imagine how exhausting it's going to be when we're chasing *two* monkeys around, every single day."

"Yeah, but we'll get a nanny, so that'll be a huge help."

My breathing halts. I don't necessarily agree with Jonas' assumption that we'll get a nanny. We haven't talked about that, so I don't know why he assumes it. But either way, I'm thrilled to hear him *finally* talking about our future life with our babies. He's never done that before. Not once. "Oh, we're getting a nanny, are we?"

"A night-nurse, too," he says. "Why not? At least for

the first year, until the babies are both sleeping through the night, we'll want all the help we can get."

I blink several times, expecting Jonas to add something like, "I mean, assuming you agree." But he doesn't. "Jonas, don't you think staffing decisions of this nature should be co-decided by your wife and the mother of your two babies?"

Jonas furrows his brow. "Why wouldn't you agree? Anyone who can afford to hire a nanny and night-nurse for twins would do it. Why would anyone suffer sleepless nights unnecessarily?"

"*Suffer*?" I say, indignation flooding me. I sit up. "I don't consider caring for my own children myself any form of *suffering*."

Jonas rolls his eyes. "You know what I mean."

"I don't, actually. Explain it to me."

He sighs. "Incessant sleep deprivation, the absence of time for self-care, the absence of time for the parents to be alone and meaningfully connect . . . all those things don't need to be part and parcel of the parenting gig. It's not a badge of honor to experience the first year of parenting as sleepless chaos."

"Is that so?"

"It is. If you're worried about a nanny taking your place, then don't be. Josh and I had Mariela, in addition to our parents, and we absolutely adored her. But loving Mariela didn't mean we loved our mom any less. It didn't mean we were less bonded to our mother. Mariela was simply another family member to love. Our mother was irreplaceable."

I bite my lip. Why didn't I immediately realize Jonas would think about parenthood through the lens of his own childhood experiences, every bit as much as I'm thinking about it through the lens of mine. If only we'd talked about this stuff sooner, I would have known his ideas are drastically different than my own. But, hey, at least we're talking about this stuff now, rather than after the babies come.

"You saw Gracie today," Jonas continues, correctly surmising my skepticism from my facial expression. "She was a hurricane. Well, imagine *two* little hurricanes tearing through our house, day in and out. I guarantee you'll be grateful to have another pair of hands and eyes living here—especially someone who's known and loved the kids from day one."

I purse my lips, trying to figure out why I'm feeling so resistant to Jonas's vision of our parenting future. But all I can think about is how hands-on my mother always was, and how close we've always been as a result. Would my close relationship with my mother have been affected if I'd been co-parented by a paid nanny?

"As long as we're talking about this stuff," Jonas continues. "I suppose I should mention I intend to ask Diana to become our live-in housekeeper, after the kids are born. At least, for the first few years. If she's not willing to take that on for whatever reason, then I'll want to find someone who will."

I can't help smiling. "Okay, on that particular thing, I'm not going to fight you. God knows, I have no particular desire to do housekeeping, especially according to your exacting standards."

Jonas sighs with relief. "Good. We'll have a live-in housekeeper for sure. A nanny for sure. And a night-nurse to be negotiated."

"I never said the nanny's not for sure. I need to think about it. But as long as we're negotiating here, then I demand a personal butler. Once I'm a mother, I'll need someone to feed me grapes at a moment's notice."

"Request denied. Nobody's going to feed my sexy wife grapes but me. I'll be your butler."

"Will you wear nothing but a bowtie? On your cock, to be clear."

Jonas laughs. "I'll wear a bowtie anywhere you want." He touches my cheek. "Baby, that's my entire point. Let's get the help we need so we've still got energy at night to play butler-fucks-the-lady-of-the-house."

I roll my eyes. "Love, if the day arrives when I don't want to jump your bones every night, bowtie on your cock or not, then, okay, hire a nanny and a night-nurse and a housekeeper and a sex therapist, too. Whatever might be needed to help me get my mojo back. Because I love our sex life as much as you do. All I'm saying is let's see how it's going once the babies are here, before we assume we'll need an army of people on the payroll."

Jonas is quiet for a long moment. "Okay. We'll wait and see."

"Other than the housekeeper," I add. "Please, feel free."

He sighs. "I just don't want to lose *us* when the babies enter the picture. We're so fucking happy. I want to keep it that way."

I touch his cheek. "We'll be even happier, Jonas. Will things be exactly the same as they are now? No. They'll be different. But if we wanted life to stay the same with the babies here, then what would be the point in having them?" I snuggle into him. "This is going to be fun, honey. It's going to be a blast. You'll see."

He kisses me, and I slide my arm around him,

cuddling him close. When my cold feet slide between his legs, however, Jonas jolts and yelps.

"Your feet are like ice!" he says.

"Sorry. My circulation isn't great right now."

"Aw, baby." He gets out of bed, rummages in a drawer, and returns with a pair of fuzzy socks, which he slides onto my feet. "Better?"

"Much. Thank you."

He returns to me in the bed and takes me into his arms.

"Aw, you sacrificed your own warmth for mine. Scoot closer. I'll warm you up." I hug him to me and rub his back, warming his cold skin. "Tell me more about your big ideas for our family of four."

Jonas kisses my forehead. "I was thinking, when the kids are two or three, we should get a puppy."

I can't keep myself from smiling. "A *puppy*?"

"Every little kid should have a puppy."

"Did you and Josh have one?"

"No. Did you?"

"No."

"Case in point. Happy, normal kids have puppies. I've seen it in movies."

"Puppies track dirt into the house. Would you be able to handle that?"

"Hence, the live-in housekeeper."

"Ah. And just like that, it all makes perfect sense." I run my hand through his hair. "What kind of puppy?"

"Whatever you want."

"A Maltese named Kiki?"

"Fuck no."

"You said whatever I want."

"Anything but that."

"You have to admit it'd be hilarious."

"There's not enough hilarity in the world to make me say yes to a Maltese named Kiki."

"A yellow lab?"

"Kinda obvious."

"So much for me picking."

"We've got time. There's no rush."

I can't wipe the smile off my face. What a difference a day makes. "What else do you have planned for our little family, Super Dad?"

Jonas is thoughtful for a moment. "When the kids are babies, we'll take them hiking every weekend. I'll put one kid in a baby-backpack and the other in a carrier on my chest, and off we'll go to climb and conquer."

My heart is crashing with joy. "Sounds like we'd better get a good hiking dog, then. When the time comes."

"Good thinking."

"See? This is why we need to talk about these things, Jonas. Because we make better decisions *together*."

"So true."

He kisses me deeply, and suddenly, further conversation is impossible. We're both too aroused to talk. He slides his hand between my legs, finds his target, and slips his fingers into my wetness. For several minutes, he massages me expertly, working me in a way that usually gets me there quickly. In fact, by this time, I normally would have had an orgasm by now.

Something is off.

For the first time since Jonas showed me what my body can do in Belize, I don't feel like my body will get there, no matter what Jonas does.

As I'm having the thought, Jonas opens my thighs

and begins crawling between them, clearly intending to lick me. But I don't feel right. Suddenly, I feel too fatigued to continue.

"No, honey," I whisper, touching his shoulder to halt him. "It's not going to work."

"I'll keep going until it does."

I shake my head. "I'm too exhausted, I think."

He returns to my face and cups my cheek in his palm. "Are you in pain? Should we go to the hospital?"

I shake my head. "No. I promise I'm not in pain. I'm seven and a half months pregnant with twins and spent the afternoon playing with a tiny blonde hurricane. I think this is perfectly normal, all things considered." I try to smile, but my cheeks feel heavy with the effort. "Please, don't freak out. This isn't a preview of our future, okay? But I think I need to take a rain check."

"You look pale, Sarah. I think we should go to the hospital, just to be safe."

"Sweetheart, I just need to get some sleep. I'd tell you if I felt anything weird."

Jonas' features are tight and pinched with worry. "Okay, we'll go to the doctor, as soon as you wake up, okay? I'll leave a voicemail now, telling them we'll be coming."

"Okay. That's fine."

He lies alongside me again and pulls me close.

"What about names, Super Dad?" I ask. "Have you thought about that?"

"No. You?"

"Jeremiah and Jack."

"Oh, I like both. Which one is Crazy Monkey?"

"Jeremiah, of course."

"I figured. Jeremiah definitely sounds like the crazy one."

I'm swooning. I didn't realize how much I've been aching to talk to Jonas like this. My heart feels like it's going to burst with joy, even as my body feels like it's slowly slipping into slumber.

"What about girl names?" he asks. "I know you're positive we're having two boys, but just in case you're wrong . . ."

"Marisol and Luna," I say. "But we'd call Marisol 'Sol.'"

"The sun and the moon."

"Yup. Because they'd be our whole world."

"Perfect."

"I'm open to suggestions, though."

"Nah, I'm sold. We're done. The hardest thing will be picking, if it turns out we get one of each."

"Well, that was easy." My heart is leaping.

"You know what?" he says. "I think we should find out the genders in the morning."

"Really?"

"That way, we'll know which set of names we'll be using—or if we have to pick one from each set."

My heart is racing with excitement. "You're sure?"

"I'm sure."

I throw my arms around his neck, kiss him, and snuggle close. "Oh, Jonas. *Thank you.* I'm counting the minutes till we find out!"

"Me, too, sweetheart." He kisses the top of my head. "Now, get some sleep. You've had a busy day and we've got a big day tomorrow."

"We sure do—a big, exciting, *happy* day."

5
JONAS

I'm jolted awake.

It's the dark of night.

"Oh my God," Sarah says.

Something in her tone sends a shiver down my spine. I sit up, my heart clanging fiercely, and reach for her. I feel warm wetness next to me in the bed. Did Sarah knock over a glass of hot tea?

"Sarah?"

She gasps. *"Oh my God.* Oh my God. Jonas!"

I turn on the lamp on the nightstand and discover Sarah's heaving body twisted atop bloodied, crimson sheets. My heart explodes in my chest. "Oh my God, Sarah," I sputter.

Blood on the sheets.

Sarah looks down, sees the blood pooling between her legs, and lets out a bloodcurdling scream.

I fumble for the phone, my heart leaping wildly in my chest.

Blood on the sheets.

"Nine-one-one. What's your emergency?"

Sarah's wailing in my ear.

"We need an ambulance," I blurt. I spit out the address.

"What's your emergency?"

Sarah's in a full-blown panic. "Please God, no," she cries. "No, no, no!"

I take a deep breath. *Blood on the sheets.* I can't link my thoughts together. *Blood on the sheets.* "My wife—there's blood," I gasp. "Blood on the sheets. So much blood." My voice is not my own. "She's my *wife.*"

Blood on the sheets.

Sarah's sobbing uncontrollably.

"Hang on, baby," I say, grabbing her hand.

"Jonas," Sarah cries. "The babies."

Blood on the carpet.

"I'm dispatching an ambulance right now, sir. What's your name?"

Blood on the white tiles. "Hang on, baby. They're coming right now."

"What's your name, sir?"

"Jonas Faraday. Please hurry."

"What's your wife's name?"

Blood on the sheets.

"Hang on, Sarah. They're coming."

"Your wife's name is Sarah?"

Sarah shrieks something incoherent.

"They're coming, Sarah."

"Your wife's name is Sarah?"

"Yes. Sarah Faraday. Please, hurry. It's an emergency. She's pregnant with twins. There's so much blood. Oh my God, no." A tidal wave of emotion is threatening to overwhelm me, but I stuff it down. *Blood on the sheets. Blood on the carpet. Blood on the white tiles. Blood on the sheets.* My life's come full circle. This is how it started, and this is how it ends.

"The babies, Jonas. Please, God, no."

"Why is there blood on the sheets?" the woman asks.

Because everything I touch turns to blood.

"Is there blood because your wife is in *labor*, or because she's been *injured* somehow?"

Sarah lets out another pained wail.

"I squeeze Sarah's hand. "Sarah, are you in labor?"

"I don't know!" she shrieks.

"We don't know what's happening—there's blood all over the bed—so much blood—we were sleeping, and then we woke up and, oh my God, there's so much blood."

"Okay, I understand. Help is on the way. Tell your wife help is coming. Tell her she's got to try to stay calm."

Blood on the sheets. Blood on the carpet. Blood on the tiles. Blood on the sheets.

A sob lurches out of me.

"Jonas," the operator says sharply. "Listen to my voice. You need to stay calm for Sarah. Do you understand?"

I don't reply. Sarah's screaming. I can't breathe. I can't talk. I glance down at the bed. The puddle of blood underneath Sarah's hips is getting bigger. It's gurgling out of her. Her thighs are covered in slick, red wetness. The sheet is soaked through.

"Tell Sarah help is on the way," the operator says.

"Help is on the way," I blurt. I tighten my grip on Sarah's hand, but she doesn't squeeze back. Her eyes are closed.

"The babies," Sarah whimpers. She's becoming still and quiet.

"I hear a siren," I say into the phone, my heart leaping. "They're close." I grip Sarah's hand again, but she doesn't grip back. "They're coming, baby."

"Save the babies," Sarah says. Her eyes are still closed. She's not thrashing around anymore. Her face is pale.

"Sarah? Sarah!"

She opens her eyes and looks at me calmly. "Tell them to save the babies."

My stomach convulses. Shaking, I cup the phone to my mouth, turn my head away from Sarah, and whisper-shout, "I can't live without my wife. Make sure you tell them to save Sarah no matter what."

"They're going to do everything they can for all of them," the operator says.

"You need to tell them: *I can't live without my wife.* Make sure they understand the situation. Nothing matters without her."

The operator says, "They'll do everything they can—"

Sarah's passed out now, so there's no reason not to shout at the top of my lungs. "Make sure to tell them to save my wife!" I scream, on the cusp of sobbing. I'm gripping the phone with white knuckles in one hand and Sarah's limp hand in the other. "Please, I'm begging you to tell them to save my wife—save my Sarah—no matter what."

6

JONAS

"Blood pressure ninety over fifty," the paramedic says. He's holding an oxygen mask over Sarah's face. Another paramedic is bent over her, securing an IV to her arm. They're crowded around her, monopolizing her, edging me out. I'm sitting down by her feet, clutching her ankle, bug-eyed, practically convulsing with anxiety and dread. This can't be happening. Surely, I'm going to wake up any minute, warm and calm next to Sarah in our bed. I'll grab her and hold her close and tell her I love her, and she'll run her hands through my hair. *And everything will be fine.*

Sarah mumbles something that sounds like, "Jonas." So, I lean past the paramedic and shove my face into Sarah's. Her eyes are wide with terror. She's pale—holy fuck, she's so fucking pale. The last time she looked like this she was lying on a bathroom floor at her university.

"I'm here, baby," I say. I grab her hand.

"The babies." The words are muffled by the oxygen mask, but I know what she's saying. Her body lurches with a sob.

"Sit back a little, sir."

I lean in, an inch from her face. "Everything's going to be okay."

"The babies," Sarah whimpers. Her face contorts into sheer agony. "The babies, Jonas."

"Sit back, sir. *Right now.*"

"No matter what," Sarah says. "Promise me."

I choke back a sob. Grip her hand and squeeze. But I don't promise. Because I never make promises I don't plan to keep.

Sarah's hand in mine goes limp.

"Heart rate dropping," the paramedic next to me says.

I sit back and stare at Sarah's unconscious body in front of me. Blood is pooling onto the stretcher between her legs, oozing, spreading. Her legs are drenched in blood, all the way down to the fuzzy socks on her feet. The socks I put on her to keep them warm a few hours ago.

"Sarah?" the paramedic prompts, but she doesn't reply. "Stay with me, Sarah."

He leans into her, right up to her mouth. I can't tell if she's talking to him or if he's listening for sounds.

"Sarah," I whisper. "Hang in there, Sarah. *Please.*"

The back doors of the ambulance suddenly swing open, and the paramedics push Sarah's stretcher out the back, where a throng of people in scrubs appears.

One of the paramedics shouts a rapid-fire laundry list of information to someone at the front of the procession.

"Hypovolemic shock," someone says as they whisk her away.

"Suspected abruption," another one of them says.

I jog behind the armada surrounding Sarah, my heart beating wildly, as they whisk her along the length of a hallway. My movement isn't conscious. My legs aren't my own.

"Twins," I hear someone say.

"Transfusion," someone else says. "Unconscious."

"Anesthesiologist."

"Abruption."

"Stat."

"Get him out of here!" someone shouts. And I know they're talking about me.

"Sir, you're going to have to wait out here," a petite woman in scrubs says to me, as Sarah disappears through swinging doors.

"I should be with her."

"Mr. Faraday, your wife has likely had a placental abruption. With the amount of blood she's lost, there's no question we need to deliver the babies immediately."

"She's only seven months along!"

"She's being wheeled into the operating room for an emergency C-section. The lives of your wife and babies are at serious risk and there's no choice but to deliver the babies right now."

I pull on my hair. "*Now?*"

"There's no other option. We're very concerned about the amount of blood your wife has lost."

A sob lurches from my throat. "Tell them to save my wife."

"The doctors will do everything they can. We'll update you as soon as the situation has stabilized." The woman in scrubs motions down the hall. "There's a sitting area down there on the left. We'll come give you an update as soon as we know anything."

I'm frantic. "If there's a choice, tell them to save Sarah."

"I'll tell them. They're putting her under general anesthesia now. Go to the sitting room and wait."

Oh my God. Did I tell Sarah I love her before she fell asleep? My heart wrenches inside my chest. I can't remember if I told her I love her before she fell asleep.

"We had an appointment with the doctor in a few hours," I say lamely. "At eight. Because I was worried."

The woman in scrubs motions to a nearby nurse. "Shannon? Can you show Mr. Faraday to the sitting area? I think he needs someone to escort him there."

A nurse comes over and puts her hand on my forearm. "Come with me."

I look down at the woman's hand. It looks tiny against my arm. This woman is half my size, if that. I could toss her down the hallway like a rag doll, push my way through those swinging doors, find my Sarah, and hold her warm hand one last time. I could tell her I love her, in case I didn't do it earlier.

"Come on, Mr. Faraday. I'll sit with you for a while," the nurse says. She pulls on me, and I let her lead me away from the swinging doors. "Do you have someone you can call?"

My legs are rubber underneath me. I feel like I'm gliding on walking on someone else's legs. When the doctor comes out to tell me Sarah's dead, I know exactly what I'll do. I'll bolt out the front doors of the hospital and run onto the nearby freeway and hurl myself into oncoming traffic. Maybe I'll get lucky and a big rig will be driving along at just the right moment. Or maybe I'll hurl myself off the nearest bridge.

Where's the nearest fucking bridge?

Oh, shit. It's the same one I drove off to kick off The Lunacy.

Fuck me. That won't work. Fuck! It's not high enough!

The nurse pulls me to a chair, and I sit. My teeth are chattering. I didn't tell Sarah I love her. I'm sure of it. Fuck. I put socks on her feet and babbled about a fucking puppy, and a fucking nanny, but I didn't say, "I love you."

I put my hands over my face and bend over in my chair. Will I have the chance to say goodbye to her? Or will my last words to her be about a fucking night nurse?

"Do you need some water?" the nurse asks.

"No."

As long as it's quick and effective, that's all that matters. I'll wait until a bus is coming and step off the curb at the last second. And that will be it. I'll join Sarah, for eternity. The only place I want to be.

"Is there someone you can call?" the nurse says. "A family member?"

I nod, pull out my phone, and wordlessly push the button for Josh.

"Jonas?" my brother says. His voice is groggy. Clearly, I woke him up.

I can't speak. My teeth are vibrating too much to form words.

"Jonas? What's wrong?"

I make a garbled sound.

"What happened?"

"Blood on the sheets," I blurt. "Blood on her *socks*. And now, I have to sit out here and wait."

"Is something wrong with Sarah?" His voice spikes with sudden panic. "Where are you?"

I try to say the name of the hospital, but I can't control my sobs. Quickly, the nurse takes the phone from me and talks quietly to my brother.

Blood on the sheets.

Blood on the tiles.

Blood on the carpet.

Blood on the sheets.

Blood on her socks.

I'll never outrun the blood. I tried, but I was a fool. It's my destiny.

The nurse hands me the phone, so I bring it to my ear.

"I'm coming right now, Jonas," Josh says. "Sit tight till I get there. Listen to music."

"Her socks were soaked in blood, Josh."

"Don't do a goddamned thing except listen to music. Do you understand me? Don't think worst-case scenario. Don't think about flinging yourself off a fucking bridge or walking into traffic." His voice breaks. "Don't give in, brother. Don't you dare even walk outside. Just listen to music and close your eyes and do your visualizations and don't think about a goddamned thing but the music and the fact that Sarah is going to be okay, and so are the babies." He almost loses it at that last thing. "She's Sarah Fucking Cruz! She's going to be okay."

"If I lose her," I begin.

"Don't think that way!" he screams. "You hear me? You need to be strong for Sarah. You're a husband and father now, and that means you don't get to fall apart."

I feel like he just slapped me across the face with a two-by-four. "Okay."

"You got it?"

"Yeah. Come now, Josh. I need you."

"I'm coming right now."

The call ends, so I drop my phone in my lap.

"He's coming?" the nurse asks.

I forgot the nurse was sitting here. "Yeah. Josh always comes when there's blood."

The nurse looks confused. "Are you going to be okay sitting here by yourself till your brother gets here, or do you want me to sit with you?"

I hold up my phone. "I'm going to listen to music."

"Okay. I'll be over there behind the counter if you need me." She puts her hand on my arm. "Mr. Faraday, I know they're doing everything possible for your wife and babies."

My wife and babies. My chest tightens. Like Josh said, I'm a husband and father now. Well, I was, anyway. For a brief, shining moment in my life, I was a husband to the world's most perfect woman, and a soon-to-be father picking out names.

But not anymore.

Now I'm alone.

Again.

The woman is gone now, so I scroll through my music library. But what song could possibly say what needs to be said at a time like this? Is there a song called, "I don't want to wake up if she's not next to me?" Is there a song that says, "Everything I touch turns to blood?"

Song titles are whizzing past my eyes.

My vision is blurring.

Suddenly, I stop scrolling. I've found the perfect song —the one that says precisely what needs to be said. "I'll Follow You into the Dark" by Death Cab for Cutie.

My fingers are shaking as I press play and bring the phone up to my ear, since I don't have my earbuds. And the moment the haunting voice begins, I know I've picked the song that's speaking my truth. God help me, when Sarah goes into the Dark, then I'm going with her.

7
JONAS

"Mr. Faraday?"

I stand and so does my brother. *This is it.* This man in blue scrubs is going to tell me my wife is dead. And then I'm going to bolt out the front door of the hospital and fling myself into traffic.

"Your babies have been delivered—they're being rushed to the NICU."

"Are they okay?" Josh asks. He's squeezing my arm. Holding me up.

"They're alive and headed to the NICU. With this much blood loss by the mother, they're likely anemic and in shock—and their lungs will probably need some form of assistance. Doctors in the NICU will assess them and administer whatever care is required. Once they're stabilized, the NICU doctors will tell you more about their condition."

Josh looks at me, and when it's clear I can't speak, he returns to the man and speaks for me. The same way he's always done whenever I'm rendered mute.

"And Sarah?" Josh asks.

I close my eyes, anticipating the life-changing words I'm about to hear.

"She's still in surgery," the man replies. "They're working hard to stop the bleeding. The situation is very dangerous, but doctors are doing everything they can."

I open my eyes and force air into my lungs.

"Mr. Faraday, your wife had a placental abruption," the man in scrubs says. "And now she's developed a condition called DIC. This means she's bled so much, she's lost the ability to clot her own blood. This is common with abruptions and it's a very serious situation. The doctors are doing everything they can."

"But she's going to be okay," Josh declares. It's a statement, not a question.

"We'll keep you apprised as the situation develops."

I lower myself into a chair behind me and put my hands over my face, while my brother sits next to me and puts his arm around my shoulders.

"Your wife will be in surgery for several more hours," the man says. "Would you like me to take you to the NICU so you can meet your babies? I've received the go-ahead from the NICU for you to come on down."

"Yeah," Josh says. "Of course."

I drop my hands from my face and stare at Josh blankly. Why can't he read my mind, as usual? I want to stay here, just in case Sarah needs me.

"Come on, Jonas," Josh says softly. "You're a father now. Your babies need you." His phone buzzes and he glances at his screen. "Kat's mom has arrived at our house to watch Gracie, so Kat's on her way to pick up Sarah's mom now. They'll be here soon." He pulls on my arm. "Come on, Jonas. Let's be the first ones to see your babies before they get here."

Exhaling, I nod and stand, even though I'm not sure I'll be able to command my legs.

"Lead on," Josh says, gesturing.

"Has anyone told you the genders yet?" the man asks, as he begins walking toward the hallway.

"No," Josh answers.

"Girls," the man says. "You have two baby girls, Mr. Faraday. Just about four pounds each."

Josh looks at me, his eyes pricked with tears. "You're a girl-dad, Jonas." He wipes his eyes. "You've got two baby girls."

My lips are trembling. Surely, he's expecting me to react positively to this news. But the truth is I can't think about anything or anyone but Sarah.

A few minutes later, we reach the NICU. And that's where we find my tiny daughters nestled inside Plexiglas incubators, each of their bodies attached to monitors and ventilators.

"I didn't know a human could be that small," Josh says as we stand shoulder to shoulder over the incubators. He continues, "Gracie looked like Godzilla compared to these two"

I'm too mesmerized by my daughters' little fingers and toes to respond.

"Man, they don't even look real," Josh marvels. "They look like animatronic puppets."

He's right. They do.

"Excuse me," Josh says to the nearby NICU nurse. "Where's the guy who's working the remote control on these puppets?"

"He's behind that curtain over there," the nurse says, motioning. She beams a smile at him, the way all women do.

"Well, tell him he's doing a bang-up job," Josh says. "These puppets seem incredibly lifelike."

Baby A in front of me is thrashing wildly, her tiny limbs outstretched and strained, while Baby B in the incubator closest to Josh is serene and quiet. Both girls are wearing little pink caps and diapers that look three sizes too big for their tiny torsos.

I reach my index finger down to Baby A, and her hand rests against it, barely covering the tip of my finger. At the touch of her soft skin against mine, a fierce protectiveness rises up inside me. "Hi, Luna," I say softly. She jerks her arms and legs wildly in reply. "Are you the Crazy Monkey who's been doing Zumba on your mommy's nerves?"

"Luna?" Josh asks. "I like it. Yeah, she's definitely Crazy Monkey. Just look at her—she's your mini-me."

Against all odds, I can't help smiling at that.

"And who's this?" Josh asks, motioning to the serene baby in the incubator in front of him.

"That's Marisol," I say. "But we're going to call her Sol." Right on cue, Sol throws up her little arm as if to say, "Here!" And Josh and I chuckle. "Sarah says we'll call them Sol and Luna because they're the sun and moon. Our entire world." Tears well up in my eyes. "Oh, fuck, Josh."

"She's going to be okay. Focus on the babies. Come on, Jonas. Be a daddy." He strokes Marisol's little leg. "Hello, Little Miss Sunshine."

"Little Miss Sunshine," I repeat. "I can't imagine a more perfect name for her. Sunshine Faraday. That's what I'm going to call her."

"It suits her." He chuckles. "I guess we need another couple pairs of pink sparkle boots, huh?"

Right on cue, Luna kicks her little thighs wildly.

"Pink sparkie boots!" Josh says, speaking for Luna. "Yippee!"

I can't help smiling again. "I already love them," I whisper. "More than I thought possible."

Josh shoots me a crooked smile. "Welcome to fatherhood."

I touch Luna's tiny toes, suddenly desperate to feel her tiny body pressed against my chest. "When will we be allowed to hold them?" I ask a nearby nurse.

"As soon as they're off the ventilators. Hopefully, no more than a few days—maybe even tomorrow. Their lungs seem to be doing pretty well."

"That's great news," Josh says. He grabs Sol's hand. "You and your sister are little beasts, aren't you, Little Miss Sunshine?"

"Switch with me, Josh. I don't want Sunshine to think I don't love her." We trade incubators, and stroke Marisol's soft feet. "Hi, Little Miss Sunshine," I say, my heart leaping and panging the same way it did when I was touching Luna.

"Hi, Luna," Josh whispers, laying his large hand on her tiny chest. "Nice to meet you, Crazy Monkey. I'm your Uncle Josh."

"If I'm Uncle Jo Jo, then you're sure as hell not going to be Uncle Josh," I say. "I'm thinking Uncle Joshie Woshie has a nice ring to it."

"Oh, hell no."

"Oh, hell *yes*. Karma's a bitch, motherfucker."

The nurse behind us clears her throat.

"They won't be able to say that, anyway," Josh whispers. "It'll come out like Unkie Jshwshsh."

"Sarah and I will work on it with them, every day for the rest of their lives until they get it," I say. And the minute those fantastical words leave my mouth, my heart wrenches in my chest like I'm being stabbed with a rusty blade. Why am I letting myself envision a future in which Sarah and I get to teach our children to say "Uncle Joshie Woshie" together?

"She's gonna be okay," Josh says, reading my mind. "She's the strongest person I know."

I blink back my tears. "If she doesn't pull through . . ."

Josh's jaw muscles pulse. "She will."

"But if she *doesn't* . . ." I swallow hard. "I'm going with her."

Josh clenches his jaw. "Jonas, look at me. That option is unavailable to you now." He motions to the babies. "They need you now."

I look down at my tiny daughters, processing what my brother said to me—and with instant clarity, realize he's right. Holy fuck. *I'm a father.* These miniature people are *mine.* Forever. No turning back. And I can't let them down.

All of a sudden, I feel like I'm standing at a fork in the road. Am I going to be the kind of father who blows his brains out while his kid is making him a turkey burger downstairs? Or am I going to be the kind of father who climbs any mountain and slays any dragon for his baby girls—even if that mountain or dragon happens to be himself?

"I'm not going anywhere," I choke out.

"Good. Focus on your babies."

"I will." I swallow hard. "But, Josh, if Sarah doesn't pull through—"

Josh grabs my shoulders. "Sarah's going to be fine. You know how I know that? Because she's Sarah *Fucking* Cruz, the biggest badass I know besides *you.*"

8

SARAH

I'm standing inside a massive cave on the lip of a towering waterfall, peering into the dark abyss below me. A warm, driving rain pelts me from above, drenching my skin and hair and clothes. If it weren't for the headlamp on my helmet, I'd be enveloped by utter blackness without reprieve.

I can't move.

I can't speak.

I'm in pain.

Is this rain-battered cave a gigantic metaphor for my own demise—a construct my mind has created to make death understandable to me? No, I don't think I'm dead, because every inch of my body hurts. *Juepucha culo.*

If this is death, though, then I'm officially pissed because the brochure said I'd feel nothing but eternal serenity all the dead-long day.

The rain is gaining in intensity. I look down and discover I'm holding my sons, one in each arm, swaddled in blue blankets. I peer at them through the dark, my headlamp barely cutting a swath through the driving rain

—but I can't make out their tiny faces. Hey, hold up. Aren't my babies supposed to be in my belly right now?

I look down and the rocks beneath my bare feet crumble away into the darkness below. I step back, trying to find firmer ground, but the rocky ledge beneath my feet continues shifting.

I tilt my face up and let the warm, sheeting rain pound me in the face.

Wait.

How is it raining *inside* a cave?

I stick out my tongue. The rain tastes salty and metallic. The smell of blood fills my nostrils. I jerk violently and scramble to focus my headlamp on the bundles in my arms. My light illuminates a crimson-soaked blanket in my right arm and another in my left. Dark, wet, viscous blood is dripping off the bundles and onto the rocks below me, making me gag. I try to shriek, but nothing comes out of my mouth.

I have to save my babies from this torrent of blood! I look down toward the dark water below and my knees knock uncontrollably. That's a long, dark, scary-as-shit way down. I can't do this. *I need Jonas.*

"Sarah," Jonas' calm voice beneath me says. "I'm right here." A small orb of light illuminates the surface of the black water below and Jonas' hand extends into the orb. And yet, I hear his voice directly into my ear. "Come back to me, my precious baby," he chokes out. "Don't leave me. I need you."

My sweet Jonas needs me. It's all I need to know. I take a deep breath, hug my babies to me, and hurl myself off the edge of the waterfall. But as I fall, I lose my grip on my babies. I try to scream as they float away from me, but I can't make a sound.

Ink-black water floods my mouth and rushes down my throat, before strong arms grab me and pull me up, up, up past the surface of the dark water.

I open my eyes and shriek, "*The babies!*" But nothing comes out of my mouth.

I'm in a darkened hospital room. Jonas is seated next to my bed, his strong arms draped across me. His fingers woven into mine. There are tubes and wires attached to me.

"Sarah," Jonas whispers, obviously overcome with emotion. "Oh, thank God."

"The babies," I say—or *try* to say. I can't make sound come out of my mouth.

"They're in the NICU," Jonas says. He strokes my face tenderly. "Two little girls who look exactly like their beautiful mommy."

A surge of pure love floods me, but I can't seem to keep my eyes open. The pain is too great. I'm too tired. I'm slipping away. I reach toward my husband, trying to hold onto him, trying to stay with him in the light, but I'm too weak to resist slipping back into the darkness.

"Sarah?" Jonas whispers hoarsely. "*Fuck.* I love you, Sarah. Don't go, baby." His voice breaks. "Please know that I love you so much and need you to come back to me."

All of a sudden, I'm standing at a jewelry counter with Jonas.

"S-A-R-A-H," Jonas says to the saleswoman, handing her a platinum bracelet to engrave.

"And you, miss?" the saleswoman asks me.

I'm disoriented. "I don't know," I choke out. "I don't know what I'm supposed to do."

"Think about our love," he coos, his nose nuzzling my ear. "Let our love lead you back to me, Sarah."

"I don't know if I can make it back to you," I admit. "I'm so tired."

"You have to come back. Please, Sarah."

"I don't know if I get to decide."

"If not you, then who?"

"Well, you know. *God.*"

"Fuck God."

"*Jonas.* Sh. You can't say that." I look around, paranoid someone will overhear him.

"I mean it," Jonas says. "God's been an asshole to me my whole life and I'm sick and tired of his bullshit." His nostrils flare. "*I'm* God now, and my first order of business is decreeing my beloved Sarah shall come back to me."

"I'll do my best."

I look down. I'm holding a huge plastic cup filled with liquid that looks like lemonade. My wedding band is on my finger and my engraved platinum bracelet on my wrist. Samba music blares in my ears.

I look to my left and there's Jonas, swigging from a big cup and shaking his gorgeous ass to the infectious beat of the music, his engraved platinum bracelet on his wrist, as usual. Before us, a parade of floats and sparkling, shaking asses passes by.

Ah, yes. I remember this. We're in Rio de Janeiro for Carnival during my second year of law school. On this particular night, we're both drinking *caipirinhas* till we can't feel our faces or toes.

As the parade of shaking asses continues moving past us to the high-energy beat of the music, Jonas wraps me in his arms, gropes my backside, and grinds his hard-on into me. "Tell your ass I'm coming for it later!" he shouts over the loud music, before throwing his head back and howling like a drunken wolf.

I burst out laughing. God, I love Drunk Jonas. Especially when he's getting turned on by a parade of gyrating Brazilian asses.

A taxi pulls up in front of us to let some people out, and Jonas grabs my arm and pulls me through the open door. "Come on, baby," he says, squeezing my bottom as he guides me into the backseat. "Prelude officially over. Your ass is *mine.*"

When we arrive at our rented beachfront bungalow, Drunk Jonas drags me onto our moonlit deck overlooking the sand, bends me over the railing, yanks my skirt up and my panties down, and bites my ass so freaking hard, I'm rendered momentarily mute from the delicious pain.

A second later, his erection plows into my wetness with astonishing force—so hard my knees give way—and I yelp at the sensation. This is not the way Jonas normally does things—this is pure animal force—a bit sloppy, even —and, holy fuck, I like it. He's ramming my G-spot with his massive erection, while groping every inch of me like he's frisking a felon, and it doesn't take long before my body begins clenching from deep inside.

People are walking on the moonlit beach in the distance, but Jonas doesn't give a fuck if anyone sees or hears us in the dark shadows of our deck, and neither do I. He grabs my hair and yanks my head back, growling in my ear as he fucks me, biting my neck, groping my breasts, ripping me in two—and, all the while, whispering to me about how he's going to fuck me till I "pass the fuck out." And through it all, I'm thinking an incoherent stream of syllables that, roughly translated, mean something akin to, "Make me your bitch."

When I climax, Jonas doesn't. As usual, booze has given my hunky-monkey husband superhuman-stamina. After pulverizing me for what seems an awfully long time, he pulls out, roughly turns me around, puts his hands on my face, and blurts, "I fucking *love* the *fuck* out of you, Sarah Cruz!" And then, without warning, he reaches down, picks me up at my knees, throws me over his broad shoulder, my ass cheeks hanging out there for the world to see, and strides into our bungalow.

He hurls me onto the bed onto my belly, rips off my clothes, and spanks my naked ass so hard, I stop breathing for a brief moment; and then he gropes and licks and bites my backside—every square inch of it from sea to shining sea, without exclusion, all the while grunting and moaning and extolling the virtues of my assets with exuberance.

"Do it, baby," I groan. Jonas has surprisingly never pushed to penetrate my final frontier. And since I've never offered, it's simply never happened. But right now, I'm feeling like a minx—a minx who can't feel her cheeks or toes—and I'm ready to try this final sex act with him. "Jonas," I slur. "*Do it.*"

Without another word, he leaps off the bed and bounds to his suitcase in the corner. I hear Jonas fumbling with something—a bottle of lube, I think—and when he returns to me, his fingers slide into my ass crack and straight up my ass with surprising ease.

"Relax, baby," Jonas whispers, his lubed fingers confidently working me. "You're gonna love it."

My breathing has become shallow. Every muscle in my body is tense with anticipation, even as my clit flutters with excitement. Will my body be able to cash this particular check, after all?

"Relax," Jonas coos, his confident fingers skimming up and down my crack. "I'm going to make you come harder than you ever have, baby."

I'm suddenly wondering when was the last time I pooped? Oh my God. Is he going to fuck the poop out of me?

"Poop," I blurt.

Jonas laughs. "*Relax.*" He rubs my back and leans down into my ear. "*Relax,* baby."

I feel him crawling on top of me to mount me—his fingers enter me again—and then, oh boy, yep, there's no mistaking what's just happened. He's in. The man just staked his flag in my moon. How do I know this to be true, given my lack of experience with this particular sex act? Oh, I dunno. Maybe because both my eyeballs just popped out of my head and rolled onto the floor.

Jonas moans loudly, clearly enjoying whatever sensation my tight ass is providing, and, although I'm not yet sure if my body's completely on board or not, the sound of his unadulterated pleasure makes my body spasm from a whole new set of muscles.

"Okay?" he asks, gasping. He's moving gently, but I'm still feeling every inch of him.

My reply is nonverbal. I clutch the bed cover, trying to decide if I'm experiencing something good or bad. Oh man, this is a whole new sensation.

He shifts slightly, and his erection suddenly finds my G-spot from an angle I've never experienced before. And that's it. I'm zinged with pleasure that's so intense, I growl like a bear in heat.

"Am I hurting you?" he chokes out.

"Good," I gasp out. "Oh my God. *Good.*"

He reaches around to fondle my more traditional lady parts, and Holy Taboo, Batman, that does the trick. After a few minutes of dual stimulation, I climax with the most intense orgasm of my life, just like he promised. The pleasure is so intense, in fact, I burst into tears.

Jonas immediately pulls out of me. "Did I hurt you?"

I shake my head and slur something that sounds like, "Beans."

He kneels next to me on the bed. "Why are you crying?"

I shake my head. I don't know why the hell I'm crying, so how can I explain it to him?

"Sarah, talk to me. Are you crying from pleasure or pain?"

I turn my head to look at him, resting my drunken cheek on the pillow. "Yes."

"Good or bad?"

I smile through my tears. "*Good.*"

He hoots at the ceiling. "Fuck yeah."

"Get yours," I choke out. "Bring it home."

"Oh, I already got mine, right along with you." He laughs. "When you came, you squeezed my dick so tight, it almost shot off and rocketed out your mouth."

"*Jonas!*"

He laughs hysterically.

"Even for you, that was pretty crass." I roll my eyes. "Just 'cause a girl lets you fuck her up the ass doesn't mean she doesn't want to be treated like a lady."

He sighs happily and flops onto the bed next to me. "Good times in Rio were had by all." He looks at me with half-mast eyes and puckers his lips at me like he's a blowfish kissing me through the air. "Sarah Cruz," he whispers, before blowing me another kiss. "My precious baby." There's another long pause—so long, in fact, I'm not sure if he's passed out or if he's merely thinking deep, drunken thoughts. Well, hmm. It seems like the party's over. Okay. He must have passed out.

"Goodnight," I whisper.

"And guess what *else* I am?" Jonas suddenly says.

"What the fuck?" I open my eyes and look at him with sleepy eyes.

"Guess what *else* I am, My Magnificent Sarah?" He flashes me a toothy smile.

"Um." I twist my mouth. "What else besides *what*?"

"Besides drunk."

"Oh. Gorgeous?"

"Well, yeah. That goes without saying. I'm Jonas Fucking Faraday. Women beg me to fuck them because I've got sad eyes and luscious lips and because I'm a fucking woman wizard." He snorts. "But guess what *else*?"

"Silly?"

"Never."

"Creepy?"

"Always. But what *else*, My Beautiful Intake Agent?"

I smile broadly. He only calls me that when he's drunk, which he so rarely is. "Intense?"

"You're a terrible guesser. You're starting to annoy me, you know that?"

"Well, jeez, hell if I know—oh, wait, I know. *Drunk*!"

He exhales, annoyed. "That was the first thing I said."

"Oh."

"The question is what *else*, numnuts."

I burst out laughing and so does he.

"You're not supposed to call your beloved wife

numnuts. That's what a 'bro-ski' should call his fraternity brother."

"I wasn't in a fraternity."

"Okay, then your actual brother."

"Josh was in a fraternity. That's how he met his best friends, Henn and Reed. Josh has always known how to make friends and get people to like him."

I laugh. "I was simply saying you should call your *brother* numnuts, not your wife. And, by the way, you know how to make friends and get people to like you, too."

"No, I don't. You're the first best friend I've ever had, who wasn't my brother, numnuts."

I'm practically crying with laughter. "Don't call your wife, numnuts! That's the kind of thing to call your brother. And by the way, you're my best friend, too."

"Jesus, Sarah! Don't mention my brother when I'm getting my fuck on. Talk about a boner-killer."

"What the fuck! You just went on and on about how your brother knows how to make friends."

"I did?"

"Yeah, numnuts, you did. And you've already gotten your fuck on, numnuts. We're done now."

"Oh. For now, anyway. Numnuts."

We both scream with laughter and call each other "numnuts" several more times, which only makes us laugh some more. Who knows if we're being objectively funny, but in this moment, we both think we're the two funniest people in the world.

After we've finally calmed down, there's another long silence. More deep thoughts, I presume. I throw my arm over his broad chest and close my eyes. Oh, how I love my hunky-monkey-drunky husband with the big ol' dick. I sigh happily. I hope my butt doesn't hurt too much in the morning—but if it does, it was well worth it.

"You know what I am?" Jonas says out of nowhere.

I open my eyes as best I can. "Drunk."

"That is correct. But what *else* am I?"

"Dude. Just tell me already."

He sits up and grins down at me. "I'm *hungry*."

Before I can even process what he means by that statement, he turns my limp body onto my back, spreads my thighs wide and begins licking me voraciously for, oh, a solid forty-five seconds or so. Until, suddenly, with a loud gorilla-grunt, my husband heaves his drunken body next to mine on the mattress and promptly passes the fuck out.

9
JONAS

There's only one visitor at a time allowed in Sarah's room in the ICU, unfortunately. And for the past two days, I've grabbed the lion's share of that time. And so, when a nurse pokes her head in and says Sarah's mom is hoping to have some time with her daughter, I wrench myself from Sarah's unconscious body, kiss Gloria on her way in, and head into the hallway.

I'm intending to grab Josh and Kat from the waiting room to invite them to visit the babies with me in the NICU. But when I get in there, I'm surprised to see some new faces in there, along with Josh and Kat: Henn and his girlfriend, Hannah; plus, two of Kat's four brothers—the two older ones who live in Seattle, along with their wives.

I greet everyone tersely and thank them for coming. But quickly, my full attention falls squarely on Henn. "Can I talk to you privately for a second?" I ask him.

"Sure."

I lead Henn across the hallway and into an empty

examination room, which is where I close the door and address him with blazing eyes.

"Any new activity?" I ask.

"About . . .? Oh. The Club? No. That's not why I came here, Jonas. Hannah and I flew in to show our support."

"The best support you can give me right now is to assure me you're still monitoring the situation closely—"

"Of course, I'm monitoring things. And so is Special Agent Eric. We're both confident we totally shut them down. But if not, and the organization is somehow rebuilding, we're confident whoever's in charge now has absolutely no idea you and Sarah took them down."

I run a hand through my hair. "I know you keep saying that, but—"

"Hey, guys." It's Josh, entering the small room. "What's going on, Jonas? Everything okay."

"Jonas wants some reassurance I've been keeping an eye on things," Henn explains. "And I told him I have been. Of course."

Josh exhales. "You don't need to be worrying about that right now, Jonas."

"If not that, then what?" I shout, instantly at full volume. "Should I worry about Sarah? The babies? The fact that I'm this close to total and complete *obliteration* and there's nothing I can fucking do about it?"

Josh puts his hand on my shoulder. "Jonas, calm down. You're trying to pick a fight with me because—"

I shake his hand off me. "Because you're acting like a condescending prick." Without conscious thought, I shove my brother's chest forcefully, and he stumbles back, looking shocked. And that does it. In a flash, two days' worth of adrenaline, anger, fear, panic, and exhaustion overtake me. And suddenly, I can't think of anything I want to do more than beat the shit out of my brother.

I lurch at Josh, intending to shove him again, but he jerks sideways and shoves me from the side. At which point, we lunge toward each other, both our tempers unleashed.

"Whoa, whoa, whoa!" Henn shouts, wedging himself between us. "Stop it, guys!"

"Beating me up won't change anything!" Josh shouts, his blue eyes blazing. "Not that you could beat me up, even if you tried."

"Watch me," I spit back. "One punch, and you'll be out cold."

"Stop it, guys!" Henn says. "Stop. *Jesus.*" He gathers himself. "Here's an idea. Instead of behaving like walking clichés—tortured heroes who think they can vanquish their demons through pointless violence—how about you do something totally outside the box, like, I dunno, talking about your feelings with people you trust and asking for help? How about that?"

Josh and I stare at each other for a moment, our chests heaving, as Henn continues wedging himself between us . . .until, suddenly, Josh bursts into laughter.

"Wait a goddamned minute," Josh says. "You mean to tell me pointless violence won't fix this situation?"

"Unfortunately, not," Henn confirms. "Sorry about that."

"Well, shit, that sucks," Josh says. He looks at me and shakes his head. "Come on, Jonas. Truce. Unclench your jaw. Unflex your arms. Take a deep breath."

I take a deep breath, as instructed, but remain silent.

"Are you going to attack me again or not?" Josh asks.

"I need to know if I can turn my back on you without suffering bodily harm."

I shrug. "Turn around and find out."

Josh puts his hand on my shoulder and smiles. "*Talking lets the feelings out.*"

It's a lifelong inside joke between us—something we've been saying to each other since our childhood therapy sessions.

I exhale. "I'm sorry. I think I'm losing my mind"

"Understandably. You're sleep deprived and scared to death."

"It's no excuse. Sorry."

"We're all good." He squeezes my shoulder. "What do you say we introduce Uncle Henny to his beautiful nieces? They got off their ventilators an hour ago, while you were with Sarah."

"*They did?*" I blurt. Even in my present state, the news is actually making me smile.

"Check your texts once in a while, brother."

"What are we waiting for?" I say, suddenly feeling amped and excited. "Let's go see those cuties, breathing on their own."

"Real quick," Josh says, halting my movement. And when I turn to look at him, he slaps his face, *hard*. Which, of course, prompts me to slap mine with the same unbridled fervor.

"What the fuck?" Henn mutters.

"It's how my brother and I have always signaled we're ready to 'move on' after any sort of display of feelings," Josh explains.

"*That* was a display of feelings?" Henn says.

"In the world we grew up in, yes," Josh says. He winks at me. "You ready to show Henn your babies?"

"Fuck yeah."

"Would you mind if we grab Hannah on the way to the babies?" Henn says. "The whole flight here she was talking about wanting to see them."

I pause with my hand on the doorknob. Of course, I know Henn and Hannah live in LA, not Seattle. But it hadn't occurred to me before now they must have dropped everything to fly here, when they heard the news.

"You and Hannah flew to Seattle to be here for Sarah?" I ask lamely, still processing their kindness.

"Yeah, and for you," Henn says. "We caught the first possible flight, the minute we found out."

"Thank you," I whisper.

"Of course," Henn says. "We're *family*."

A lump rises in my throat. This is new to me. I'm used to Josh dropping everything to help me, as needed. But until this moment, I didn't realize I had friends who'd do that for me, too. Now that I think about it, though, if Henn or Hannah were the ones in need, I'd move heaven and earth to help them.

"We're family," I whisper. "I feel that way, too. Thank you." I open the door to the small room and clear my throat. "Wait till you see the babies, Henny. You won't believe how much they look like their mother."

"Yeah," Josh agrees. "Lucky for them."

10

SARAH

My mind is careening through time and space, soaring through the patchwork quilt of memories that comprise The Love Story of Jonas and Sarah.

Suddenly, the memories stop flickering past me on a dime.

Apparently, I've decided to linger in one particular memory.

Thailand.

Jonas brought me to this beautiful country three weeks ago to celebrate my recent law school graduation, and, thus far, the trip has been pure magic. We've visited Jonas' favorite caves and climbing spots. We've island-hopped. And for our last stop, we're hanging out in Bangkok for a few days.

By sheer coincidence, Josh's good friend, a record label owner named Reed Rivers, happens to be in Bangkok tonight, too. Apparently, he's attending a VIP nightclub appearance by one of his hottest artists. A hip-hop star named 2Real. And since I'm a huge fan of hip hop in general, and especially 2Real, my sweet husband has kindly agreed to grin and bear it and take me to his show.

When we first step inside the glittering nightclub and make our way to the VIP lounge upstairs, I feel physically dizzy from the sheer spectacle of the place. It's like someone put a Las Vegas nightclub into a blender with Asian décor and strobe lights. Or, hell, maybe it's all the champagne coursing through my veins that's making me feel this dizzy. Because Jonas and I sure downed quite a bit of it earlier over dinner.

As Jonas chats with Josh's buddy, Reed, I take a seat on an empty couch and survey the crowded nightclub below. There's a stage down there, where 2Real will appear soon. And the very thought is making me breathless with excitement.

"Is this seat taken?" someone asks, and when I turn to look, it's motherfucking 2Real himself!

"Yes!" I shout. "I mean, no. Please. Sit. Hi!"

Chuckling, Will sits down, extending his hand to me. "I'm Will," he says, using the given name I've seen on his Wikipedia page, rather than his famous stage name.

"Nice to meet you, Will," I say. "I'm a huge fan. I'm Sarah Faraday. My brother-in-law is Reed's good friend from college, Josh Faraday."

"I love Josh! We hung out in Vegas last year. He actually did me a huge favor recently. Good guy."

I snicker. "If I had a dollar for every time I heard someone say Josh Faraday did them a huge favor, I'd have a stack of hundred-dollar bills as high as my head."

He leans toward me, obviously trying to hear me above the loud music in the club. "You said you're Josh's *sister*?"

"No, his sister-*in-law*," I shout. "My husband is Josh's twin brother, Jonas." I point toward Jonas, who's standing about fifteen feet away, still chatting with Reed. And even after all this time, I can't help swooning at the sight of my gorgeous husband.

Will studies Jonas for a moment. "He looks a lot like his brother."

"Yeah, they're fraternal twins. Their personalities are really different, though." There's a pause in the conversation, during which the full force of this surreal situation slams into me: *I'm chatting with the guy whose song is my frickin' ringtone right now.* "'Crash' is my ringtone!" I blurt, referring to his incredibly catchy song that's been at the top of the music charts for weeks. "They play it during my spin class all the time, and I sing along to every word, even the super-fast rapping parts." Oh God, someone put a gag on me. I'm a babbling fool. And yet, I can't keep myself from adding, "I guess you could say I'm a world-class spin-rapper." Oh God, no. That was a bridge too far.

Will leans his ear toward me. "You said you're a world-class *badminton* player?"

I burst out laughing. "No, although that would have been a much cooler thing to be. I said I'm a world-class *spin-rapper*—because I rap all the words to your song during spin class." I roll my eyes at myself. "Basically, I just revealed myself to be a total dork, thanks to my nerves."

"Why are you nervous?"

I motion to him, like "duh."

"Don't be," he says. "I'm as big a dork as you are."

"Impossible."

"I am. Ask me anything. You'll see."

"*Anything*?"

"Anything."

"Wow." I consider for a moment. "Has the reality of your astronomical success measured up to the fantasy of it, or has any part of your success come as a surprise or disappointment to you?"

Will raises his eyebrows. "Wow. I guess we're done with flattery and small talk, huh?"

I wince. "Not what you meant by 'ask me anything'?"

He throws his head back and laughs. "No, it's cool. I just didn't realize I'd sat down next to the Latina Oprah."

"Oh God, I'm so sorry."

"No, it's all good. I hate small talk, anyway. Did I get that right, by the way? Are you Latina?"

"I am. My grandmother came to the US from Colombia."

"Cool." He glances at Jonas while sipping his drink. "How long have you been married?"

"A year and a half."

He smiles. "So, does the reality of marriage live up to the fantasy of it, or is there some part that's come as a surprise or disappointment?"

I grin at him. "Marriage to my amazing husband *far* exceeds any fantasy. He's my perfect match and I'm the luckiest girl in the whole world."

He looks surprise. "Wow. I've never heard a woman talk about her man like that before."

"Really? Wow. I feel sorry for whatever women you've been talking to."

"My ex-girlfriends, mainly."

I shrug. "Sounds like a 'you' problem, then. I hope you don't mind me saying that."

"The truth is the truth." Will swigs his drink. "It's

okay. I don't have the time or attention-span for a girl-friend these days, anyway." He rolls his eyes. "As I've recently proved in spades."

"Hey, at least you know that about yourself now, so you don't give anyone false expectations. My husband is fond of saying 'under-promise and over-perform.' I think that'd be a good rule of thumb for you, considering how crazy your life must be right now."

"Damn, you're smart *and* beautiful?" He looks at Jonas again. "Too bad you're married. You're exactly my type."

"Thank you. But, yes, I'm very, *very* married to the most amazing man in the world."

"Congratulations."

He sounds sincere, actually. Not sarcastic or rude in the slightest. But, still, I feel the need to say, "If you want me to move so you can talk to someone else who might—"

"No, no. I'm enjoying talking to you. Once we got past the small talk, anyway." He winks.

"Speaking of which, you never answered my question."

"No?"

"No. And you did say I could ask you anything, you might recall."

"True. But I think I'm going to need another drink if I'm going to go that deep." He motions to a cocktail wait-ress and orders drinks and shots for both of us. "So, while we're waiting on those," he says, "I think we should come up with your rapper name. You can't be a world-class spin-rapper without one."

"True."

"M.C. Oprah?" he asks.

"I'd get a cease-and-desist letter from Oprah's legal team before I could say 'Wave your hands in the air.'"

He laughs. "Lil Big Talk?"

"So, you think I'm a total blowhard? That's what you're saying."

He chuckles. "No. 'Big Talk' as opposed to 'Small Talk,' because you don't have time for that shit. It's a compliment."

"Ah. Well, thanks, but I still think it sounds like I'm a blowhard."

"Never."

A guy approaches Will, obviously a fan, and Will graciously shakes his hand and leans in for a selfie on the guy's phone. I glance at Jonas with Reed, thinking maybe I should get up and let this fan talk to Will for a bit. But when I return to Will, the fan is already walking away.

"Okay, back to your rapper name," Will says. "It's got to be good. You're *world-class*, remember. It can't be fucking bush league."

"Dude, I know. But I'm drawing a blank. I need your expertise."

Will purses his lips. "What's your maiden name?"

"Cruz."

"*Boom.* You could do the one-word name thing. Eminem. Kanye. Jay-Z. *Cruz.*"

I gasp. "Oh, I've got it! I could be O-A-P Cruz! I've got an O-A-P tattoo that could be on my album cover!"

"Boom. Love it. We're done."

The waitress returns with our drinks and we both down a shot together.

"So, what's O-A-P stand for?" Will asks.

I blush crimson, as I realize I've drunkenly said something I shouldn't have.

"That's a secret," I say, putting my index finger across my lips. "Something only my husband knows." I snicker. "But trust me, it's badass."

Will raises an eyebrow. "Intriguing. At least, tell me where's the tattoo?"

I shrug. "A place only my husband will see."

"*Damn, girl*. Your husband's a lucky motherfucker."

"It's not luck. He's a god among men. A sex god.."

Will chuckles. "Okay, well, whatever OAP stands for, it's definitely the right call for your rapper name. OAP Cruz, it is."

"Phew. Glad we got that settled. You never know when a world-class spin-rapper might be called to duty."

"Exactly. The emcee's got to know how to introduce you."

"Truth. Speaking of being called to duty, aren't you supposed to perform tonight?"

"Yeah, in a little bit. We like letting the crowd get really drunk first. That way, if I fuck up, they don't even notice."

I laugh. "I saw you on *Saturday Night Live* last month, Will. Your days of fucking up, if they ever existed, are long over."

He grins. "Are you *sure* I can't convince you to divulge what O-A-P stands for?"

"I'm sure."

He taps his ear. "Whisper it right here, OAP. I promise I won't tell a soul."

"Nope."

Will flashes me his most charming smile. "What if I tell you about all my tattoos? I never tell people about them, but I'll tell you." Without waiting for my reply, he rolls up his sleeve and points to a tattoo of an elaborate flower on his forearm. "This is my mom's favorite flower. I got it here so I can always bring my momma flowers no matter where or when I see her." He rolls up his other sleeve and points to a dragon with a huge heart. "I got matching hearts with my girl back in high school because I thought we'd last *forever*." He chuckles. "But then she slept with my best friend so that was that—so I added the dragon to camouflage it." He flashes me his most seductive smile. "Okay, your turn."

"Thanks for sharing. But I'll never tell."

"Damn, OAP. You're killing me."

"Says the guy who never answered my question, despite saying I could ask him 'anything.'"

"Oh yeah. I forgot about that. Told you my attention span was for shit these days. What was the question again?"

"You know what the question was. You're just stalling for time."

Will bursts out laughing. "OAP Cruz doesn't fuck around! Ha!" He throws back another shot before leaning forward, running his hand through his hair, and saying, "Okay, Latina Oprah. Here's your hard-earned scoop. The honest answer is that the reality of my success has been a mixed bag. There's been money, women, fame, travel, and as much weed as a man could ever want. So that part is fan-fucking-tastic. But it's also lonely as fuck to be me, as cliché as it sounds. Soul-crushing, at times."

"I'm sorry to hear that."

"It's my own damned fault, mostly. I recently cheated on my girlfriend, Carmen, and she dumped me. Rightfully so. And ever since, I can't stand small talk with strangers, even more than usual. Honestly, the only interesting conversation I've had lately with a new person was with this world-class spin-rapper I met in Bangkok. I sat down next to her because she looked so much like Carmen, I couldn't believe my eyes. But when I found out how cool she was, and also, sadly, that she was happily married, she only made me think about how much I blew it with Carmen, even more."

As I'm staring at Will, mouth agape, not sure what to say, his large bodyguard who's been standing nearby, strides over to Will and says something into his ear. So, while they're talking, I glance at Jonas to check in. To my surprise, he's staring at me with blazing eyes while Reed looks at his phone—and when our eyes meet, Jonas raises his eyebrows, apparently asking me if I'm okay. I nod and raise my champagne glass to him, confirming I'm good, that I'm enjoying myself, and he nods, his jaw muscles pulsing. I know Jonas trusts me completely, as he should. But I also know he's a possessive man who's probably not enjoying watching me engrossed in conversation with a handsome superstar.

"So, tell me, OAP Cruz," Will says, drawing my gaze away from Jonas. "What makes your husband so fucking amazing? I'm assuming he's rich as fuck, since he's Josh Faraday's brother. And that probably doesn't hurt. But what else is so fucking amazing about him?"

I bristle. "My husband's money has nothing to do with the reasons I love him."

"How do you know that for sure, unless you also loved him before he was rich?"

"We could live in a mud hut, and I'd still be head over heels in love with him. Two weeks ago, we camped outside a cave in Mae Do and had as much fun together as the times we've stayed in luxury."

"I'm sorry. I was trying to be funny."

"You failed at your attempt. You were rude."

"I was. Sorry." He smirks. "You're definitely Latina. All fiery and shit."

"*Any* woman of *any* heritage would be offended to be called a gold digger, Will. Any woman with self-respect, anyway."

His smile broadens. "Damn. I shouldn't admit this, but watching you get pissed is really fun."

"You're right. You shouldn't admit that. It makes you sound like a jerk."

"Okay, so tell me what makes your husband so great, so I can strive to become more like him and less of a jerk."

I shrug. "He's kind and generous—and I don't mean he's 'generous' with his money, though he is. I mean he's generous with his heart and soul. He's also funny and weird, in the best ways." I snicker. "And on top of all that, Jonas worships at the altar of 'sexual excellence,' which he calls *sexcellence*. Talk about a complete package."

Will's face lights up. "Sexcellence? Holy fuck, that's sick! Can I steal that for use in a song?"

"I don't see why not. Jonas abhors hip hop, so he'll never know, anyway."

As Will clinks my glass, Reed and Jonas appear at the side of the couch.

Reed says to his artist, "It's showtime, 2Real." As Will rises from the couch, Reed addresses Jonas and me. "Do you two want to watch 2Real's show from the VIP section at the foot of the stage?"

"Hell yeah!" I exclaim, leaping up from the couch. But when I look at my taciturn husband, it's clear we're not on the same page. "Actually, never mind," I say. "I think we'll watch from here."

Reed shakes his head. "Come on, Jonas. The show will be much better downstairs."

"Go on, Sarah," Jonas says. "I don't want you missing out."

We go back and forth briefly, with Jonas ultimately insisting I head downstairs with Reed to watch the show, up close and personal amid the rest of 2Real's rabid fans, while he remains here, quite happily, to enjoy the show at a comfortable distance.

"Will you take Sarah downstairs to the VIP area and make sure she's safe?" Jonas asks Reed.

"I'll do one better than that," Reed says. He addresses me. "How'd you like to watch the show with me, from the wing of the stage?"

"I'd love it!" I squeal. "Oh my gosh, thank you!"

"Keep a close eye on her," Jonas says to Reed. "She's had a lot to drink, and this place is packed to the rafters."

Reed points to the large bodyguard who's been keeping tabs on Will. "Barry will be with us the whole time. I promise Sarah will be safe and sound."

Jonas squeezes my hand. "Have fun, baby. But be smart. You've been drinking."

"And now I'm drunk on love!" Laughing at Jonas' eyeroll, I throw my arms around his neck and kiss him. "Thank you for bringing me here. I know how much you hate nightclubs and hip hop."

"Anything for you. Have fun."

"It's now or never, Sarah!" Reed calls to me, as he begins walking away with Will and the bodyguard. "See you on the flipside, husband!" With that, I kiss Jonas' cheek and take off as fast as my tipsy legs will carry me, laughing with glee as I go.

11

SARAH

Reed told me 2Real collaborated recently with a wildly popular Thai group on a new song. Hence, the reason Reed and 2Real came to Thailand in the first place—to promote that song. And now, all five members of that Thai group are performing one of their hits to open the show, as 2Real stands in the wings with Reed, his bodyguard, and me, awaiting his cue to head onstage.

As the performers do their thing, I glance toward the balcony and spot Jonas' muscled frame among the few people remaining up there. I wave excitedly at him from behind Will's shoulder and Jonas smiles and waves back, letting me know he's every bit as thrilled to be standing up there, away from the action, as I am to be in the thick of it.

The song ends and one of the performers onstage says something in Thai before yelling, "2Real!"

As the crowd goes wild, Will bounds onstage. And two seconds after that, a bass-heavy beat hurtles all performers, including Will, into glorious action.

"This is their collaboration!" Reed yells to me. "It'll be released worldwide next week!"

"I love it!" I shout back. And it's the truth. In fact, the song is so catchy, I can't help bopping and dancing to it like a madwoman, even though I only understand Will's portion of the lyrics. As I'm dancing, I happen to glance up at my husband in the balcony, curious to see his reaction to the song, and the smolder I see on Jonas' face takes my breath away. He's watching me, not the show. And, clearly, he's thoroughly enjoying my body's happy, drunken gyrations.

The song ends and the crowd explodes, prompting me to wrench my attention off my smoldering husband and back onto the stage.

"You ready to 'Crash' into me?" Will shouts, and, of course, the crowd goes apeshit. And even more so when the famous beat begins, and Will begins rapping his now-ubiquitous rapid-fire lyrics.

Given my status as a world-class spin-rapper, I sing and rap along to every word, even the most challenging, spitfire rap refrains, and even more so when Will turns around and locks eyes directly with me.

When Will sees me rapping enthusiastically along with him, he smiles broadly before turning back around to face the audience. And I must admit, I feel thrilled he got to see me put my money where my mouth is, given my big talk earlier on the balcony.

A few minutes later, as Will's famous song reaches its bone-vibrating final chorus, Will stops rapping and singing, but, instead, lets the famous beat continue without him.

"Keep that beat going, man," Will says, apparently talking to his sound engineer. He says, "I want to thank you for making this song number one around the world."

The crowd cheers.

"To thank you," Will continues, "I've got a special treat for you tonight. Something that's going to blow your fucking minds, so keep those cameras recording!" The few people who haven't been recording 2Real's show until now, begin doing so. At which point, Will says, "You're not going to believe this, but there's a world-class *spin*-rapper in the house tonight."

Oh, shit.

"In fact," he says, "she came all the way from Seattle to help me with this performance tonight."

Oh, fuck. *No.*

"So, give it up for . . . O-A-P *Cruz*!"

As the crowd explodes, Will turns around and beckons to me, his face split in two with his wide smile. When I shake my head, mortified, Will strides toward me in the wings, his arms outstretched. And that's when I feel Reed's hand on my shoulder and his mouth against my ear.

"Don't leave him hanging out there," Reed says. "Go on." He gives my back a nudge, and the next thing I know, I'm sliding my hand in Will's and striding to center stage with him.

As I take my position, I look up toward the balcony, desperate to see Jonas' calming face, but stage lights are blinding me.

"Let's do this, OAP Cruz!" Will bellows. He hands me a microphone and leans into my ear. "First verse. Wait for my cue." He pauses for a moment, letting the music progress toward something specific, while I stand frozen and waiting. Finally, whatever cue Will has been waiting arrives. Will points at me and shouts, "Okay, OAP Cruz! This is it! One. Two. One-two-three-four."

Right on cue, the words fly out of my mouth, much to the thrill of the audience. When the chorus arrives, Will and the members of the Thai hip hop group join me, and when the second verse rolls around, Will and I fall into an easy back-and-forth rhythm, alternating our vocals as if we've been performing a synchronized duet of this song for years.

When the song ends, and the crowd loses its collective shit, Will grabs my hand and raises it in the air. "O-A-P Cruz, everyone!" I glance up toward the balcony, eager to share this insane moment with Jonas, but, still, I can't see a damned thing through the blinding stage lights.

I begin scurrying offstage toward Reed and Barry, like a chicken with my head cut off, but Will grabs my arm. "No, come with us." Dutifully, I follow him and the Thai group to the opposite side of the stage, since, apparently, I'm one of them now. And suddenly, I'm standing in a small dressing room getting high-fives and hugs. Amid the raucous celebration, someone hands me an open bottle of booze, so I take a big swig because I'm a fucking badass spin-rapper, and that was one of the most electrifying things I've ever done in my goddamned life!

"Thank you so much," I squeal to Will, when his attention finally turns to me. "I was petrified, but it wound up being so much fun!"

He laughs. "You fucking *rocked* it, OAP. Oh my God."

The unmistakable smell of pot suddenly fills my nostrils. I look around the tiny room and one of the Thai guys is blowing a huge puff of smoke out his mouth and passing the joint to his bandmate.

"Give it here," Will says. He takes a long drag and offers it to me.

"No, thanks. Pot only makes me sleepy."

"Not this shit. This shit's gonna give you the best sex of your life."

"It's laced with something?"

"No, it's only weed. But the good stuff."

Fuck it. I take the joint from him and inhale deeply, and my body immediately feels like it's melting. Warming. Tingling. "Holy shit," I say. "I feel like I just got wrapped in a vibrating Snuggie."

Will chuckles. "Just wait till tonight when your husband starts going down on you. You'll have the best orgasm of your life."

"Well, in that case . . ." I take the joint from him and inhale again. Even more deeply this time, and everyone in the room laughs.

"If you really want to have the time of your life tonight," Will says. "Mix that with molly. You won't believe how good you'll feel."

"No, no," I say waving him off. I know Kat took ecstasy several times in college. But I've never done it and don't intend to start now, while I'm awaiting the results of my freaking bar exam.

"Hey, Chakrii," Will says to one of the Thai guys. "You got some more of that ex from the other night?"

Chakrii reaches into his pocket, pulls out a baggie full of little white pills, fishes out two of them, and hands them to Will.

"No, thanks," I say. "I don't want to die in Thailand."

Laughing, Will grabs my hand and lays the two pills in my palm. "Take them with you for later, in case you change your mind. One for you and one for your husband."

I push the pills back at him. "I won't change my mind about not wanting to die."

Will rolls his eyes. "This isn't an after-school special, Sarah. This is pure MDMA. It's not laced with anything. I took some the other night and had a great time. All it's going to do is make you and your husband feel pure, unadulterated ecstasy for a few hours. Perfectly safe."

"Jonas makes me feel pure, unadulterated ecstasy every night," I insist. "It's the culmination of human possibility." Oh, shit. The weed on top of the booze is beginning to hit me so hard, I'm not sure if I said the word 'human' right. "Hyoomuhn," I mutter, trying to correct my pronunciation. But I think I just made it worse.

Will laughs. "Combine that molly with that particular strain of weed, and you're going to have the time of your life tonight."

12

SARAH

As Reed hugs and high-fives everyone in the dressing room, I gaze at the lights in the ceiling and murmur, "Pretty lights."

Reed puts his arm around my shoulder. "You crushed it, OAP Cruz."

I look at Reed and blink slowly, thinking, *Did your hair always look this soft?*

"What the hell does OAP stand for?" Reed asks.

"That's a secret," Will interjects, appearing at my side. He puts his index finger across his lips, reminding me not to spill my precious secret, and winks.

"I'll never tell," I confirm. "That's only for Jonas to know."

There's laughter among the members of the Thai hip hop group. One of them strides over to Reed, Will, and me, holding his phone. And that's when I see myself on his phone, having an epic rap battle onstage with 2Real.

"Ha!" Reed says. "You're going viral, OAP."

My gaze drifts from the video of myself to Reed's shirt. The fabric looks supernaturally soft. Is it? I touch

Reed's sleeve and confirm it does, indeed, possess an otherworldly kind of softness. "Supernaturally soft."

"*What*?" Reed says. He leans into me, apparently trying to hear me over the loud din in the dressing room. And when I repeat the phrase again, only this time elongating the vowels because it feels so good to roll them on my tongue, Reed immediately rolls his eyes, turns to Will, and bellows, "In the two minutes I left her alone with you, you gave her fucking *ecstasy*?"

Will taps my arm, attracting my slow gaze to fall on him. "Pretty eyes."

"Did you take one of the pills I gave you, OAP?"

"One. The other one is for Jonas."

Will laughs and addresses Reed. "Yeah. Apparently, I did."

"Fucking hell, Will!" Reed shouts at the top of his lungs. "I promised Jonas I'd take care of her."

"She'll be fine. It's really good stuff and she only took one."

Reed is beside himself. "Jonas is the opposite of his brother in every fucking way! He doesn't party like that. Ever. He's always been anti-drug, as long as I've known Josh."

"Jonas will thank me after he takes the other pill and has the best sex of his life."

"No, he'll want to kick your ass." Exhaling, Reed grabs my hand. "Come on, Sarah. It's time for me to bring you back to your control freak of a husband."

"Jonas is the only one who gives me orgasms," I say flatly.

Reed glares at Will, who's laughing, before returning to me and saying, "Do me a big favor, Sarah, and don't say a word to Jonas, until I'm long gone, okay?"

"Jonas is perfect."

"Not a word, okay?" With that, Reed drags me to the door of the dressing room. When he opens it, to my surprise, there's Jonas! My beloved husband who gives me orgasms! Except, oh no, he's ranting at the top of his lungs to the bodyguard, Barry.

"I'm not going to be patient and wait!" Jonas screams. "Not when my goddamned wife—"

"Jonas!" I sing out, floating toward him. "Did you see my rapping duel with Will?"

Jonas doesn't return my smile. In fact, he looks pissed as hell. "I did. Let's go." He nods at Reed in farewell, grabs my hand, and starts pulling me away.

"Wait, love. I want to say goodbye to all my new best friends! They've been so nice to me."

"Reed, do me a favor and say goodbye to everyone for Sarah."

"You got it," Reed tosses over his shoulder as he practically sprints past Barry into the dressing room.

"Jonas, wait," I insist, pulling my hand out of Jonas' grasp. "I want to say thank you to Will for bringing me onstage and giving me the chance to—"

"You've already said too much to Will." He glares at me before adding, "*OAP Cruz.*" With that, Jonas snatches my hand back and resumes dragging me away toward the front doors of the packed nightclub, as I rack my chemical-infused brain to understand his anger.

Our progress toward the front door is slow, in turns out, not only because the crowd is dense, but because people keep hurling themselves at OAP Cruz to tell me I'm amazing and ask for selfies.

"No selfies," Jonas keeps saying, without stopping for the nice people.

"Jonas, you're being rude," I say. "Let me stop and—"

"Sarah, we need to get out of here right fucking now."

"So grouchy," I mutter. But when my eyes train on his gorgeous forearm as he pulls me along, and I feel a sudden, outrageous zinging between my legs that inspires me to shout, at the top of my lungs, "Let's go fuck in the bathroom!"

"I think you're grossly misreading my mood."

Oh man. He's *really* pissed. Which only makes him look even hotter to me. Damn, he's sexy when he's angry. "Come on, *cariño*," I coo. Jonas can never resist me when I speak Spanish. "Let me rub my naked body against yours. I want to roll around in a big pile of feathers with you."

Jonas stops dead in his tracks, his eyes wide. "Are you *on* something?"

I giggle and nod. "Will said—"

"*Stop.* Quiet." He looks around, his blue eyes blazing. "Don't say another fucking word until we're safely in our hotel room. Do you understand me, Sarah? Not a fucking word."

I bite my lip. "*Word.*"

To my shock, Jonas grabs my shoulders and leans into my face. "This isn't a joke. We're in Thailand, remember? This isn't Seattle. Don't say another fucking word."

I touch his blazing face. "You're so hot when you're mad. I'm so lucky you're all mine."

His chest heaving, Jonas pulls my hand off his face and drags me toward the front of the crowded club.

A moment later, we're outside in the balmy night, being mobbed by fans of OAP Cruz again. And a moment after that, we're sitting in the back of a taxi, whisking away into the Bangkokian night.

I run my fingertips up Jonas' soft forearm and lean my

cheek against his broad shoulder, my skin tingling and my clit pounding with almost unbearable arousal. I slide my hand between his legs and stroke his package, desperate to feel him harden beneath my fingertips, but he abruptly grabs my hand and pins it against his outer thigh. "No. Stop," he says. "And don't say a word until we get to our room at the hotel."

"But Jonas," I begin. And that's when my hunky monkey husband places his palm over my mouth, and keeps it there, until we're pulling up to the front of our hoity-toity hotel.

In short order, Jonas shuttles me into the hotel lobby, and all the way up to our suite. At which point, he shuts the door behind us with a loud bang, whips around to face me with blazing eyes, and shouts, "What the fuck, Sarah?"

Uh oh. I've only ever seen my husband angry like this once before: three years ago in Las Vegas, when Jonas and I paid a visit to Oksana Belenko and her son, Max—and I wound up going off plan and scaring Jonas half to death.

"What are you on?" he demands to know, his arms flailing wildly.

"Ooooh, you're so sexy when you *gesticulate,* baby," I purr. Jonas and I always make each other laugh by saying non-sexual words in a sexual tone. Surely, if I get Jonas laughing now, he won't be mad at me anymore and we can finally get down to having some dirty fun. I step toward him, cooing, "*Gest-iiiiii-cyooooo-late.*"

But he's not amused. Or turned on. He's nothing but enraged.

"Sarah, for the love of fuck," he says. "*Focus.* What did you take? Did you smoke weed?"

"I nod. With all my friends in the dressing room,

because that's how world-class rappers celebrate after a kickass show." I smile but Jonas doesn't. "I also took the little white pill Will gave me," I confess. "And now, all I want to do is feel your naked skin against mine."

Jonas grabs my hands, stopping me from pulling up his shirt. "Was it Ecstasy?"

I nod and giggle. "He gave me a little white pill for you, too. Wasn't that nice of him? He said if we both take it, we'll have the best orgasms of our lives."

He's livid. Furious. Beyond enraged. He grabs the pill I'm offering him in a huff, marches into the bathroom, and flushes the toilet. When he returns, he looks capable of murder.

"Did you take anything else?" he demands.

"No."

"You don't have any other pills on you? Any weed?"

I shake my head. "I've got nothing but love for you."

He doesn't believe me. He digs his hands into my pockets, and then into my purse, looking for something that's not there.

"Why waste time being so mad, baby?" I purr. "When we could be fucking right now."

He grips my shoulders. "This is Thailand, Sarah. Cops here are notoriously corrupt, always looking for a bribe, especially from Westerners. You never know who's snitching to them, either—taxi drivers, hotel clerks. If they zero in on you, they can frisk you or make you do a pee-test, and then, God help you. You're totally at their mercy."

I place my palm on his heaving chest, feeling so aroused I think I'm going to explode. "Baby, channel all that rage into railing me before this high wears off. Will said the molly, combined with this special kind of weed, will give me the most insane orgasm of my life, and I want to experience that."

Holy shit. I thought my explanation would make Jonas less angry and more inclined to give me what I want. But clearly my plea has only enraged him even more. In fact, if Jonas were any other man looking at me this way, I'd surely cover my head with my arms reflexively, in anticipation of getting the shit smacked out of me.

"How the fuck did it come to pass that you talked to that motherfucker about *orgasms*?" he booms, his face every bit as lethal as the time we left The Club's office in Vegas and Jonas let me have it for leaving him on the other side of a locked door.

"With *you*," I clarify. "He promised I'd have the best orgasm with *you*. My husband. A god among men."

The "external jugular vein" in Jonas' neck—which I can confidently identify thanks to my run-in with a certain Russian hitman in a bathroom—is bulging like crazy. He grits out, "You told Will—and then the whole fucking world—about OAP."

Oh, fuck. I suddenly understand the root source of his rage. Giving me pleasure is Jonas' religion. My orgasms sacred and only for him. Which means, in his eyes, I committed careless blasphemy tonight.

"I'm sorry," I say. I reach for his face, saying, "To punish me for my sins, how about you fuck me until I can't move?"

He grabs my wrist to stop me from caressing his cheek. "You divulged something that was supposed to be sacred between you and me, Sarah. Something you promised was only for *me*."

I gasp, realizing what I've done. "I didn't tell Will

what OAP stands for," I insist. "He has no idea what it means. I promise."

"I don't believe you," he says simply, pulling my hand from his face again. "I don't believe a word coming out of your mouth right now.'

My jaw hangs open. Jonas has never said that to me before—that he doesn't believe something I've promised him—and I don't know how to respond. Again, I try to reach out and touch his face, desperate to reassure him. To make him understand how sorry I am. How much I love him and want to please him. But he's not having it. After shooing my hand away, repeatedly, he finally turns away from me in a huff and disappears into the nearby bathroom.

When he returns to me, he's holding a waist-tie from a hotel bathrobe. Grunting like a caveman, Jonas tosses me onto my back on the bed, yanks my hands over my head, and roughly ties both wrists to the headboard. "You fucked up tonight, Sarah." He crawls on top of me and straddles me, his face ablaze. "And you're going to repent for what you did."

Well, hot damn.

If my husband wants to make me stop feeling aroused, then tying my wrists to the headboard and demanding retribution for my sins is the wrong way to go about it. In fact, this entire situation—the way he's manhandling me with smoldering rage in his eyes—is only making me even more desperate for him to fuck the living hell out of me.

"I'm having an orgasm," I gasp out, as tiny flutters of pleasure ripple through my clit and everything attached to it. "Oh, fuck, I'm so turned on, Jonas. *Fuck me.*"

Jonas' breathing halts. I've never had an orgasm like

this before, without any direct stimulation, and it's clearly taken him aback that I'm having one now. Suddenly, I feel his hard dick bulging against my thigh from behind his jeans. Jonas shudders as he looms over me, his Adam's apple bobbing. Obviously, I've succeeded in turning him on, whether he likes it or not.

"Let's talk about my sins later," I purr, writhing and straining against my bondage. "After you fuck me, as hard as you can. Come on, baby, before this amazing pill wears off."

Jonas closes his eyes and exhales. "*Fuck.*" With a loud groan, he slides off me and grabs his computer—and a moment later, the chaotic, thumping sounds of "Psycho" by Muse blares in the room.

"That's it, baby," I coax, like I'm luring a rabid gorilla into a cage. "Fuck me like a madman, love."

Jonas pulls his shirt off and throws it onto the floor, revealing his beautiful physique and tattoos. He says, "I knew that fucker was going to hit on you the minute we walked into that VIP area. You grabbed his full attention the second he saw you." His bare chest heaving, Jonas unbuttons his jeans, causing his hard-on to spring out. He yanks off my G-string and roughly unclasps my bra. "But, still," he says, "I let that motherfucker sit on that couch and flirt with you, and order you drinks, and show you his goddamned tattoos, because I thought I could trust my wife."

"Of course, you can trust me," I whisper, gyrating with arousal. "Always."

"Can I?" His nostrils flare. "*OAP?*"

My stomach drops into my toes, even as my clit flutters wildly. "I told him I'm madly in love with you," I insist. "I told him you're my everything. And you are, Jonas."

The rage on my husband's face morphs into pain. "You told another man something that's sacred to me. Something we both agreed was only for *me*."

I exhale, panic suddenly flooding me. "You think I said more than I did," I gasp out. "You think I was trying to be sexy with him, but, no, it was the opposite. I was being silly. I said, 'Well, I have a tattoo that says OAP, so maybe my rapper name—'"

The pain on his face explodes into intense rage, yet again. "You told that motherfucker about your OAP *tattoo*?"

Fuck. Shit. What have I done? "Only that I have it!" I blurt. "I never told him *where* it is or what it means." I moan as my body ripples with another wave of intense pleasure. "Oh, fuck, Jonas, I messed up. I get it. But, please, fuck me now and talk later. I'm so fucking turned-on, I'm going to explode."

His entire body trembling, Jonas yanks my loose bra up and off my breasts, but he can't take it completely off, due to my bound arms. With my breasts bared to him, he voraciously licks my hard nipples, while slipping a couple fingers inside my panties and inside me. "You wanted him," he says, as his fingers begin working me into a frenzy.

"No! Of course not! I only want you, Jonas. Forever and always."

"You wanted him to want you, though. You wanted that validation."

I open my mouth to deny it but close it again. Is he right about that?

As the Muse song barrels into its final chorus, Jonas

continues touching me. Sending my arousal higher and higher. Oh, God, the pleasure he's giving me with his fingers is almost unbearable.

He bites my neck. "You were stranded in the dark and *I* brought you into the light."

"Yes."

"*I* delivered you unto pure ecstasy for the first time, Sarah."

"Yes."

"And every fucking day since."

"Yes."

"And not because you took some fucking pill."

"Yes!" I let out a tortured sound as another orgasm wracks through me. This one far more powerful than the last.

As my body warps and releases, Jonas climbs on top of me and straddles me, his cock straining toward his abs. "You gave that motherfucker a piece of yourself tonight, Sarah. A piece that wasn't yours to give because it was all mine." He opens my legs, his blue eyes blazing. "And now, I'm taking it back."

With that, he plunges himself inside me, causing me to cry out in pleasure.

"I don't want *artificial* ecstasy," Jonas grits out as his body fills mine, over and over again. "I only want the fucking truth."

"Yes," I eke out. "Yes." He's never pounded me like this. And it feels amazing. So much so, I'm soon throttled by another powerful orgasm—one that seizes my entire body.

As my body begins warping and clenching, Jonas pulls out of me, still hard as a rock and looking like a ferocious beast. His cock straining, he slides his fingers inside me again and begins strumming a spot deep inside me.

"I can't," I sputter. I know what he's trying to do, because he's tried before.

"Relax," he whispers. "Focus on the pleasure I'm giving you and nothing else."

"I can't," I gasp out.

"You can. Close your eyes and let go. You're closer than you've ever been."

"It feels like I'm going to pee."

"You're not. Let go. You're so close."

I arch my back and whimper, feeling dangerously close to losing control of myself in a whole new way. But something stops me. Even now, when I'm out of my head. I clench and hold it in, unwilling to trust Jonas with this one last thing, despite all the times he's coaxed me to try to get me there. I groan and whimper. Arch my back and strain against my bondage. But, ultimately, when I come again, it's the same kind of orgasm as the last one. Which is fucking amazing, yes. But certainly not the new frontier Jonas has been trying to reach with me for some time now.

As I climax, Jonas grabs his cock and comes all over my stomach, growling like grizzly bear as he does. When he's done, he wordlessly gets up and grabs a towel from the bathroom. In silence, he cleans me up and unties my wrists. At which point, I sit up and throw my arms around his neck.

"I'm so sorry," I say. "I didn't mean to betray your trust. But I see now that I did. I promise I'll never do it again. I swear it on my life. Please forgive me."

He embraces me, thank God, and holds me close. But, still, he hasn't spoken a word.

Finally, he pulls back from our embrace, looks me dead in the eyes, and says, "When you were lying on that bathroom floor at U Dub in a puddle of blood, I was terrified I'd lost you forever. And seeing you flirting with that motherfucker, knowing you'd told him sacred, intimate details about our life together, made me feel that same terror again."

I furrow my brow. "You couldn't possibly have thought you were in any real danger of losing me to another man. I fully understand your anger and hurt, but you couldn't possibly have thought I was in any danger of leaving the club with Will."

"You don't understand."

"Explain it to me."

He takes a deep breath. "I felt the danger of you tearing a hole in the fabric of our cocoon-built-for-two. Our cocoon isn't something to take for granted, Sarah. It's not something you can assume. You have to hold it sacred and respect it, at all times."

I furrow my brow. "I do."

Jonas shakes his head, obviously feeling frustrated at my lack of understanding. He sighs. "What do you know about Judo?"

"Um. Not a lot. I know it's a martial art."

He takes a deep, steadying breath. "Judo is one of the few martial arts that by definition involves no equipment or weapons of any kind. It's hand-to-hand combat, Sarah. Two combatants attempt to subdue each other through nothing but the forces of balance, power, and movement. It's about harnessing human power and strength in its purest form." He takes my hand. "For me, sex with you is like Judo—and it's my life's mission to become a tenth-degree black belt."

I open and close my mouth, not sure where he's going with this.

"A Judo master would never use a shotgun or knife, not even a stick, to subdue his opponent," he says. "Because weapons of any kind are antithetical to the basic tenets of the art form—an affront to the *purity* of it."

A lightbulb goes off in my head. "I get it."

"I don't know if you do, Sarah. I want your orgasms to come from *me* and only me—my cock, fingers, and tongue. The forces of balance, power, and movement. Not the fact that you get off on making me jealous. Or making another man want you. And certainly not because you took a little white pill." He shakes his head. "What if I'd succeeded in finally making you squirt for the first time tonight—while you were high on fucking *Ecstasy*? What glory would there have been in that for a Judo master like me? And even more importantly, how could I have duplicated that for you in the future? I know you probably think I'm overreacting. But this is me, Sarah. This is who I am. And I can't be any other way."

"I love you, exactly as you are, Jonas."

"I know that. But tonight, you didn't *respect* me. And I need you to fully comprehend how much I need that respect from you. If other married women talk about sex and orgasms with men and in nightclubs, and their husbands don't give a shit, then good for them. But that's not the way our marriage works because *I'm* the husband in this marriage, *and* I can't fucking handle it. Not by a long shot."

I blink and tears squirt down my cheeks. "I understand. I totally blew it. Please forgive me."

He slides his palms on my cheeks. "You're the only

person I've ever loved with all my heart and soul and everything I am. It's the greatest feeling in the world to love you this way, but it also means you've got the unbridled power to destroy me. You could crush me, Sarah, and I wouldn't be able to save myself."

I'm trembling under his touch. "I promise I'll be much more careful and respectful of your heart, forevermore. Please believe me."

His beautiful blue eyes soften. "I do." He kisses my cheek. "You were *amazing* on that stage tonight, by the way. Even when I was furious about your introduction and plotting Will's murder, you still managed to turn me on and blow my mind."

I bite my lip. "I did?"

"Fuck yes. Every person in that club tonight fell head over heels in love with you. Including me, all over again. You're the goddess and the muse, OAP Cruz. And after tonight, the whole world knows I'm the luckiest bastard in the world."

13
SARAH

"Dada?"

"He'll be right there, any minute now," Kat replies to ten-month-old Gracie. We're standing together near the entrance of the baggage claim area, awaiting our husbands' arrival from Peru. And little Gracie, who obviously needs a nap, has been growing increasingly restless in her mother's arms. Kat gives her baby an animal cracker to calm her down, and then says to me, "When I get Josh home, right after putting Gracie down for a nap, I'm going to lock him into our bedroom and attack him."

"I'll be doing the same thing at my house, sister."

"Josh won't know what hit him," Kat adds. "I'll be all over that man like Jack the Ripper on a London hooker."

I giggle. "I'll be all over Jonas like a black bear on a camper eating a bag of potato chips."

"I'm gonna be all over Josh like luck on a charm."

"Like track marks on a junkie's arm," I say.

Kat laughs. "Like a Speedo on Michael Phelps."

"Shoot," I say. "That's a tough one to beat."

Kat and I play this silly game whenever our husbands travel for work, which they do fairly often these days, as they continue building their joint empire. But whereas our husbands' work trips usually only last a few days, this climbing trip lasted a whole three *weeks*, during which Kat and I both missed our husbands in a whole new way.

"So, you concede?" Kat asks. And when I nod, she holds up Gracie's fat little fist, shakes it in victory, and pretends to speak for her baby. "Mommy did it!" Kat says in a little voice. "She beat Auntie Sarah's booty in a battle of wits!"

"It was a fluke," I say, feigning annoyance.

"Dada!" Gracie shrieks, drawing our attention. And sure enough, there they are—the Faraday twins, both of them sporting ripped muscles, beaming smiles, and Sasquatch beards.

Squealing happily, I ditch Kat and Gracie and sprint toward my husband, leap into his arms, and begin peppering his beautiful, bushy face with a thousand kisses. After three weeks without Jonas, I'm a bucking bronco of sexual heat. Not to mention, while Jonas was gone, and my period came and went, I realized I didn't want to start the next birth control packet. That, indeed, I'm ready to start trying for a salsa-and-Plato-infused Faraday baby. Since our wedding night, Jonas has always said he'd let me take the lead on deciding our timing. In fact, he's repeatedly said I don't need to ask his permission or check in with him, that he'd be perfectly happy to be surprised. So, last week, I bit the bullet and didn't start my pills, figuring I'd take Jonas at his word and surprise him with the exciting news when he returned from his trip.

"I missed you so much," I gasp out, still peppering his face with kisses.

"I'm never leaving you again," Jonas replies. He's holding me up by my ass, receiving my frantic kisses like they're giving him life.

"Did you have fun?" I ask breathlessly.

"I did." He squeezes my ass. "Except for the fact that I was miserable without my daily fix of *albóndigas*."

I run my fingers over his furry chin. "I love the beard."

He rubs his whiskers against my chin, making me laugh. "Let's have some fun with it before I shave it off."

"Hell yeah."

After one last, passionate kiss, I slide down from his strong embrace and we head over to Josh, Kat, and Gracie by the baggage carousel.

"Welcome home, Josh."

I hug my brother-in-law in greeting, and he kisses my cheek.

"If you ever find yourself doubting how Jonas feels about you," Josh says, "then ask me to tell you some of the amazing things he said about you during our trip— every fucking day, a hundred times a day, for three fucking weeks."

I laugh. "He missed me, huh?"

He rolls his eyes. "I wanted to push that fucker off the mountain."

We retrieve the guys' huge backpacks from the baggage carousel and head out to Kat's Range Rover, with Josh, Kat and Gracie walking arm in arm in front of Jonas and me through the parking lot.

"I have a surprise for you at home," I say playfully, pressing myself into Jonas as we walk.

"I hope it involves you riding on my beard."

"It does, actually. In part."

"*Hallelujah.*"

———

As Josh and Kat peel away from our driveway, no doubt racing off to fuck like rabbits, Jonas and I sprint inside our house, panting and growling like rabid dogs. The minute we get inside, Jonas hurls his massive backpack to the floor, grunting like a gorilla, and begins ripping my clothes off like they're on fire.

When he gets to my G-string, he yanks it off with a loud groan, unlatches my bra, and slams me against the closed front door, mauling me with breathtaking intensity. Before I can even move to disrobe him in return, Jonas' fingers are deep inside me, touching the precise spot that ramps me up like lightning.

He leans down and buries his face in my breasts, like a kid bingeing on cookies, and nuzzles his nose into my cleavage. "Holy fuck, I want to physically *eat* you." He sucks furiously on one of my nipples. "I'm never leaving you again."

I reach down to open his jeans, and when his massive erection springs out, its tip already shiny and dripping with wetness, I growl at the sight of it.

"Jack in the box," I say, swirling my fingertip over the delicious bead of moisture pooled on his tip.

"Only if you're the box."

He licks my neck and spreads my legs with his muscular thigh, positioning his hard-on to plunge inside me.

And, suddenly, I realize I should probably warn him that my eggs are going commando these days, despite what he's said in the past about me taking the lead. Before leaving for the airport, I set up a cute way of telling Jonas the situation. But I set it up in our bedroom, not realizing we wouldn't even make it past the front door when we got home.

"There's something I want to show you in the bedroom," I gasp out.

"Show me later," he mutters.

He pulls his fingers out of me, obviously intending to replace them with his cock, and I'm too horny, too excited, to say anything but "okay."

As soon as the word escapes my lips, my husband plunges himself inside me so deeply, my eyes bug out of my head like one of those stress-relief-squeezy things. As he fills me up, I let out a long, loud, moan of relief and excitement, and so does he. Oh God, it feels like it's been forever since Jonas' body has been inside mine, a lifetime since I've smelled his masculine scent, eons since I've watched his beautiful features contort from pleasure. Holy fuck. This feels so good, my deepest core muscles are already tightening sharply, getting ready to release.

"I went off the pill," I gasp out. Yes, he's told me repeatedly he's ready whenever I am, but, still, the last thing I want is for Jonas to have a change of heart about that *after* the deed is done and a baby might be on the way.

Jonas shudders with arousal and kisses me even more enthusiastically. But unless I missed it, he hasn't replied to my shocking pronouncement.

"Did you hear me?" I gasp out, as his cock practically impales me against our front door.

"Yeah."

"And?"

"It's great news."

With that, he begins thrusting into me with even more enthusiasm, so I wrap my legs around his waist and grind my body into him, positioning myself so his shaft rubs against me in just the right way. I touch his rippled muscles and run my hands through his hair and clear my mind, and a moment later, I'm throttled by white-hot bliss. The kind that makes me scream in ecstasy.

"You're a fucking symphony, baby," he grits out. "My favorite sound in the world."

When I'm done convulsing and screaming, I'm surprised to see Jonas has pulled out of me, still fully erect and straining. He scoops me up, brings me to our couch, and lays me down before sinking onto his knees before me and eating me with fervor. As he consumes me, as his beard and chin, lips, tongue, and fingers, send me closer and closer to heaven, we both let out loud moans of pleasure. Until soon, warm waves of pleasure throttle my every nerve ending, yet again.

When I'm done climaxing, Jonas turns my body over and slaps my ass-tattoo—the one I got for him in Thailand as an apology of sorts after pissing him off in that nightclub. "*Propiedad de Jonas Faraday.*" That's what the tattoo on my ass cheek says. *Property of Jonas Faraday.*

"Mine," Jonas says, which makes sense, considering what's stamped on my ass. With that, he scoops me up, throws me over his shoulder like a caveman, and begins walking down the hallway toward our bedroom.

"Shake it for me," I say, my face dangling mere inches from his gorgeous, naked ass. And, of course, my husband humors me, like he always does.

In our bedroom, Jonas lays me down on the bed, his

hard-on straining. He commands, "Do a backbend for me."

"Huh?"

"A backbend. We're gonna do something called The Arch." He licks his lips. "I couldn't stop thinking about doing it with you while I was gone."

I've learned to follow Jonas' lead through an almost endless exploration of sexual positions over the past two years, and I've never once regretted it. And so, without hesitation, I get into position.

"Like this?" I ask. I'm in a full-blown gymnast's back-bend on our bed, with my head dangling and my palms and soles flush on the bed.

"Actually, no, that's not what I meant—although, Jesus Christ, Sarah, that's hot as fuck." He admires me for a long moment. "*Damn*. I want to eat you like that before we move on to what I had in mind."

"Jesus, Jonas. I'm a wet noodle from those two orgasms. I won't be able to hold this position for much longer."

Jonas laughs. "Okay. Another time. Now lower your shoulders back down onto the bed, but keep your legs, back, and butt raised high."

"Huh?"

He guides my body into position. "Like this. There you go. Perfect."

"Can't we just, you know, fuck like normal people and maybe do this position later tonight?"

"Fuck no. If we're possibly going to make a baby, then let's do it in style. Now, put your arms out to the sides to stabilize yourself."

"*Stabilize* myself? What the hell?"

Without answering me, Jonas kneels on the bed

between my legs, so that his penis levels off with my raised pelvis. He slides a finger inside me to find his target and then, without further ado, enters me, pulling my pelvis into him as he does.

"Oh, wow," I say, as Jonas begins rocking back and forth in rhythmic gyrations. "This feels incredible."

"It's sort of like The Butterfly," he says, "but with an added bonus."

I wait a moment for him to explain the added bonus. But he doesn't. And soon, I'm so close to orgasm, I can't speak.

Up until now, Jonas has been supporting my raised pelvis with both his hands, but now he brings one hand to my clit while deepening his thrusts—and the effect is mind-blowing. In fact, the pleasure is so fucking intense, so disconcerting and disorienting, I'm suddenly bathed in sweat and shrieking uncontrollably.

Jonas comes inside me, and two seconds later, I come, too, before falling onto the bed in a sweaty heap.

Jonas lies alongside me, his blue eyes on fire. "You were so close this time," he says. And, of course, I know exactly what he's referring to—his continuous quest to make me squirt. He asks, "Right before you came, did you feel like you had to pee?"

"Yes."

Jonas exhales with excitement. "Okay, when you feel that next time, I want you to push through it and let go."

I shake my head. "I'm not willing to piss all over you while getting fucked. Especially not while hopefully making a baby."

"You won't piss all over me. But so what if you do? You have to train yourself to push through that discomfort. I promise, there'll be exponential pleasure on the other side of it—a new kind of pleasure you can't fathom."

"I can't fathom there being anything better than what you already do to me."

"Exactly my point. *You can't fathom it*. But trust me, it's awaiting you. You simply have to trust me completely and surrender."

"I already trust you completely."

"No, you don't. Not yet. You're close. But you're still holding back."

"Not wanting to pee for your pleasure isn't the same thing as not trusting you completely."

"*It won't be pee, Sarah*. Trusting that, accepting that there's nothing that could possibly scare me off, being willing to be completely vulnerable, *that's* what's going to deliver Orgasma the All-Powerful to the next level. The next peak." He kisses my neck. "Remember that roadblock you felt when we first started going for full-bodied, G-spot orgasms, instead of clitoral ones?"

I nod.

"And then remember how hard it was at first to get *both* clitoral and G-spot orgasms working for you, all at once? Well now, all we have left to climb is this one remaining peak. Let me help you get there."

I can't help smiling. "Okay. I'll try."

"Good girl." He pulls me into him, and we snuggle for a long moment, until, suddenly, Jonas blurts, "What the fuck?" He laughs. "You're such a dork, Sarah."

I look to where Jonas is pointing and remember the metaphor I arranged for him earlier—the silly thing I giddily set up to tell my husband I'm ready to make a baby. Chuckling, I say, "'No great genius has ever existed without some touch of madness.'"

"You don't get to quote Aristotle to justify *that*. What the hell is that?"

"You don't get it? It's a riddle. A secret code."

"I understand the eggs and tadpoles—eggs and sperm. But what are those pink and blue things?"

"Peeps."

Jonas looks at me like I'm an escaped mental patient.

"Marshmallow Peeps," I explain. But when he looks nonplussed, I add, "*Egg* plus *sperm* equals *baby chicks*."

"I still don't get it. Those are marshmallows."

"You never had marshmallow Peeps in your Easter basket?"

"No. Josh and I never got Easter baskets. At least, not after our mom died. I'm sure she got them for us, but I was too young to remember."

"Oh. Well, that's sad. I didn't mean to bring up a sad memory. I was trying to be funny."

"It's funny. Very funny."

"It would have been funnier if I didn't need to explain it. I know how much you love grand gestures and metaphors. I thought I'd give you one, for a change."

Jonas pulls me to him and kisses my head. "Thank you. It's a *grand* grand gesture. Actually, if you must know, I've always had a marshmallow-chick fetish. I was too embarrassed to tell you about it before now."

"Too embarrassed to tell your Beautiful Intake Agent about a fetish? Sweetheart, trust me, I've read about much weirder fetishes than that."

We both laugh and cuddle close.

"Do you think we made a baby?" I whisper.

"Nothing would make me happier. But if not, try, try again. And again and again and again."

"Count me in."

He kisses the top of my head. "It's funny. I was raised to think it'd be a fate worse than death to get someone 'knocked up' and get myself tied for eternity to some woman who was only interested in getting herself some guaranteed child support."

"That's funny?"

"Well, not funny 'ha ha.'"

"God, I hate your father," I murmur.

"Yeah, he really did a number on me. Even more so on Josh, though." Jonas runs his fingertips down my naked back. "But that's what makes this moment even sweeter for me—knowing that, despite all the brainwashing my father tried to pull on me, all the ways he tried to convince me I'm not worthy of love or happiness or a family, I'm here with you now, knowing for sure you love me for me, hoping so much we just made a baby . . . and wishing with all my heart and soul I had more than one eternity to be tied to you."

14
JONAS

For four days, Sarah's been in a near-constant, deep slumber, a quasi-coma, her blood pressure critically low, her heart rate shockingly slow, her body struggling mightily to overcome the horrific blood loss and complications she suffered after that first horrible night. Sarah's opened her eyes and stared at me blankly several times these past four days—she's even spoken to me briefly, too—and each time, I've practically choked on my heart with excitement and relief. But each time, she's quickly slipped away again, leaving me more bereaved than ever, certain I'd just witnessed Sarah's last words.

My fingers entwined in Sarah's, I close my eyes and listen to the beeping of the monitors attached to her, racking my brain to think of something new to say to her. But I feel like I've said it all, at least a thousand times. *Please, come back to me. I love you. I'm right here. The babies and I need you. Come back to us.* Has she heard any of it? Is my voice leading her back to me? God, I hope so.

The song playing on my computer is "Sky Full of

Stars" by Coldplay—the song I started listening to on a loop since forcing myself to ditch that Death Cab for Cutie song about following Sarah into the dark. It's a song of hope—the one I want playing when Sarah finally wakes up. The doctor says she could turn the corner at any time now . . . or never wake up at all. Either outcome is on the table, so I haven't dared turn the music off or leave her side. And always, I talk to her. Tell her how much I love her. Beg her not to leave. I tell her about the babies and how much they look like her. And when I can't stop myself, I cry my eyes out.

Sighing, I touch Sarah's cheek. "I love you so much, baby," I whisper. "I'm right here. Come back to me."

Her eye twitches. Or did I imagine that?

"Sarah?"

She rustles. Her eyes flutter open.

"Sarah," I whisper-shout, my heart clanging. "Hey, baby. Welcome back." I know she's opened her eyes before, so this might be another false start. But, still, I can't help hoping it's a good sign.

"The babies?" she whispers.

"Two little girls." I've told her this before, of course. "They both look like you."

A weak smile spreads across her pale face. "They're okay?"

She's never talked this much before. By this point, she's usually gone again. Does this mean she's finally back for good?"

I nod. "Sol and Luna, just like you said. Sometimes, we call Sol 'Sunshine' or 'Sunny.' Even your mom calls her that. Blame Josh. He started it."

Sarah grins. God, she's so fucking pale. "I love it. *Preciosa*."

My heart is racing. Bounding. Leaping. But I try to contain myself. "The names fit both of them to a tee, baby. Sol is a little light. And Luna is already concocting her villain origin story."

Sarah smiles weakly. "Healthy?"

I grab her hand and kiss it. "Yes. Tiny but healthy. They're off the ventilators now. Breathing great. The doctor said they'll be here a few months, probably, to strengthen their lungs. But then they'll be able to come home with us." *With us.* Please, God, let this be a true statement. A wave of emotion threatens, but I stuff it down. I don't want Sarah knowing how close she came to leaving the babies and me. That's the last thing she needs to know about right now.

"Is Luna our Crazy Monkey?" she whispers.

"Of course." I bite my lip, but it's no use. Tears are squirting out of my eyes. "She looks exactly like you, but I think she got my personality. I'll apologize to her profusely about that when she's old enough to understand how unlucky that is."

Sarah blinks and tears fall down her cheeks, mimicking mine. "She's one lucky monkey."

I can't hold back anymore. I lean down onto my wife's chest, clutch her to me, and sob my eyes out.

"I've been so scared," I choke out. "So fucking terrified I'd lose you."

She makes a cooing sound. "Sweet Jonas."

A nurse bolts into the room and immediately begins checking Sarah's vital signs. Wiping my eyes, I leap up and pace around the room, simultaneously electrified with hope and filled with dread. Is Sarah here to stay this time? Or will this turn out to be some sort of last gasp—a brief moment of lucidity before the darkness comes to claim her for good?

"Can I see the babies?" Sarah asks the nurse.

"As soon as the doctor says you can. You're going to need to stay in bed for another day, I'm guessing." The nurse looks at me. "Maybe grab her mother from the waiting room? She's been begging to switch places with you for a while now." She flashes me a look of chastisement, but I don't care what she thinks. In fact, she can kiss my fucking ass. I've lived this *exact* moment before, after Sarah was stabbed—and I know *precisely* what happens next: Gloria bursts into the room, throws herself onto Sarah's prostrate body, and promptly steals Sarah away from me to recuperate at her house, without either of them giving me so much as a backward fucking glance.

"Don't go, Jonas," Sarah says. "I want you here. My mom can wait."

My heart bursting, I resume my seat at Sarah's bedside, take her hand, and whisper to her.

"The doctor is on her way," the nurse says. "I'll be right back."

I watch the nurse leave. And the minute she's gone, I smile at Sarah and say, "I've got something to show you." Wordlessly, I stand and pull off my T-shirt, revealing the new tattoo on my chest—the one I got last night while Gloria was sitting here with Sarah and the NICU was closed to visitors. It's a galaxy of twinkling stars surrounding a glittering sun and moon inked over my heart.

I sit, take her hand, and place her palm on my bare chest, right over my heart. "The sun and moon are Sol and Luna, of course. But you're the *sky full of stars*. My universe." I choke back a sob. "I'm so fucking relieved you've come back to me."

————

This right here, sitting with Sarah in the NICU, each of us holding one of our babies, is all I've dreamed of doing since the moment I first laid eyes on our daughters five days ago.

"You make a much prettier co-parent than Josh," I say.

Sarah wipes her eyes. "Oh, I dunno. Josh is awfully pretty."

"Don't let him hear you say that. His ego is big enough."

She looks down at the bundle in her arms. "Josh came down here a lot, huh?"

I nod. "I'm sure the girls think their parents are Josh and Gloria. I spent most of my time with you."

She swallows hard. "I'm so sad you had to go through that, Jonas. You must have been so scared."

"I was terrified. But I had the girls. They helped keep me strong."

Sarah gazes at Luna in her arms. "You're an amazing person. A lesser man would have been broken by everything you've been through in life."

I furrow my brow. "I *was* broken, until you came along."

Sarah smiles. "No, love. You were badly *sprained*. That's the thing that amazes me about you. You never break. You're the strongest person I know." She blinks and tears squirt out her eyes. "I hate knowing I've brought you even more pain in your life, when all I've ever wanted was to turn your sad eyes happy."

"You have. Sarah, look at me." I widen my eyes. "See? Today is the happiest day of my life. This moment, the best yet."

She smiles. "But do you need to talk about anything? I mean, all of this must have been horribly traumatic for you. Do you maybe want to talk about it. If not with me, then with a therapist?"

I look down at Luna. "No, I'm good. Honestly, I don't want to think about that night ever again—except to remind myself, if I'm ever stupid enough to need reminding, that I'm the luckiest man in the world." When I look up, Sarah is crying. But thank God, it's clear she's crying tears of joy.

"Let's switch," she chokes out. "I want Sol to get to know me, too."

I call a nurse over and she helps us make the switch. And a moment later, I've got Luna in my arms, while Sarah is cuddling our little bundle of Sunshine.

"Gracie never felt so tiny," Sarah says.

"That's because Gracie was at least twice their size," I reply. "These two don't even look human. They look like baby monkeys."

"They do." Sarah touches the top of Sol's head. "Ooo ooo eee eee," she says softly, mimicking a monkey's call. She looks at me. "That means 'I love you' in monkey."

I laugh and look down at Luna in my arms. "Ooo ooo eee eee, little one. I love you."

A lump rises in my throat, but I stuff it down. If this moment isn't the peak of happiness—the divine original form of love-ness—then I don't know what is.

Sarah looks down at the baby in her arms. "I never imagined myself as a mother. I didn't know if I was cut out for the job. But sitting here now, I feel this over-whelming maternal instinct kicking in. Like if anyone ever tries to hurt my baby monkeys, this momma bear would go Latina on their ass so fast, they wouldn't even have time to notice all the mixed metaphors in that sentence."

I laugh. "God, I love you."

"And I love you." Sarah sighs happily. "Never in a million years did I think things would turn out this way when your application landed in my inbox."

"Oh, I did," I tease. "How else could it have turned out?"

Sarah bursts out laughing, making me laugh, too. And for a moment, I'm overwhelmed with gratitude that I get to hear that glorious sound again—the sound of Sarah's infectious laughter. I get to see the twinkle in her brown eyes. *I get to see her holding our child.*

"What?" she says, reacting to my facial expression.

"I'm just feeling grateful," I manage to say.

Sarah flashes me a smile that makes my heart feel like it's physically expanding in my chest. "I love you, Jonas."

"I love you, too, Sarah. More than I ever thought possible."

15
JONAS

It's the dark of night.

Sarah moans next to me in our bed, and I open my eyes, wrenched from a sex dream. I've had a lot of them lately, due to the fact that we're only two weeks into our six- to eight-week moratorium on post-natal sex. And this particular dream was white-hot, featuring Sarah squirting in ecstasy all over my mouth and her thighs, followed by me licking it up enthusiastically. But nothing, not even the hottest sex dream of my life could keep me from flying into action at the first sound of discomfort from Sarah.

"Sarah?" I blurt, grabbing her arm. "Are you awake? Are you okay?"

"I'm fine, honey," she says soothingly. "I've got to pump again. My boobs are rock hard.."

A wave of relief floods me. Sarah's made great strides in her healing since we came home from the hospital, but I still hold my breath every time she shows even the slightest hint of distress or discomfort.

Sarah turns on the lamp on the nightstand and looks down at herself in the dim light. And it's plain to see the front of her white nightgown is soaking wet and plastered to her chest. Which means her dark, erect nipples are visible through the wet fabric of her gown.

"And . . . I'm hard," I say.

"Based on your moans while you were sleeping, I'm guessing you already were."

"True." I hop out of bed. "I'll get your pump."

"Thanks, love. It's on the chair."

I retrieve Sarah's pump from a corner armchair and return to the edge of our bed with it, stopping short of handing her the pump.

"What are you waiting for?" she asks, her arms outstretched.

"Okay, hear me out," I say, a wicked gleam in my eye.

"No, Jonas."

"It's perfectly natural. I don't see why the world sees it as such a taboo thing."

"*I* see it as a taboo thing. Now, give me the pump and get your depraved ass back into bed."

I hand her the pump and slide back into bed. "You honestly don't think it'd be a little bit hot?"

"Not at all. Do I think it's Freudian as fuck? Yes. Twisted? Yes. Maybe even illegal in some states. But hot? No."

"Liar. Part of you thinks it'd be hot."

"Jonas, you know I love saying yes to you and all the ways you enjoy exploring my body. But this little fetish of yours isn't going to get fulfilled."

"It's not a fetish. I simply want to see what it tastes like. It'll be one and done."

"If you want to taste it, then take a sip from a bottle after I'm done pumping."

"I'm not craving the milk itself. Not at all. I'm craving the sensation of sucking warm fluid out of your body. The fact that your tits can create nourishment that sustains life turns me on like crazy."

Sarah looks at me like I'm demented.

"What's so weird about that? I'm obsessed with your body. We both know that. So why wouldn't I want to do that once? It's no different than being obsessed with making you squirt."

"It's very different." She motions to her breasts, which are now being rhymthically pumped by her machine. "Squirting is inherently sexual. This is *not*. These are for the babies."

"Yes, I know that. I'm not saying I want to make it a regular thing. Consider it a bucket list item."

"This is so fucking Freudian."

I shrug. "Call it what you want. But watching you do that gets me so fucking hard."

She rolls her eyes. "Well, I'm sorry to disappoint you, but I'm not going to breastfeed my husband. So, suck on *that*."

"I don't want to *breastfeed*. This wouldn't be some sort of twisted role play. I'm a grown-ass, horny man with a hard-on who wants to give his wife's nipple a good, strong suck and get a sweet, warm surprise that will hopefully give me a little preview of the cum I'm going to lick off you when I finally get you squirting one day. That's a sex act, baby, all the way."

"I think three weeks without sex is doing crazy things to your head."

"Not at all. Well, yes. But that's not what's driving this. It's simple biology. *Science.* Did you know oxytocin, the hormone that releases during orgasm, is the same hormone that releases during breastfeeding? Do you think that's pure coincidence? Absolutely not. *'Nature does nothing in vain.'*"

"You're saying Plato had a breastfeeding fetish, too?"

"That was Aristotle. And I might have used that quote a little bit out of context."

She giggles.

"All I'm saying is nature, or God, or whatever fucking genius designed you must have had a damned good reason for making breastfeeding feel *orgasmic.*"

Sarah bites her lip—a telltale sign I've scored a point with her, however small. So, I decide to stop talking for a few minutes, to let whatever small headway I might be making sink in. With my cheek on my pillow, I stare at Sarah's breasts for a long moment, absolutely mesmerized by the sight of them releasing milk.

Finally, I say, "Watching you do that is so fucking hot."

Sarah rolls her eyes. "I'm being milked like a cow. *Moo.*"

"No, you're Mother Earth. Hotter than ever."

"This isn't normal. If we asked one hundred people on the street, they'd all say what you want to do is totally weird, if not disgusting."

"Well, good thing none of those hundred people are married to me then, huh?" When she says nothing, I turn onto my back and grab my hard dick. "With that skin of yours, I bet you'd taste like the finest latte if you let me do it."

She giggles. "More like a caramel macchiato."

"Don't tease me."

She smiles and closes her eyes, still holding the pump to her breasts. And, suddenly, the enormity of my assholery crashes down on me. The woman is exhausted. On pain meds. She's been dragging her aching body to the hospital every day since we've been home for hours on end to visit the babies and bring the nurses the milk she's pumped. She's still bleeding profusely and will be for several more weeks. And now, on top of everything else, she has to deal with her horny-ass, depraved husband begging for a little suck?

"I'm sorry," I say. "I shouldn't have pushed. I was trying to be playful. But I think I missed the mark."

She opens her eyes. "No, it felt playful. Don't worry. I'm just extra tired these days."

I pull up her nightgown to reveal her angry C-section scar and kiss it gently. "Do you need anything? Your wish is my command."

"Some water would be great."

"Coming right up, my bodacious queen."

Sarah giggles. "Thank you."

I slide off the bed and start walking toward the doorway.

"Maybe a couple Oreos, too?" Sarah says behind me.

"You got it. With some oat milk for dunking?"

"You know me so well."

"Jonas," she says softly behind me, so I turn around in the doorway. "I love that you're completely yourself with me. I love that you honestly tell me what you're thinking. What turns you on. Please, always do that. I might push back or not completely understand, but I never want you to censor yourself with me. Ever. I love you. All of you. I hope you know that."

Warmth fills my core. "I do, Sarah. Do you think I'd beg to suck milk out of your tit if I didn't?" With that, I wink at my adorable wife, turn on my heel, and practically skip to the kitchen, well aware I'm the luckiest man alive.

16

JONAS

I'm sitting at my kitchen table, eating a bowl of cottage cheese, doing something I haven't done in years: watching porn on my laptop.

Sarah and I visited the babies in the hospital this morning, exactly as we've done every day since Sarah came home from the hospital four weeks ago, and now I'm alone in the house while Sarah hangs out with Kat.

When I first sat down at my computer, I wanted to do some research on bondage. Both the "how to" of it and what, from a psychological standpoint, makes it such a draw for so many people. Why? Because I've realized, if I want to push my wife past her current sexual boundaries and hang-ups, if I want to coax Sarah out of her comfort zone, then I need to join her in that pursuit. It's only fair, right? And I did give her that box of goodies, after all. So why not learn how to use them all to maximum effect?

Unfortunately, however, my research on bondage didn't last long. Once I stumbled upon a video entitled "Watch a hot woman squirt!", that was it for me. I've watched nothing but squirting videos ever since.

I take a big bite of cottage cheese and gaze at the boisterous fuckery happening on my computer screen. I'd clicked on this particular video because it was entitled, *She's a Squirter, Fellas!* But it's turned out to be fucking useless. The way the man and woman are positioned would never in a million years stimulate the woman's G-spot enough to make her squirt, let alone orgasm at all, unless the guy's dick happens to be bent like a crowbar. Which means this woman is a spontaneous squirter, which means this video won't help me with my little Mount Everest, or it's a total fake.

I click out of the video, mid-fuck, and scroll through the other search results on the side of the screen. A video entitled *How to Make a Woman Squirt Every Single Time* catches my eye. I click on it and an average-looking guy with no discernible muscle tone appears on-screen.

"Hey, guys," the dude says. "Do you want to make your woman squirt?"

"Fuck yes," I say out loud.

"Do you want to do it every single time, like clockwork?"

"Absolutely."

"Well, through years of practice and experimentation, I've figured out a method for making any woman squirt, every time, without fail. It took me years to perfect this technique, but I did it. And now, I'm demonstrating my secret technique for you. Just click on the video link below to watch step by step instructions—Venmo, Paypal, and credit cards accepted—and you'll be well on your way to gliding down your own personal Slip 'n' Slide."

My gut tells me the guy's full of shit, but I can't resist. I click on the pay-per-view link, make my payment of a hundred bucks, and immediately click on the new video that pops up.

"Hey, guys. Thanks for tuning in," Mr. Squirt-Master says to the camera. "In this video, I'm going to show you precisely how to make *any* woman squirt, no matter who she is—whether she's experienced with squirting or a total newbie. It doesn't matter if your woman has never even had an *orgasm* before. My technique, if performed correctly, will make her explode with cum. I'm talking every woman. Every time. No matter what."

"Just get to it, fucker," I grumble.

"The best part? I'm not just going to merely tell you about it—I'm going to *show* you on three real women, so you can see *exactly* how it works."

"Another fake," I mutter. But, still, I keep watching.

"Before we get to the women, however, let me talk you through the technique on this model of a vagina."

Mr. Squirt-Master pulls out a rubber replica of the interior of a vagina and proceeds to finger it, talking in explicit detail about his "surefire" technique. A couple times, I rewind the video and watch him explain something again. What he's saying sounds ridiculously simple, actually, but infinitely variable, depending on a particular woman's physiology. And I'm not one hundred percent sure how this fingering technique differs from the way I give women—well, Sarah, nowadays—vaginal climaxes through G-spot stimulation. How the fuck does this differ from fingering her G-spot for an all-body orgasm? It's not clear to me.

"You need to be able to *feel* exactly what you're looking for inside there," he says, confirming what I was just thinking. "There's no way for me to explain it to you precisely—it takes a little trial and error."

Ah, so he *is* full of shit. How convenient. He knows no one can call him on his bullshit, because every guy who fails using this technique will assume he simply hasn't mastered the "trial and error" portion of it. Douchebag.

"Be persistent," Squirt-Master says. "And soon, you'll be able to do it on command."

"Sure, buddy," I murmur.

In short order, Mr. Squirt is joined on-screen by a smoking hot woman who's *way* above his paygrade.

"Guys, this is Carla."

"Hi," Carla says, waving at the camera and smiling.

I can't help wondering how much this guy had to pay Carla to do this.

"Have you ever squirted before, Carla?"

"Nope," she says. But I don't believe her for a second. Surely, squirting is Carla's *thing*.

"Do you want to?" the guy asks.

"I sure do." Carla smiles at the camera. "What woman doesn't?"

I smirk. *Well, my wife, for one.*

"Then let's do it," Mr. Squirt says.

Carla stands and undresses unceremoniously, while Mr. I-Can-Make-Any-Woman-Squirt stays fully dressed, and then the two of them sit down together on the edge of a bed.

Mr. Squirt turns to the camera. "I'm going to show you everything I just talked about, step by step. But first, I'm going to kiss her and touch her skin lightly, just to get her pussy aching for me. Once I've got her good and wet and throbbing, then I'll finger her the way I explained to you on the rubber model." He holds up his hand by way of demonstration. "To recap: I'll use my middle and index fingers right on that spot I was telling you about, and I'll stroke it in a 'come hither' motion—like this." He demonstrates in the air. He turns to Carla. "Ready to squirt all over the bed, Carla?"

"I sure am."

Mr. Squirt proceeds to kiss Carla, slowly stroking her arms and bare back and face as he does, and the woman's nipples visibly harden under the stimulation. I can almost smell her pussy getting wet for him through the screen. Or, hell, maybe she's just a great actress.

After a couple minutes, Mr. Squirt stops kissing Carla and looks at the camera. "Guys, take a note. Women really need foreplay—and lots of it. You can't just shove your hand up inside her and expect her to be ready for you. Pro tip: women respond particularly well to kissing as foreplay." He winks again.

Jesus. Give me a fucking break. I roll my eyes. Is there a man alive that really needs this explained to him? For fuck's sake, I should click out of this horseshit right now. But I don't. I can't. I'm fixated. God help me, I've gotta see for myself if Carla's gonna blow or not.

After a bit more kissing and stroking Carla's bare torso and nipples, the guy finally slides his hand inside Carla, making her moan, and, thirty seconds later, holy motherfucking shit, she arches her back and shoots so much cum out of her pussy, it's like he's shoved a fire hose up there and turned it onto high.

"Holy motherfucker," I say out loud, leaning toward the screen.

"Oh my God," Carla blurts, looking genuinely shocked at the massive stream of ejaculation erupting from her body.

Mr. Squirt looks at the screen and flashes a shit-eating grin. "And that's how to do it, fellas. *Every fucking time.*"

Carla looks at the guy and then at the camera. "Oh my God," she says softly, beaming. "Amazing."

"You wanna do it again, honey?" he asks her.

Carla nods vigorously.

And, by God, he does it to her again. Within a minute. Jesus Christ.

Okay, fuck me. This is fucking impossible. Obviously, the whole thing is rigged. A total farce. I mean, there's no doubt Carla actually squirted (*twice!*) right before my eyes —I don't think that was, like, digital special effects or something—but there's no way this was her first time. No way. Obviously, this woman's one of those rare specimens who squirts as easily as she sneezes. The woman must be able to charm her Skene's gland like a snake charmer on a cobra.

"That was pretty awesome, huh?" Mr. Squirt-Master says. He's alone on-screen now. "One hundred percent real, too. I bet some of you are thinking I'm pulling a fast one here, though? You're thinking Carla is a porn star who squirts for a living?" He chuckles. "*Wrong.* What I just demonstrated was Carla's first squirt, unless she was lying to me, I suppose. But, regardless, it doesn't matter. Because this will work on *any* woman, no matter who she is—whether it's her first time or one hundredth. The only requirement is that she's turned on, so don't skimp on foreplay. She should also want to squirt. *Consent*, guys." He winks and claps his hands together. "Okay, so for all you doubters, I'm now gonna demonstrate my technique on two more ladies. Both of whom have never squirted before."

Woman Number Two enters the screen. She's older

than Carla. Attractive in an elegant sort of way. I never would have pegged her for participating in a video like this. Quickly, she strips off her dress, revealing a hot as fuck body underneath her prim clothes, and the pair then proceeds to engage in the same dog and pony show as the guy did with Carla. And, I'll be damned, within a matter of minutes, the woman's pussy blows like a geyser right before my eyes.

Holy fuck. Hopefully, my house isn't on fire right now —because, if it is, oh well. It's gonna burn to the ground.

On to Woman Number Three, with the same result: *Thar she blows.*

In frustration, I pull on my hair. What does this little shit know that I don't? There's got to be more to it than he's said in the video—because what he's described, I'm positive I'm already doing, without success.

My hands trembling, I pull out my phone, and thankfully, Henn answers after one ring.

"Hey, Jonas," he says in greeting.

"I need you to find someone for me," I say. "As soon as possible."

"Why, hello, Jonas. I'm doing great. Thanks for asking. How are you?"

"It's this guy on YouTube. I'll send you the link. His video is pay-per-view, but I'll buy it for you."

"A pay-per-view video?" Henn laughs. "Is this video *porn*, by any chance?"

"I emailed you the link. Watch the video and find me the guy. I need to talk to him."

"Hang on. Let me open your email." There's a pause during which Henn presumably clicks on my link. "Holy shit. I was joking about the video being porn!"

"Can you find him for me?"

"I can do anything. I'm a fucking genius. Hang on." I hear the video playing in the background, followed by the sound of Henn chuckling. "This guy is showing his face, Jonas. Dig around a little bit, and I'm sure you'll find him without me."

"I don't have time to hunt this guy down and figure this shit out. I'd rather pay you to do it for me."

"Well, I'm not going to take your money to find him. I should be paying *you* for buying me this video. You've made my day." He snickers. "And Hannah's night."

I don't reply. He's obviously still watching the video, and I don't want to chat while he's doing that. It's not natural.

"Oh, hello beautiful," Henn murmurs. Which means Carla must have entered Henn's computer screen. "You want me to find this woman, too?" he asks.

"Of course, not. Just the guy."

"Just wondering."

"I'll never ask you to find me another girl as long as I live, Henn. I'm *married.*"

"Well, obviously, Jonas. I was only asking because I thought maybe this is a business matter for you. Maybe these two embezzled funds from one of your companies, for all I know. How was I supposed to know you're asking me to hunt down a squirt-master for personal reasons?"

I shake it off. "I need this guy's phone number. I want to ask him a few questions."

"So do I. Damn."

"Just find him for me."

"Only if you pass along anything really good you find out."

"Deal."

"Damn. I feel like such a pimp right now. Whoa! Carla

just blew her load all over the bed! Now *that's* what I call entertainment. Hot diggity damn."

"So you're on it?"

"Like purple on Barney. This is definitely a white-hat job. Absolutely free of charge."

"Thanks."

"Is this a thanks-for-having-my-babies surprise for Sarah?" Henn chuckles. "Most guys give their woman jewelry for that occasion, but Jonas Faraday makes his wife squirt."

Shit. I didn't even think of giving Sarah jewelry to thank her for the babies. "Most guys give their wife jewelry after she gives birth?" I ask.

"From what I've seen.

"Shit."

"Don't worry. I'm sure it slipped your mind because you were so busy being terrified your entire family was gonna die." He pauses again, and I can hear the video playing in the background. "Ooh. Enter woman number two," he mutters.

"Okay, thanks. Gotta go."

"Hang on. How are Sarah and the babies doing?"

"Good. Sarah's still not feeling great, but—"

"But she's about to start feeling a whole lot better. Ka-*bam!*"

"Shut the fuck up, Henn. You're talking about my wife."

"Sorry."

"I'm joking. It'd be hard to get pissed at a comment like that when we're watching a squirting video together."

He laughs. "True. How are the babies?"

"Jesus, Henn." I pause the video on my screen, not

wanting a woman to be squirting while I gush about my daughters. "The girls are great. They should be coming home in about three weeks."

"Awesome."

"Yeah, they have to get to the point where their lungs are fully developed. Pretty normal with preemies, I guess."

"Send me a pic."

"Hang on." I scroll through my photos, looking for a good one, as the sound of the video continues on Henn's side of the phone call.

"Woman number two just wet the bed!" Henn announces gleefully. "Oh my God. This is my favorite thing."

I find a cute photo of the babies and email it to Henn. "Just sent you a pic."

"Aw, they're so cute. They've filled out a ton since I saw them. They look like actual humans now instead of raisins. I can't wait to see them again. Hannah and I are planning to come to Seattle when Josh and Kat have baby number two."

"Did you hear it's a boy?" I ask.

"Yeah. They FaceTimed Hannah and me with the news. Kat was freaking out about having a penis inside her at all times, and Josh was like, 'What's new about that?'"

We both laugh.

"Oh, here we go!" Henn blurts. "Woman number three, step right up."

"You and Hannah should stay here when you come to Seattle."

"Cool. I'll tell Hannah to calendar it—right after I make her squirt."

"Okay, that's it. I'm hanging up. Sarah will be home soon."

"And you've got some more porn to watch?"

"Nah, I've got actual work to do. I'm a respectable member of society, if you haven't heard."

"I read that article about you guys in whatever magazine. The one about Peru? So impressive. You looked like Thor. I told Josh they made you look way cooler than him and he almost punched me in the face."

"Poor Josh. He's so used to Kat lying to him about his good looks," I say, "he's not equipped to handle the truth."

"I'll tell him you said so."

"Please do."

We share a chuckle.

"Talk to you later," I say. "Thanks for the favor."

"You're not going to ask me if I've got any news about The Club before we hang up?" Henn asks.

My stomach tightens. "Do you?"

"Nope. Nothing at all. I'm just shocked you didn't ask me about it. I think that's what the psychologists call *progress.*"

"You'll tell me if something comes up, right?"

"Indubitably."

"Then, I trust you."

"Cool. Talk to you soon, Jonas."

"Talk to you later, Henn."

"Happy squirt-questing!" he calls out enthusiastically.

"You, too."

"Oh, Jonas? Get Sarah a whole mess of diamonds. She's been through a lot."

"I'll do exactly that. Thanks for looking out."

"You bet, brother."

We say our goodbyes, and the minute we hang up, I cue up the squirting video and re-watch the entire thing. When it's over, I rise from the kitchen table, taking care not to whack my gigantic erection against the underside of the table as I go, and beeline straight for my shower, unbuttoning my jeans as I go.

17
JONAS

Sarah moans softly next to me in the bed, and my eyes spring open. A hard rain is battering the house. It's the dark of night. I don't understand that particular moan she just made. Is she in pain?

"Sarah?" I reach for her. My eyes haven't adjusted to the darkened room. "Are you okay?"

Sarah's hand skims my bare chest and then grazes the front of my boxers, right over my cock. "Jonas," she whispers softly. "*Yes.*"

Oh, thank God. I know that tone in Sarah's voice. That's pure arousal right there—which means that moan she made a moment ago was the sound of my baby having a sex dream. *Hallelujah.* These past five weeks since Sarah gave birth, her sex drive has been as dead as a doornail—and understandably so. Not to mention, the doctor made it clear we'd have to wait to have penetrative sex for six to eight weeks. So, I've done my best to take care of my sexual urgings on my own and leave Sarah to heal in peace.

But did that guttural moan signal my wife's body is

beginning to spring back to life? If so, I've got a tongue that's ready, willing, and able to give her an orgasm, if she wants one, while we continue waiting for the green light for me to use my fingers and cock.

I scoot myself closer to Sarah in the warm bed, and my rising erection brushes against her thigh. "What's going on, baby?" I coo.

"Jonas, I had a dream about you," she whispers, finding my hard cock with her palm.

And that's it.

I'm instantly on fire.

With a soft moan, I push Sarah onto her back, pull up her nightgown, and begin pulling down her big ol' granny panties with the big ol' pad in the crotch. Even if I'm not allowed to make love to my wife with my cock and fingers yet, I'm beyond hungry to eat my favorite meal, after so many weeks without.

Sarah's body stiffens. "I'm still bleeding."

"I don't care," I soothe, as I yank her undies past her hips.

She puts her hands on mine, momentarily halting the downward progress of her underwear. "It's gross."

"It's not. It's natural. I don't care."

"The sheets."

"I'll get some towels."

My cock at full alert, I get out of bed and stride toward the bathroom, navigating my way slowly in the moonlit room. Surprisingly, given all the pussy I've eaten in my lifetime, this will be my first ever bloody box lunch. With women before Sarah, bloody sex hasn't come up. And with Sarah, even though I've always been more than willing, she's always pushed back, saying it's "too gross." But this time, all bets are off. I'm earning my red wings with my wife, come hell or high water. Or blood.

I grab a couple towels from the bathroom cabinet and head back into the bedroom, stopping at my computer on the way to press play on "Sky Full of Stars" by Coldplay. Ever since I played this song for Sarah in the hospital, I've been dying to make it the soundtrack to an earth-shattering orgasm for her. And now, I've got my chance.

I crawl back into the bed and slide two thick towels underneath Sarah's hips.

"Relax," I whisper. "I want to do this. I'm turned on by the idea."

She trembles and nods and I know she's finally surrendering to arousal.

I kiss Sarah deeply, running my fingertip across her collarbone. "Just relax." My fingers slide over her erect nipples. There's a small patch of wetness in the fabric of her nightgown, over her left nipple. The sensation makes my cock twitch again.

I pull her to a sitting position, remove her nightgown, and assess her naked torso in the moonlight.

Holy fuck, she's a work of art. Mother Earth. Demeter. I lay her onto her back and lay soft kisses on her C-section scar. "*Besitos* for your booboo," I coo.

"Oh, Jonas."

I kiss the faded scar on Sarah's ribcage, the only visible reminder of what those bastards at The Club did to her in that bathroom at U Dub.

"*Besitos* for this booboo, too," I whisper. And it's clear from her reaction, she's beginning to feel swept away in the sensuous moment.

I work my way up from Sarah's ribcage to her bountiful, dripping breasts—and holy fuck, it's like her skin is covered in a thin layer of sweet cream. It's all I can do not to take her nipple into my mouth and give it a good strong suck. But I don't. Not without permission. Not until she's ready to enjoy giving me so much pleasure, despite herself.

I pull at Sarah's panties again, this time forcefully, and she arches her back to help me out.

With her undies off, I spread Sarah's smooth thighs and the unmistakable scent of Sarah, the scent I've dreamed about on a running loop for weeks, floods me. But this time, for the first time ever, that delectable aroma is tinged with something new—the one fragrance I've been hardwired to recoil from since as long as I can remember. *Blood.*

And yet, I don't recoil.

Not at all.

In this moment with Sarah, I feel nothing but turned-on and aching to chow down on her. The weight of my lifelong demons sloughing off me.

I reach gently between Sarah's legs and touch her tip. It's erect—hard and slippery against my fingertips. And soaking *wet.* Way more than usual.

Sarah moans softly at my touch. "Jonas."

Under normal circumstances, I'd probably kiss Sarah's mouth for a while massaging her clit and G-spot. But since doctor's orders prevents me from reaching inside her to work her G-spot, I lean in and lap at her pussy with the full expanse of my tongue, provoking a loud groan from Sarah that makes my cock drip with pre-cum.

The wetness against my tongue is a different texture than usual, but no less sexy to me. Also, the taste is something new—salty and sweet, with a hint of metallic. It's not unpleasant, though. On the contrary, it's deliciously primal.

I'm in the zone now.

Barreling ahead voraciously with my tongue and lips.

Taking both of us into previously uncharted territories.

There's nothing I won't do for my wife. Nothing I won't do to give her pleasure. And nothing about her that could ever turn me off. She's perfect to me. Always. In all ways. And in this moment, I'm proving it to her with my voracious hunger.

A.

That's the shape my tongue is making against Sarah's delicious, wet, salty pussy. And in this moment, it's a tribute to Sarah's *a*we-inspiring *a*ss.

Propiedad de Jonas Faraday.

That's what the tattoo on Sarah's ass cheek proclaims —that her ass belongs to me. Jonas Fucking Faraday. And it *a*lways will.

B.

This one is for my precious *b*aby. My *b*rilliant wife with *b*odacious *b*reasts. B is for my *b*eautiful intake agent. The bombshell who unexpectedly *b*lasted into my care- fully constructed life three years ago and *b*lew it all to smithereens in the *b*est possible way.

"Jonas," Sarah chokes out. She's writhing. Gyrating. Moaning with pleasure. And I'm losing my fucking mind. I'm being *b*aptized in Sarah's pussy right now. I'm *b*orn again.

Blood on the sheets.

Blood on the floor.

Blood on the tiles.

Blood in my mouth and on my tongue and chin.

I'm born again in this moment, taking away the power of the one thing that's always scared me the most. The one thing I thought I couldn't handle. But now I know—there's nothing I won't do for my baby. Nothing I can't handle, as long as I've got my precious baby by my side.

C.

This one's for my baby's delicious cunt. It's favorite meal—no matter when or how it's served. Even when it's dripping with salty goodness—the evidence of what Sarah's body went through to give life to two tiny miracles. Of course, it's also for climax. Because Sarah's about to have a lot of them.

D.

Desire.

Dreams.

My unwavering dedication to Sarah, our family, and our love.

Too many times to count, my wife has said I'm the man of her *d*reams. With each swipe of my tongue, I *d*edicate myself to making sure Sarah *always* thinks that of me. Whatever I have to *d*o in the *d*ecades to come, however I need to make Sarah understand she's my everything, my universe, my sky full of stars, I'm *d*etermined to *d*o it all. This woman is my heart's desire. The *d*ivine original form of beauty, love. And I'm *d*evoted to making sure she always knows that.

E.

Because my wife is my *e*verything. *E*ternally. And bringing her *e*cstasy, however I can, will always be my greatest pleasure.

Speaking of which . . . Just as I'm thinking about bringing Sara ecstasy, she suddenly makes The Sound—

the one that tells me she's on the bitter cusp of release. Practically growling with excitement, I grab her hips and ferociously pull her against my mouth, desperate to shove her over the edge. Oh, God. I feel like a lion devouring my prey. I feel untethered. Unshackled by social construct and rules. *And it's turning me the fuck on.*

Finally, Sarah releases with a loud scream. As she does, I grip my cock and pump myself forcefully, continuing to lick her furiously through her orgasm.

Furiously.

F.

After feeling your body rippling against my tongue and lips, I want to *fuck* your brains out, *furiously*, Mrs. *F*araday. But since I can't do that, per doctor's orders, I'm going to get you to the *finish* line again and again tonight, with nothing but my magical mouth.

G.

Well, that's an easy one. You're the *goddess* and the muse, Sarah Cruz. Also, the stars in my *galaxy*. You're *glorious*. *G*orgeous. And our love is the *greatest* love story ever told.

H.

Because I'm a *hungry* boy tonight. With a gigantic *hard-on*.

I'm frantic now.

I...I...I.

I love you, Sarah. Oh, how, how I love every fucking *inch* of you.

As I lap at her pussy, I pull Sarah's body forcefully into my face, my hand working savagely on myself as I do. And when I'm about to move on to "J," Sarah gasps for air, stiffens, and explodes with a second orgasm that sends her clit, and everything connected to it, seizing violently under my tongue.

I growl and pump my shaft as Sarah's body warps against my mouth, slurping her up and burrowing my tongue even deeper inside her, as far as it will go, enjoying the sensation of her orgasm rippling against me.

"Jonas," she gasps out. "Jonas!"

There's my J.

Jonas.

I'm the man who loves Sarah with all his heart and soul. And always will.

"Jonas, oh my God," Sarah gasps out. "That was incredible."

"I'm not done yet."

I crawl up to her mouth and kiss her fervently, and she receives me hungrily, running her hands through my hair and moaning into my lips as I continue pumping my shaft. I'm so turned on by now, I'm delirious. Throbbing almost painfully. I kiss her passionately, twirling my fingertips against her hard, slippery, swollen clit. Little circles, again and again. Until it's clear Sarah is ramping up, yet again, and barreling toward yet another powerful release.

My cock is dripping with evidence of my arousal. My heart crashing in my chest. Panting, I bring my mouth to Sarah's ear. "Baby, let me taste all of you. Just once. I want *all* of you."

Sarah knows exactly what I'm begging for. And much to my relief and thrill, she doesn't hesitate to give it to me. "Yes," she gasps out. "Do it now."

My body electrified, I lean down, take Sarah's hard nipple between my lips, and give it a good, strong suck, like my very life depends on it. And that's it. As delicious, sweet fluid floods my mouth, Sarah begins screaming at the top of her lungs in a way she's never done before, and her pussy begins rippling forcefully underneath my fingertips for a third glorious time.

"Holy *fuck*, Jonas," she says through gritted teeth. "Do it again. One more time."

I can't breathe. Can't think. I'm nothing but a vessel right now—for love, lust, adrenaline, desire. With my hand stroking my hard shaft, I take her other nipple into my mouth and give that one a good, strong suck, too, and come hard as warm milk floods my mouth again.

Oh, Jesus. As my eyes roll back into my head, I'm momentarily blinded by pure bliss.

Blood on the sheets.

Fuck yeah, there's blood on the sheets. And on my lips, nose, chin, and tongue. And I'm not scared of any of it. Not ashamed. On the contrary, I'm *free*.

I get out of the bed and scoop Sarah into my arms, adrenaline flooding me. Blood on the sheets. Blood on the tile. Blood on the floor. I'm not scared of any of it anymore. Fuck you, Blood. Blood in my mouth and on my lips. *Fuck yeah*. I've done it. I've emerged victorious. If I'd gotten to "V," that's what it would have stood for. *Victory*.

With Sara in my arms, I flip on the light in the bathroom, and turn toward the mirror.

"Holy shit," Sarah whispers, staring at our reflections.

We're both completely smeared with blood, from the tips of our noses all the way down to our thighs—as if some mad painter used our skin as his living canvas.

"It's war paint," I declare. "We won the war, Sarah. You helped me win the fucking war."

She furrows her brow. "The war?"

"Blood on the sheets. Blood on my lips. Blood on my

tongue. It was the one thing that scared me the most, and now it's the source of our pleasure. My badge of honor. The evidence of my oath to you—to do anything, always, to make you understand you're my everything."

Her features soften. She touches my bare chest. "You're a warrior, Jonas. A sexy fucking beast."

She's right. I'm a savage beast. An animal. My lips are covered in her blood and milk and her delicious juices. My chest is marked with my religion and smeared with the blood of my righteous battle.

I bare my teeth at myself in the mirror, enjoying the contrast between my teeth and bloodied face. I look like a shark. No, a *megalodon*. A beast that's prehistorically wired to eat and fuck and nothing else. And I fucking love it.

My whole life, the Blood has come after me and rendered me powerless. Since age seven, the Blood has terrified me, like nothing else. But now I've made the Blood my bitch. And I'm never going back.

My chest heaving, I grab Sarah's hand and press it against my heart, right over the spray of tattooed stars adorning my flesh. "Do you understand now?" I choke out. "I love every inch of you, Sarah, without reservation or condition. I *crave* every drop of you. No matter what. I want it all."

She swallows hard, her eyes blazing. "I understand."

"There's nothing to stop us anymore. Nothing between us. No dark spaces. No secrets. No room for doubt. We're one and the same, you and me. Your body is mine. Your pain is mine. Your pleasure is mine. *Your blood is mine.*" I take a deep breath. "'Love is composed of a single soul inhabiting two bodies.'" I'm quoting Aristotle.

But the way I feel as the words escape my mouth, I've claimed them as my own.

Sarah's eyes well with tears. She grips my neck and rests her forehead on my shoulder. "I love you."

"I love you. More than those words could ever convey."

I carry my wife into the shower, turn on the hot water, and let the water baptize both of us anew. We're reborn on this day, Sarah and me. We've taken our love to a whole new level. One that transcends who we're supposed to be, how we're supposed to love, and takes us exactly as we truly are.

"*Hoy en adelante, renaces,*" Sarah whispers, giving voice to my own thoughts. *From this day forward, you're reborn.*

"*Hoy en adelante, renazco,*" I reply. "And so are you, pretty baby."

Sarah nods and says, "*Renacemos juntos.*" We're *reborn together.*

18

JONAS

"Hello?" a male voice says in greeting.

I press my phone into my ear. "Is this Sam from the squirting videos?"

"Who's this?"

"My name's Jonas. I saw your videos and was wondering if you'd answer a couple questions."

"About the videos?"

"Yes. About the technique."

"Yeah, okay. I've got fifteen minutes for you—if you've got a hundred bucks for me."

"Seriously?"

"Yep."

I resist the urge to call him a douchebag. "Fine."

He gives me his Venmo information and says he'll wait till the money comes through. When it does, he says, "Okay, what do you want to know?"

"Can you *literally* make women squirt, each and every time you try—or is that an exaggeration?"

"Well, every time I *want* to do it, I can. Sometimes, I don't want to do it."

"When wouldn't you want to do it?"

"If we're on a friend's couch. Or in a public bathroom. Or some other place where it wouldn't be great to have to clean up a gallon of cum."

I process that for a minute. I never thought about that.

"Or if the woman's just not that into doing that particular thing. It's pretty intense, especially for someone who's not used to doing that. Some women do it for the first time and get addicted. Others do it and freak out and say never again. It really depends. If they're not down with it, I never force them, obviously."

"Why do some of them freak out? What do they say about not liking it?"

"I don't know. Women have all kinds of weird hang-ups when it comes to sex. Some don't even like oral sex, go figure. I guess when it comes to squirting, some of them are grossed out by it or whatever."

"But every single woman *can* do it, right? As far as you know, there's not a woman alive who can't do it through some physiological barrier?"

"If she's got a pussy she was born with, then she can do it. No doubt about it."

My heart his thrumming in my chest. "Have you ever encountered a really tough nut to crack?"

"Sure. Lots of times."

"But you cracked them, eventually?"

"Of course. Every time. Like I said, if I want to do it, I can. Every time."

"How did you crack the really tough nuts? And how long did it take you?"

"Timing varies. Sometimes, I need more than one session with a woman to get her there. But I always do."

"But how? *How*?"

"The key is getting her crazy turned on. Like, totally out of her head. Not thinking about anything but how good she feels. And then, *bam*. I flip the switch and enjoy the geyser."

I exhale. It's the last frontier for Sarah and me, and I want it so badly I'm going fucking insane. "Percentage-wise, how many women would you estimate are tough nuts to crack?"

He considers the question. "Take ten women. One will be easy-peasy squirting material, like the women in my video. Just squirting cum at the drop of a hat. One will be *really* hard. The kind where I'll need more than one session to get her there. Those are a special kind of fun, actually. When you finally get her ther, you feel like a fucking superhero, you know?"

"I bet."

"And then the rest in the middle will usually get there in one session, after varying amounts of time. As long as you're not in any rush, and you follow the technique, exactly as I've explained it in my videos, it's not that hard to get them there. One, two, three, squirt."

"But what's the one, two, three? That's what I need to know."

"I told you that in the video."

"But there are gaps in the information."

"I don't think so."

"I do. Explain it to me, slowly. Don't skip anything."

With a loud exhale, he complies with my request, with me asking several detailed questions along the way.

"Here's what I still don't get," I say. "How does any of that differ from what you need to do to get a woman to have a vaginal orgasm through G-spot stimulation? I know exactly how to get an orgasm through fingering the G-spot. I'm a master at it. What I can't seem to do is get her to *squirt* while she's having an orgasm like that."

"If you already know how to get an orgasm through her G-spot, then getting the squirt to go along with it is going to be like child's play to you. Most guys I talk to don't even know how to find the G-spot. All you need from there is a minor adjustment at the very end, right before she comes, and she'll explode with cum for you."

"Tell me what I'm missing."

"Time's up."

"Excuse me?" I ask.

"I agreed to give you fifteen minutes. Time's up."

"You can't be serious."

"I can give you another fifteen for another hundred."

After muttering a string of curse words under my breath, I send the douchebag the money, against my better judgment, and he thanks me upon receipt.

"Okay," he says. "You know when she's *really* turned on, and you're stroking her G-spot, and she's starting to make crazy sounds and you feel the G-spot enlarging like a water balloon?"

"Yes."

"That's the fork in the road. If you keep going, she'll have a vaginal orgasm that'll curl her toes. If you want her to squirt in that moment, though, you've got to pull her magic trip cord, right before she reaches The Promised Land."

He explains the subtle difference in what I'm feeling for deep inside a woman—what this "magic trip-cord" feels like. "If you dig your fingers into the G-spot when it's engorged like a water balloon," he says, "you'll feel it in there. It's called the Skene's gland. Feels like a tight band down there. Put it between your middle and ring fingers and kind of pull on it, like you're squeezing the last bit of toothpaste out of a tube."

"So, you're saying to *milk* her?"

"Exactly. It sounds gross, I know. But yeah. That's the movement you're going for right at the end. Down, then inside and up. If you're doing it right, you'll feel that gland fill up with fluid between your fingers, and you'll hear this kind of faint whooshing sound. Once you hear that, massage it again and again. Three or four times. And then milk the fuck out of her."

I process for a moment. "Why didn't you say any of this in your videos?"

"Because I wanted to hold a little back. Can't give away *all* my hard-earned information on the internet."

I run my and through my hair. "Okay," I say on an exhale. "Let's talk about the one in ten who's the toughest nut to crack. What would you say is the most important thing for cracking a woman like that?"

"Getting her completely out of her head. A woman like that is just hung up on something. Maybe she's been sexually assaulted or abused in the past. Maybe she's insecure about her body. Maybe she was raised to think sex is bad. I have no fucking idea. But whatever is messing with her head, you've gotta help her get over it, whatever it is, or she'll never relax enough to give you the geyser."

"And what strategies do you employ to do that?"

"Well, you gotta make her feel safe, first of all. Helps if she feels loved, but that's not my forte. I can fake it okay, though. I guess, overall, my best advice is to surprise her, if you can. Keep her guessing. Kill her with foreplay and anticipation. Mess with her head to keep her brain from telling her body to close up shop."

"Shock and awe."

"Exactly."

"I can do that."

"Oh, if you're dealing with a tough nut to crack, then edging is the name of the game. Don't let her have multiple orgasms. Let it build, so she can't control herself when you finally push her over the edge. If you do that, she'll have no choice but to squirt all over you, once you finally pull her magic trip cord."

"How do you know all this?"

"Trial and error for twenty years. I'm almost forty. Been focused on this particular thing since I was nineteen."

"How'd you first figure it out?"

"By accident. My girlfriend squirted like a backyard hose set to high on night, and I was like, holy fucking shit. *What was that?* The next time, I retraced my steps, or thought I did, and nothing happened. So, I became obsessed with making it happen again. Finally, I could make her squirt on command. But with my next girlfriend, I couldn't do it. So, I became obsessed again. And that's when I figured out how to make it work like clockwork."

"How many women have you done it to?"

"At least a couple hundred."

"Seriously?"

"Why so surprised? That's not that many women, spread out over the course of twenty years."

"No, I guess not."

"You think if a guy looks like a nerd, he can't get women, right? But the thing is, when you know this nifty little trick, word gets around and women practically line up around the block. So, chin up, dude. Master this trick and you'll get women, too."

"Thanks."

"Here's a good tip. I do this all the time, man. Say you get a match on Tinder or whatever, and the woman says, 'Sorry, I'm just not feeling it.' Tell her, 'Fair enough. But FYI, before you ghost or block me, you should know I can make any woman squirt on command.' A good half the time, no matter who she is, no matter how hot she is, she won't be able to resist saying, 'Prove it, asshole.' And then, boom. *Squirt.* Another one bites the dust. It's definitely a cool parlor trick."

I grimace. This guy is giving me hives. "So, it's a parlor trick for you?" I ask. "You push a certain button on whichever woman-computer you're in bed with and cum squirts out her chute?"

"Exactly."

"So, a squirting orgasm isn't meant to be the peak of sexual pleasure for your partner—the divine original form of ecstasy?"

"Huh?"

"I'm asking if you're addicted to squirting orgasms because it's the pinnacle of female pleasure, and that's what turns you on about it, or if you think it's a cool thing to be able to do because other guys can't get the swing of it?"

"Yeah, it's a cool thing to be able to do, man. It gets me chicks I wouldn't otherwise get, because they're curious. Don't overthink it. Just roll with it."

Shit. I've been taking advice from *this* moron? Clearly, this jackass isn't striving to be a Judo master. He's not a mountain climber like me or a guy who considers sex an art form. No, he's an average dude who stumbled upon a parlor trick that lures curious women into his bed, if only briefly. And that's it.

"Thanks for the info," I say abruptly. "I think I've got everything I need."

"You've still got a few more minutes on the clock. You don't want to ask me anything else?"

"No, I'm good. I'll combine what you've said with a few things I already know and give my woman an orgasm that will take her to the peak of female pleasure. Not as a parlor trick. But as the culmination of human possibility."

19
JONAS

"I wish this guy would drive a little faster," I mumble to Josh, glancing at our driver. I look at my watch. "Fuck."

"How does Sarah put up with you?" Josh says. "You're the most impatient man alive."

"Well, good thing you're not married to me, huh? My impatience isn't your problem."

Josh bursts out laughing. "Sure, Jonas. You're not my problem." He looks out the window of the car. We're on the freeway, heading home from the airport after another successful business meeting in Denver, where we hope to significantly expand the business. Josh says, "Come to think of it, other than the fucking part, we might as well be married. I see you every day of my life and Climb and Conquer is our baby."

"There's no such thing as marriage without the fucking part. That's called *friendship*. A business partnership. In our case, I also think the fact that we're brothers would throw a wrench in your plans for our holy matrimony."

"All I was saying is I don't know how Sarah puts up with you, as her husband. I could *never*."

I roll my eyes. "Well, lucky me, somehow, I've tricked Sarah into liking me." I look at my watch again. "I hope she's home from visiting the babies by now. If not, I'm going to have a nervous breakdown."

"Why are you acting like this? I know you hate being away from her, but, Jesus, man. Chill."

"I'm all out of chill, my brother. Today marks the finish line on our post-natal 'no sex' order from the doctor. Today, thank God, I'm finally allowed to fuck my wife again."

"Oh, well now I understand. No wonder you've been acting like a madman."

"I'm going to text her. Make sure she gets her ass home, if she's not already there."

"Oh, yeah, I'm sure she'd love receiving a text like that —commanding her to get her ass home."

"As long as it's for sex, I actually think she'll like it."

Josh's eyebrow rides up. "Sarah likes a little caveman shit, does she?"

I wink. "Under the right circumstances."

"Nice."

I pull out my phone and send Sarah a text.

Me: Josh and I landed safely. We're on our way home now. I'll probably be there in thirty minutes or so.

Sarah: Welcome home! Did your fancy meeting go well, Mr. Mogul?

Me: Really well. Price is right. Numbers crunch. Their locations are a perfect complement to our existing ones. Match made in heaven.

Sarah: Woohoo! Mr. Fancy-Pants strikes again! Does this mean we're gonna be rich, hubby?

Me: We'll be rolling in it.

Sarah: What a relief, since I married you for your money.

Me: Yes, I know.

Sarah: How many gyms will this add?

Me: 20.

Sarah: 20 more gyms? SQUIRT!

Me: LOL. That's what's finally gonna make you squirt for me? More gyms? Well, shit. If that's the case, I'm gonna buy up every rock climbing gym in the world for you, Mrs. Faraday.

Sarah: SQUIRT!!!!

Me: Oh, God. You're making me rock hard while I'm sitting next to my fucking brother.

Sarah: Tell him I said hello and congrats!

Me: I'm done talking to him. Starting now, I'm laser-focused on YOU.

Sarah: Oooh la la. Let's drink some champagne tonight to celebrate the deal. I'll pump and dump.

> Me: Oh, baby, you know I love it when you talk dirty to me.

> Sarah: Pump and dump. Puuuump and duuuuuump.

> Me: Stop turning me on. I'm already losing my mind today, knowing the doctor cleared you yesterday.

> Sarah: WOOHOO!!!!!

> Me: So . . . does that mean you're feeling ready to give it a whirl?

> Sarah: FUCK YES!! Let's do it! I'm ready for some massive cock in every hole.

I send her a meme of a guy with his eyes bugging out and she sends me laughing emojis.

> Sarah: That was a joke, sorry to say. I think you're going to have to be really gentle with me at first.

> Me: I'll take you any which way you need, baby.

"Are you still texting with Sarah?" Josh says, out of nowhere.

I snap my head up from my phone. "Why do you care?"

"Just wondering. You've been smiling and laughing like crazy. Is she telling you stories about the babies?"

"Yeah."

"How are they doing?"

"They're good." Luckily, I talked to Sarah last night about the babies, so I'm able to add a bit of truth to my lie. "The doctor said they'll probably come home next week."

"Awesome."

I return to my phone.

> Me: Shit, baby. My cock has grown at least fourteen inches since I've been sitting here texting with you. You'd better be naked and spread eagle when I get home, woman, or I'm going to throw you over my shoulder and drag you into my cave.

> Sarah: I'm at the hospital right now, singing "Twinkle Twinkle Little Star" to two tiny humans. But I promise to get naked and spread eagle when I get home tonight.

> Me: Tonight? Fuck that! Get your ass home NOW! I want to fuck my wife!

> Sarah: I can't. After my visit with the girlies, I'm going to pump some breast milk to leave for them overnight. And then, I promised my mother I'd swing by her place for dinner tonight. I thought you were coming home much later.

> Me: I changed to an earlier flight so I could FUCK MY GORGEOUS WIFE.

Sarah: Shoot. I could maybe cancel dinner with my mom, but I'm still going to be at the hospital for at least another hour.

"Fuck," I mutter. I call up to the driver. "Excuse me. Change of plans. I need you to drop me off at the U Dub Medical Center, rather than my residence."

"No problem."

"Sarah's at the hospital?" Josh asks.

"Yup."

"Aw. So you've decided to be a good daddy and race over there to say hello to your daughters?"

"Yep."

Josh snickers. "Surely, that's what's driving this sudden change of plans."

"Of course."

Josh chuckles. "I definitely see a medical supply closet in your near future, my brother."

I flash Josh a cocky grin. "I'll see the babies *and* drag Sarah into a medical supply closet. I don't see how either thing is mutually exclusive."

"Such a multi-tasker." He motions to my phone. "Maybe you'd better tell Sarah about that change of plans, so she doesn't race home to surprise you."

"Good thinking. That sounds like something she'd do."

Me: I'm coming straight to the hospital. Do. Not. Leave.

Sarah: Yes, sir. Yippee!

Me: If you leave, you'll be in big trouble.

Sarah: I am very scared of you, so therefore I will not move.

Me: Good girl.

Sarah: I have a surprise for you at home, btw.

Me: Does it involve tadpoles and marshmallow chicks?

Sarah: Nope.

Me: Thank God.

Sarah: Can't wait to see you!

She adds a heart emoji, an apple, and an eyeball to the end of her message. I quickly surmise that's her way of telling me I'm the apple of her eye. Which is sweet. But I'm not in the mood for sweet. Smirking, I reply to Sarah's cute message with four emojis of my own: a bone, a bomb, a hammer, and a heart.

Sarah: LOL. What does that mean?

Me: I can't wait to bone you, bang you, hammer you, and make love to you.

Sarah: Aw, Mr. Valentine's Day Bullshit strikes again.

> Me: Are you wearing a skirt?

> Sarah: Yes.

> Me: Good. Take off your panties before I get there. Go commando for me, baby.

> Sarah: Will do. See you soon, love.

> Me: See you soon. Can't fucking wait.

I plop my phone in my lap, just in time to overhear Josh say to our driver, "Hey, sir. Looks like you can drop me off at the hospital, too. No second stop required."

"What?" I blurt.

Josh holds up his phone. "Kat and Gracie are on their way to visit the babies." He smiles wickedly. "They said they're going to surprise Sarah and take her out to dinner." He bursts out laughing.

"Josh, don't be a dick," I say. "Tell Kat the situation and tell her to turn around."

"Hell no. I'm not gonna stop my beloved toddler from generously visiting her tiny cousins in the hospital, just so her Uncle Jo Jo the Dancing Clown can screw Auntie Sarah in a supply closet. In the interest of helping me raise my child to become a caring, considerate, empathetic human being, you're going to have to wait to bang your wife at home."

"Gracie's got a lifetime to visit her cousins. It's you and Kat who need to exercise caring, consideration, and empathy. For *me*."

Josh is thoroughly amused. "Nope," he says. "I not only told Kat I'd meet her and Gracie at the hospital, I also said I'm taking everyone out to dinner after our visit."

I try to grab my brother's phone, but he pulls it away and shoves it into his back pocket, a wide grin on his face.

"Consider this a life lesson, my impatient brother," Josh says with mock solemnity. "A chance for you to learn the art of the chill, whether you like it or not."

20

JONAS

When Josh and I bound into the NICU, we find ourselves in the middle of a raging Faraday girl-party that's already well underway. Sarah's sitting in a glider chair, holding our little Sunshine. Little G is sitting next to Sarah in another glider, holding Luna with an assist from her mom. Of course, Gracie's wearing her pink sparkly boots, which are barely hanging over the edge of her chair. And to my surprise, Sarah's mother is here too, taking photos and instructing everyone to smile.

Oh my fucking God. I love each and every one of these people, God knows I do, each in a very different way. But I must admit I had a very different kind of "party" in mind when I told our driver to take me to the hospital, instead of my empty house.

As my brother beelines to his wife and toddler, I stand rooted to my spot inside the NICU entrance. I need a minute. I wasn't prepared to be Happy-Go-Lucky Jonas right now. I was all amped up to be Fuck-My-Woman-Till-She-Screams-My-Fucking-Name-In-a-

Supply-Closet Jonas. Followed immediately by Marveling at My Babies Jonas. But this? It's going to require far too much socializing for my current mental state to handle.

"Hi, love," Sarah says to me. "I'm so excited you're here." There's a bloom in Sarah's cheeks again these days —an exceedingly welcome development after the long haul of the last eight weeks. She's even got a mischievous twinkle in her eye again, too. She says, "Kat surprised me by bringing Little G *and* my mom to visit the babies." She barely contains her smirk. "Isn't that *awesome,* honey?"

"*Awesome,*" I deadpan. "What a great surprise."

Sarah bites back a chuckle.

I cross the room toward Sarah and notice she's wearing the white sundress I bought her in Belize. "I love that dress," I say, flashing back to the memory of that dress crumpled on the floor of our tree house. I lean down to kiss her.

"Today's a special occasion," Sarah whispers into my lips. "I figured you'd enjoy taking it off me."

I'm about to whisper something suggestive to Sarah in reply, but all of a sudden, I'm getting hugged by Kat and Gloria, and kissed by Little G. Gloria tells me to scoot close to everyone and pose for a photo—and it's immediately clear that any form of stolen, covert fuckery with Sarah here at the hospital is a pipe dream.

"Take Marisol, honey," Sarah says. "I'm sure she's been missing her daddy."

I take the baby from Sarah's arms, and the minute I do, I'm so consumed with love for the little person in my arms, I totally forget about my initial motives for getting dropped off at the hospital. "Hello, my Sunshine," I coo, after getting myself settled into a glider next to Sarah.

"You've grown so much in three days." I look at Sarah. "Her growth is physically *visible*."

"Isn't it crazy?" Sarah says. "I'm shocked every single morning when I first see them."

I gaze at Luna on Gracie's lap. "They're the prettiest babies the world has ever seen—along with you, Gracie." I wink at my niece, and she tries to wink back, closing both of her eyes in an exaggerated blink.

"What do you think of your cuzzies?" Kat asks Gracie. "Are they cutie patooties, or what?"

Gracie nods.

"Say cutie patootie for me, Gracie," Sarah prompts. "Cutie patooties."

"Cootee patoooootshee."

Everyone chuckles and praises Gracie, at which point she says it again, which elicits another round of laughter.

"You funny," Sarah says.

"I funny," Gracie agrees. "I a big girl."

"You sure are, *mamacita*," Sarah says. "You're the biggest cheese in town—*La Quesota*."

Gloria giggles. "Oh, Sarah."

"Cheese?" Gracie says to Kat.

"Yep, you're the big cheese," Kat agrees.

"No, Momma. *Cheese*."

"Oh, you want some cheese?" Kat says, and when her toddler confirms that's the case, Kat replies, "I don't have any. But we're going to a restaurant in a few minutes, so you can have some then."

Gracie looks like she's about to protest. And loudly, too.

"Hey, Gracie-cakes," I say. "You want to hold Sunny now?"

Gracie's face lights up. "Sunneeeee."

"You have to be quiet and calm."

"Okay."

"Oh, you're good," Kat says to me.

At Sarah's cue, I take Luna from Gracie's lap and get Marisol settled in her arms, with an assist from Kat, and immediately start cuddling Luna in my arms. "Hi, Crazy Monkey," I whisper, kissing her little head. "Do you know I love you to the moon and back again?" I look up, intending to make a comment about how much Luna looks like Sarah, and I'm met with Sarah's teary-eyed gaze.

Sarah mouths, "I love you."

So, I return the gesture, feeling like my soul is flying around the NICU. Indeed, for the life of me, I suddenly can't remember what the fuck I was so grouchy about when I first walked into this room.

———

"Do you want pizza or chicken nuggets?" Kat asks Gracie.

"Peesuh," Gracie replies, her little face lighting up.

"Pizza, *please*," Kat corrects.

"Peesuh, pwease."

"Thank you for your nice manners, honey."

Fuck me. Okay, I'm grouchy again. And then some.

The minute we arrived at this deep-fried travesty of a chain restaurant, a restaurant with fucking kiddie menus for the love of fuck, I tried to get Sarah to pop into the bathroom with me for a quickie, but her mom was on her like white on rice about one thing or another, and absconding Sarah for some lightning-fast bathroom-fuckery simply wasn't in the cards.

And then, fuck me, the nanosecond after Gloria finally left Sarah alone, when I thought I might have a brief window of opportunity, Gracie suddenly wanted her Auntie Sarah, and nobody else, and there was nothing to do but pile into the restaurant booth, with Gracie wedged between Sarah and me.

"Oh, that's pretty," Sarah says, referring to Gracie's crayon-scribbles on her kiddie menu.

"Tank oo."

"Are you excited to meet your baby brother in a few months?" Gloria asks the kid.

Gracie smiles. "He going to be Jack."

Sarah smiles at Josh and Kat. "You went with my suggestion?"

"So much for surprises," Kat says. "Thanks, Gracie."

"Welcome," Gracie replies happily, clearly not understanding her mother's sarcasm.

"Oh, come on, Kat" Sarah says. "Surprises aren't allowed in this family."

"Jack Faraday," Josh says wistfully. "Now that's a *name*. That's a guy who drinks scotch *neat*. Jack Faraday doesn't own a *wrench*. He just uses his *teeth*."

"Whenever Jack Faraday crosses the border into a new country," Josh says, "they immediately put his face on their currency," Sarah says, and everyone laughs.

"The Pope calls *Jack Faraday* and asks him to bless his water," Josh says.

"When the groundhog comes out of his hole in February, he asks Jack Faraday what he should do," Kat adds.

"*Gravity* asks Jack Faraday for *permission*," Sarah says.

"When Jack Faraday wipes his ass, the toilet paper writes him a 'Thank You' note," Josh says, and we all roll with laughter. Even Gloria's wiping her eyes and holding her sides.

"After Jack Faraday visits the Virgin Islands, they officially rename them... the *Islands*," Sarah adds, wiggling her eyebrows, and we all lose it.

"Hey now," Kat says primly. "Speaking as Jack Faraday's mother, I can assure you Jack's going to be a complete gentleman to anyone he pursues romantically."

"It was a joke," Josh says.

"Yes, I know," Kat says. "And that's find for now. But we can't joke like this after he's born. I don't want Jack growing up, thinking he has to be the Crocodile Hunter because of his name. For all we know, he'll want to take ballet lessons and be on Broadway one day. Or he'll bring home his boyfriend, Brad. Whoever he is, I want him to feel free to be exactly that."

"Well, of course," Josh says, rolling his eyes. "All I was saying is Jack Faraday is a cool name. However his coolness ultimately manifests is perfectly fantastic with me."

Kat beams a smile at her husband. "Good. Thank you."

"Of course. The only caveat being, if he's anything like Peenie, then I'll disown him."

Kat bursts out laughing. "Well, duh."

From what I've seen, this is a regular inside joke among the Morgan clan. And I think I know why. I met Kat's craziest brother, Keane, aka Peen, aka Peenie Weenie, at Josh and Kat's destination wedding in Hawaii a couple years ago, so I'm well aware the guy's got a larger-than-life personality. According to Kat's older brother, Ryan, with whom I'm pretty friendly, the Morgan clan doesn't call Keane Morgan their family's *black* sheep. He's their *neon* sheep. The family actually adores their quirkiest member, precisely because he's so weird. But, still, one of their favorite sports is razzing him, even behind his back. Much to Keane's pleasure, as I recall.

"We really do love the name Jack," Kat is saying to Sarah, when I tune back into the conversation. "You're *sure* you and Jonas don't mind us stealing it? I know it was one of your top picks for a boy."

"It's yours," Sarah says. "We're done making babies."

Oh, my heart.

I gaze at my wife, my heart panging for her. Of course, she's right. The doctor recently told us our chances of getting pregnant again are practically nil. And even if that weren't the case, I've already told Sarah I'd never want to try for a third baby. Not after the way Sarah's life hung in the balance this time. Regardless, however, it breaks my heart to remember the way Sarah broke down in tears in her doctor's office, when she first heard the news.

"Oh! I just thought of a Jack Faraday joke!" Sarah's mom, Gloria, says. Is she trying to distract her daughter from thinking about that day in the doctor's office? I'm guessing yes. Gloria continues, "I promise I won't say this sort of thing, after Jack is here. But I think it's a good one." She pauses for dramatic effect, her pretty face aglow, and finally says, "When Jack Faraday visits the Queen, she curtsies to *him*."

Everyone laughs.

"Good one," Josh says. "Now I see where OAP Cruz gets her sharp wit."

As Sarah says something to her mother, and the women engage in conversation, I get my brother's attention.

"Hey, do me a favor and stop calling Sarah 'OAP' all the time. You don't even know what it means."

"Of course, I do. Why do you think I say it all the time? Because I know it annoys you."

My heart is racing. Did Sarah lie to me when she told me she didn't tell Will what OAP meant?

"How do you know?" I manage to ask.

"Reed told me, after Will told him." He chuckles. "I think it's hilarious."

Motherfucker. My heart is crashing in my chest. I'm gonna track down that motherfucking piece of shit "2Real" and pummel his goddamned, fucking face for blabbing Sarah's secret. Sara was drunk and high and mesmerized by Will's superstardom, so I really can't blame her too much. But Will? Yeah, I'm going to murder that motherfucker.

"Other *Asshole's* Property," Josh says, interrupting my rambling thoughts.

"Huh?"

He leans forward and whispers. "Other *Asshole's* Property. That's what it stands for, right?"

I swallow hard. "Yes. That's it."

Josh chuckles. "I don't know why you're so touchy about it, honestly. I mean, so what if 2Real had the hots for Sarah? Obviously, he was paying an indirect compliment to *you*." He winks. "*Asshole.*"

"Oh, I thought of another Jack Faraday joke!" Gloria says, drawing our attention to the women's conversation. She pauses, briefly. And then, "Jack Faraday's *grocery list* is a *New York Times* bestseller!"

Everyone chuckles and praises Gloria's effort, including Sarah. Thankfully, whatever sadness washed over Sarah a few minutes ago is gone now.

"The ball is in your court, Jonas," my brother says. "Are you going to let Gloria show you up like this?"

Shit. He's right. I love my mother-in-law with all my heart, but she's not known for being funny. And I don't normally join in when our usual foursome is having a group 'clever-fest' like this, since I'm always fourth in the pecking order when it comes to being funny. But this time I actually think I've got a pretty good one.

"All right. I'll play," I say. "The doctors tried to circumcise Jack Faraday, but their scalpels kept breaking."

To my surprise, everyone bursts into hysterical laughter, even Gracie, who clearly doesn't understand the joke.

"*Intentional* humor from Jonas Patrick Faraday?" Josh says. He glances out the window of the restaurant. "Are there frogs falling from the sky? Is it Judgment Day?"

"So, will this legendary Jack Faraday have a middle name?" Gloria asks.

Josh looks at his wife for permission, and she motions to him like she's giving him the floor.

"As a matter of fact," Josh says. "We've decided our awesome son with the coolest name ever will bear the name of the most awesome, coolest person we know." He grins at me. "He'll be Jack *Jonas* Faraday."

My jaw drops open. "Thank you," I choke out. But it's all I can manage.

"You bet," Josh says. "We both think we'll be lucky if Jack grows up to be even half as awesome as his Uncle Jo Jo the Dancing Clown."

"Unkie Jo-Jo-da-danseen-clahn," Gracie mutters, as she continues coloring with crayons on her menu. And for the first time ever, I don't mind her calling me that nickname in the least.

21

SARAH

My mom is sweet.

And I love her.

My mom is nurturing and kind.

I have to keep reminding myself of these positive and loving affirmations, so I don't throttle her. After dinner at the restaurant, while we were waiting for the check, my mom insisted on riding home with Jonas and me in our car, even though Kat was the one who'd picked her up and brought her to the hospital in the first place, because she said she was worried about me. She said I looked flushed and flustered. And that, clearly, I'd overdone it for the day, contrary to doctor's orders.

In reality, of course, I was feeling extremely horny at that moment, because my impatient and excited husband had started stroking between my legs underneath the table, in anticipation of finally getting to fuck me when we got home. I told my mother I was fine. That Jonas was going to take the best possible care of me. But no matter what I said, she wouldn't back down. And now, unfortunately, Jonas and I will have to wait for God knows how long until my mother is gone to finally get to jump each other's bones.

"Let's get you out of that dress and into your pajamas, *mi hija*," Mom says as we enter the house.

"No, Mama," I say, because there's no way in hell I wore my delicious-anticipation sun dress from Belize so that my darling *mother* could rip it off my body tonight. *Jeupucha culo.*

"Well, let me get you some herbal tea, then," Mom says. "Where's your thermometer, *cariña*? I'll take your temperature."

I settle onto the couch. "I'm fine. And if not, Jonas will take extra good care of me—just like he always does. Because he's my *husband*, Mom."

"Yes, I know that. But Jonas just returned from an important business trip today and I'm sure he's exhausted. Let Jonas get himself de-stressed and settled while I tend to you."

There's no use in fighting her. The woman is hard-wired to smother me with love.

"Okay, Mama. Some tea sounds good."

As my mother scurries off to the kitchen, I look around the living room, wondering where Jonas went. But I've no sooner had the thought than Jonas appears with my pump, his eyes burning like hot coals.

"Thank you, love," I say with a wink. As we both know, the sooner I pump and get my mother the fuck out of here, God bless her, we'll be free to ravage each other.

With a return wink, Jonas exits the room, leaving me on my own to pump and receive the well-meaning smothering I'm about to receive.

An hour and a half later, when Jonas strides through our front door after driving my mother to her house, I'm sitting on the couch where my mother left me, watching a show. When he reaches me, Jonas wordlessly grabs the remote control from my lap, turns off the TV, pulls out his phone, and emphatically presses a button. A moment later, "Radioactive" by Imagine Dragons starts blaring through our sound system. And I know that's Jonas' way of telling me his boner is radioactive at this point—on the cusp of going fucking nuclear if he doesn't *finally* get to fuck his wife.

He guides me onto my back on the couch, clearly intending to fuck me right here and now.

"Hold on," I gasp out. "I've got something I need to show you first."

"The only thing I want you to show me is the inside of your pussy," Jonas mutters. He slides his hand between my legs as he kisses my neck. His hard-on is spearing my hip. His skin is practically sizzling with arousal.

"I'm *dying* to show something to you," I insist. "I won't be able to fully relax until you've seen it."

Jonas freezes, exhales, and bows his head. As my husband knows, I can only come when I'm fully relaxed and not thinking too much, even after all this time. "Sarah," he murmurs. "It really can't wait?"

"It can't. Come on."

I sit up, grab Jonas' hand, and pull him toward a nearby hallway. Our destination? The nursery. The magical room that's finally ready for our daughters' arrival any day now.

As we walk, Jonas presses a button on his phone, stopping the blaring music, and mutters, "It's times like this, I wonder if you love me at all."

I giggle. "I do. With all my heart."

"You have an evil way of showing it," he teases.

"Poor baby."

By the time we reach the closed door of the nursery, my stomach is fluttering with a thousand butterflies. For the last four days, while Jonas has been away on his work trip, I've worked almost nonstop on this surprise. During that time, I've constantly fantasized about the look on his beautiful face when he sees my work. Hopefully, reality will meet my fantasies about this moment.

"My surprise is in the nursery?" Jonas says.

Since the answer is obvious, given that we're standing at the nursery door, I reply with, "Close your eyes." When he complies, I take a deep breath, open the door, and lead the great love of my life into the room.

22

JONAS

I don't know how Sarah managed it, but she did: I'm not thinking about my throbbing dick anymore. Not feeling grouchy I'm not presently fucking her. I'm too moved by Sarah's incredible surprise, too over-whelmed with the clanging of my heart, to think about sex in this moment.

I'm stunned. In awe at what she's done to the walls of the baby's room.

I've always known Sarah is a talented artist.

But this? This mural she's painted onto the lavender walls of the nursery is a masterpiece.

Every wall is littered with twinkling stars. A giant moon and yellow sun, both of them smiling broadly, adorn two opposite corners—while an array of colorful scenes and images fill in the rest. There's so much good-ness here, so much symbolism and love bursting from every inch of this room, I can't focus for long on any one image.

"Sarah," I whisper. "It's incredible."

Sarah squeezes my hand and points upward, drawing

my attention to three phrases scrolling across the tops of three contiguous walls. Reading aloud, she whispers, "*Love is the joy of the good... the wonder of the wise... the amazement of the gods.*"

Goose bumps erupt all over my body. "It's perfect."

She strokes the tattoo on my forearm bearing these same words. "We're the greatest love story ever told, Jonas. Our love is the envy of the gods. I want our daughters to feel that love every time they're in this room." She turns me around and points behind us, to the top of the fourth wall. Reading aloud, she says, "*You're the divine original form of you. Our family is the divine original form of love.*"

I open and close my mouth, incapable of conjuring words for what I'm feeling.

She turns me back around and directs my attention to a painted scene on one of the walls. It features a big, blue, shaggy monster with one enormous eye and a huge goofy grin. He's standing on a flowery hilltop, next to a slightly smaller, yellow monster with long eyelashes, red lips, and a noticeably huge ass, while two little-girl monsters with colorful bows on the tops of their shaggy heads frolic in the flower fields surrounding them.

"We're a family of monsters," I say?

She laughs. "I prefer to call us beasts. But, yeah. Whoever we are, however we don't fit in, we're never afraid to show it. We love each other, no matter what."

"I love it."

Sarah points to the next wall, where a muscled knight in shining armor sits gallantly atop a powerful white steed. A dark-haired queen in a flowing white dress sits behind the knight, squeezing him tightly, her cheek pressed against his broad back and little pink hearts flowing out of her chest. Two dark-haired princesses in flowing pink and yellow gowns ride alongside the knight, each one riding her own brown pony.

"You're my knight in shining armor, Jonas," Sarah says. "And I have no doubt the girls will always consider their daddy their knight in shining armor, too."

As I fight back tears, Sarah points to another wall. This time, there's a cartoon version of me with ridiculous He-Man muscles, a whoosh of Prince Charming hair, and a chin that's three times larger than the real thing. Cartoon Jonas is shirtless and positioned in the classic thinker's pose, a platinum bracelet on his wrist, and a book covered with a big, red heart in his hands. Two little babies are nestled in one of my muscled arms, opposite the book in my hand, and a cartoon version of Sarah with flowing hair lies on the ground at my feet on her stomach, gazing up at me with little hearts floating up from her chest. Like me, she's wearing a prominent platinum bracelet on her wrist.

"You're *teaching* all of us what true love is," she explains.

I shake my head. "This one should be the other way around. I didn't know what love was until you came into my life."

"Neither did I," she says simply. "Not this kind of love, anyway. I can't wait to see you with the girls, honey. They're going to love you so much."

"Oh, Sarah. This is incredible. Thank you."

"There's more."

She points to another wall. In this painting, I look like a realistic version of me, more or less. I'm not a beast. There's no gleaming armor or white horse. I'm wearing a simple T-shirt and jeans, smiling at the viewer, standing on a cloud. Sarah's behind me, way off in the distance, on another cloud, gazing at me and holding a baby in each arm. Once again, little red hearts flow from her chest and float up into the starry sky.

"Why am I standing away from you all on a cloud?" I ask. "Is this the afterlife?"

Sarah giggles. "No, it's the ideal realm. You're the divine original, just the way you are. We're off to the side admiring you, because we're so proud of you. As the girls grow up, you're going to inspire them so much, Jonas— the same way you've always inspired me."

My chest tightens. This is too much. I move to embrace her, but she holds up her hand.

"One more, *mi amor.*"

Sarah turns me around. This time, the wall is adorned with a towering, snow-capped mountain, topped at its highest peak by our little family. I'm holding Sarah's hand and raising it to the sky in triumph, and our dark-haired little girls are standing on either side of us, holding each of our hands. Pink and red hearts float above all four of our heads and mingle with the stars.

"In this one, we're climbing and conquering together," Sarah says. "Our family is the culmination of human possibility."

23
JONAS

I'm hard as a rock as I continue marveling at Sarah's artwork on the walls.

My body is a riot of need, love, and eight weeks of pent-up lust.

Words aren't enough. Not nearly enough.

The only way to express myself in this moment is with my body.

I pull Sarah's white dress above her head, and she gleefully lifts her arms to help me out.

I didn't envision making love to Sarah again after all this time in the nursery. Obviously. But now that I've seen Sarah's breathtaking tribute to our love, I can't do anything but drop to my knees, right here and now, without a second to spare, and worship at Sarah's altar.

With Sarah standing naked and glorious before me, I peel my clothes off, sink to my knees before her, slide my palms to her bountiful ass, pull her into my mouth, and begin eating my favorite meal.

Sarah wobbles in place and digs her fingertips into my shoulders at the touch of my tongue and lips, which causes rockets of arousal to shoot into my hard dick. In short order, she begins gyrating her pelvis along with the movements of my mouth, and, just like that, I feel like I'm being shot out of a cannon and straight into pure bliss.

My wife tastes brand-new to me. She's a revelation. A mystery unraveling, but only for me. And yet, she also tastes like coming home. I swirl my tongue over and around Sarah's sensitive flesh, aiming to take her higher and higher into the stratosphere. I've read women can be more sensitive sexually after giving birth, and I intend to find out, right here and now, if the theory is true.

Sarah's clit is hard and slippery under my tongue, exactly the way I've been dreaming about it for so many weeks. It's crack cocaine to me. The sweetest candy. And I can't get enough. Everything about Sarah's pussy, as well as this moment—the sounds Sarah's making, the way she's gripping my head to steady herself, the sweet taste of her, the fact that my cock feels like it's going to fucking explode from so many weeks of anticipation—every-fucking-thing is so erotic to me, so intoxicating, I feel physically high as I lap and lathe and worship and coax.

Finally, Sarah makes a sound that tells me she's damned close, so I slide my fingers inside her to her G-spot and begin stroking that sensitive bundle of nerves in concert with the movement of my mouth. I've learned, if I start touching her too early when I eat her, her orgasm won't be as powerful. Give her a while to ramp up before touching this spot, and she goes off like the Fourth of July.

In short order, she's growling loudly with extreme arousal. Her knees keep buckling, but she's using my head to steady her. Weaving her fingers into my hair and gripping the strands like her life depends on it.

When I feel her G-spot engorge like a motherfucking water balloon, I gently dig my fingers into the middle of the balloon, the way Sam the Squirt-Master instructed, and holy fuck, I feel something new there! The magic trip-cord Sam described! How have I not felt this hidden treasure buried here before? Or if I did feel it, how did I not understand its significance and function? Shame on me.

As Sarah's sounds become increasingly desperate, the wobbling of her knees more and more frequent, I follow Sam's next instructions to a tee, and, suddenly, I hear the damnedest thing. A *whooshing* sound described by Sam.

Shit. Sarah's not quite ready to come yet. If I were a douchebag like Sam, a guy who gets off on being able to perform a parlor trick, rather than giving my woman a transcendent orgasm, I'd put the cart before the horse and pull Sarah's trip-cord right now. But, obviously, that's not the way I do things. As much as I've been dying to conquer this final frontier with Sarah, I only want to do it if it enhances her pleasure, along with mine.

I keep licking and stroking without mercy, until, finally, her core tightens sharply around my fingers. She whimpers with pleasure . . . and moans loudly . . . and it's only then that I finally pull her magic trip-cord.

Eureka.

As Sarah lets out the sexiest scream of her life, as waves of pleasure throttle her core, warm liquid gushes out of her pussy and into my mouth.

Sarah crumples onto the floor, writhing like a fish on a riverbank. "Oh my God," she gasps. "Did I just pee on you?"

I laugh with glee. "No, baby. You *squirted* on me. Now, open your legs so I can lick up the rest."

"I did *what*?" she shouts.

"You had a squirting orgasm. Lie back, so I can finish licking up my prize."

She doesn't lie back. She's obviously processing what just happened.

"That wasn't a squirting orgasm," she says. "I had an orgasm, and then stuff squirted out of me."

I furrow my brow. "Yeah, exactly. That's a squirting orgasm."

"But I thought . . . Jonas, no. I had an orgasm, and then you did something weird inside me, and I couldn't keep myself from peeing."

"It wasn't pee." I run my finger through some of the liquid on her inner thigh and stick it into my mouth. "Definitely not pee." I repeat the exercise and bring my finger to her mouth—and to my surprise, Sarah takes my offering. As she tastes my finger, Sarah makes a face that says, "Could use a little more salt." But ultimately, she smiles reluctantly and says, "Definitely not pee." She bites her lip, contemplating something.

"You didn't like it?" I ask.

"I'm not sure," she answers. "It felt different than I thought it would. It was like I'm a vending machine and you pressed the right button and Ding Dongs came out. I thought squirting would happen when I reached the next level of the video game, so to speak."

"The video game being pleasure?"

"Yeah. I didn't know it would happen when you pressed a button on a vending machine."

"You're saying it didn't enhance your pleasure?"

"I don't know. The orgasm felt amazing, but it freaked me out to have stuff squirting out of me. I felt self-conscious. I felt . . . ashamed."

My heart sinks. "Sweetheart, you've got nothing to be ashamed about. It's perfect natural."

She presses her lips together. And once again, I'm reminded there's a figurative knot inside my wife's brain in terms of her sexuality. And that unraveling is my life's greatest addiction.

"I tell you what, my love. We'll leave further exploration of this particular mountaintop for another day. I won't press the button on your vending machine, ever again, unless you ask me to do it."

Her shoulders soften. "Thank you. I'm sorry. I know how much you wanted this."

"No, what I want is to give you every possible form of peak pleasure. All I want to do is make you feel so fucking good, your body does things you didn't even know it could do." I rub her thigh. "You know what I think? Now that your body knows it can squirt, now that we've broken through that mental barrier for you, I won't even need to press that button again. One day, you'll have an orgasm so intense, you'll squirt from sheer pleasure, and not because I've pressed any kind of button on your vending machine."

"That's what I want."

"Then that's what we'll wait for. If it doesn't happen again, so be it."

It'll happen again. And soon. I know it in my bones. But why make Sarah feel any kind of pressure or expectation?

She smiles. "Thank you."

"No, thank you. Trust me, figuring out the puzzle that is Sarah is my favorite sport."

She giggles and grabs my straining shaft. "Come here, love. Let's put this beautiful cock to good use, shall we?"

My chest heaves. "Lie back, love."

After she obeys my command, I stroke her pussy for a bit, getting her ramped up again. And when she's wet and writhing, I raise her thighs to my shoulders, slide her hands above her head, and sink myself inside her, taking care to be gentle, even though my body aches to plow the ever-loving hell out of her. The moment my body invades hers, Sarah lets out a sexy gasp, followed by a long exhale.

"Good?" I ask.

"So good," she replies. "You can go harder. I'm good."

I groan with relief and pleasure and start rocking back and forth with more enthusiasm, and, instantly, I feel like my very molecules are vibrating with the unique pleasure I've only ever felt when fucking Sarah Cruz. Oh, God, eight weeks without this glorious sensation has felt like eight years. Heaven itself couldn't possibly feel more blissful than this.

I slide Sarah's hands above her head across the carpet and pin them there, keeping my fingers interwoven with hers. My hips are gyrating in a way that ensures my shaft rubs against Sarah's clit with each thrust. My lips and tongue are hungry against hers.

In short order, I feel Sarah's innermost muscles tighten sharply around my cock. But the muscles don't release. She's on the bitter cusp. A tick shy of untethering completely.

I kiss her even more passionately, swirling my tongue in rhythm with the rocking of my hips, before moving on to kiss and bite her neck. After kissing my way to her ear, I whisper that she's the goddess and the muse. Hotter now than ever before. "You're Mother Earth," I whisper. "You're Demeter." I tell Sarah her sweet pussy owns me. That it's sweeter than ambrosia. I tell her she's so fucking gorgeous, so fucking addicting, she's my drug. An illicit drug that's in this moment being mainlined straight into my veins.

"I can't live without you," I whisper, my voice strained as I fight to stave off my own orgasm. "You're my everything, Sarah. Oh, God, I've missed fucking you."

With a guttural growl, Sarah comes hard underneath me, giving me permission to finally let go, as well. As Sarah's body ripples around my cock, my own body is racked with pleasure so intense, so profound and merciless, I'm momentarily blinded by bright colors and shimmering lights.

Still shuddering and shaking, I collapse on top of Sarah, and then lie still for a long moment, trying to catch my breath.

"Holy fuck," I mutter.

"Holy fuck," she agrees.

I roll off her and lie next to her on the carpet. "I thought I was having a stroke for a second there."

Sarah snickers. "Sex with me was as good as you remembered?"

"Better. You're a whole new level of hot."

She weaves her fingers in mine. "You were just sex starved."

"True, but it wasn't only that. You didn't feel a difference?"

She pauses. "No, I did. I know what you mean." She turns her head to look at me. "Isn't it kind of depraved we just did that in the girls' nursery?"

"Not really," I say. "It's not like they're here. It would be depraved if they were sitting in their cribs watching us, obviously. But this? All we did was christen the room by doing the same thing we did to bring them into existence in the first place, while surrounded by your beautiful artwork."

"You really like it?"

"I love it beyond anything words could ever convey." I roll onto my side and touch her face. "There's something I need to tell you. I should have told you about this before, I know, but I didn't want to upset you."

She looks concerned. "You're scaring me, Jonas."

"Nothing to be scared about. This is a good thing. I think if you take a moment and really think about it, you'll—"

"You hired a nanny, didn't you?"

I exhale. "Yes. She'll be starting in two weeks."

Sarah bolts to sitting. "Jonas P. Faraday! We talked about hiring a nanny and I said *no*."

I match her sitting position. "No, you said, 'We'll see.'"

"That was code for no fucking way, but I don't want to fight about it right now, and you knew that."

"In my defense, I hired her while you were lying unconscious in a hospital bed. When I was scared shitless I'd have to raise the girls, on my own. And I didn't seek her out. The perfect nanny fell into my lap, literally the perfect person, and I couldn't *not* hire her. I couldn't risk losing her, especially when I thought I might have to raise the girls alone."

That throws Sarah for a loop. "Who is she?"

"Mariela's cousin. A woman named Rosario who's been working as a nanny for a family in LA for years. When you were still fighting for your life, I called Mariela, just to hear her voice. Because I needed someone I could cry to, and she'd understand. And that's when Mariela told me about her cousin, Rosario. She said her cousin was about to start working for a new family in New York, since the kids she'd been helping with in LA were getting too old to need her. Mariela said if I made Rosario an offer, right then, she thought Rosario would drop the new family to work for us. But I had to act fast. So, I did."

"Okay, that explains why you hired her back then. But I'm fine now. You've had plenty of time to tell her there's been a change of plans."

"Why would I do that when I'm positive you're going to agree with me at some point and want a nanny. I'm sure of it. And when that happens, whenever that is, it'll be too late for us to get Rosario. By then, she'll be bonded with the new kids in New York, and she won't want to leave them. Mariela said she's very loyal and falls deeply in love with the children in her care."

Sarah takes a deep breath, clearly trying to calm the anger she's feeling. "When does she think she'll be starting this job with us?"

I swallow hard. "A couple days after the babies come home, so your mom can help us out for a few days first, like you wanted."

Her dark eyes blaze. "Jonas P. Faraday. When were you planning to tell me about this?"

"At the last possible moment. It's a testament to my love and respect for you I'm telling you now, with this much notice."

"You're trying to steam-roll me."

"Not at all. I'm trying to help you because you're stubborn and don't realize how hard twins will be. I'm still going to have to work long hours, you know. And you said your goal is to get back to work within a year, right? So, okay, then let's have Rosario with us from day one, so that the girls already love her when that time comes."

Sarah pulls a face that lets me know I've scored a point. It's not a surprise. I know she's been struggling to figure out how she's going to juggle career and motherhood.

"How about this?" I say. "Let's have Rosario come live with us and help out for a month, as a trial run. While she's here, she can help out as little or as much as you decide. Totally up to you. If you're not seeing the point in having her with us after a month, then I'll admit I was wrong about this, give Rosario a fat severance check and send her on her way to the next family."

Sarah chews the inside of her cheek. But finally, she says, "Okay. On two conditions. One, you never pull anything like this again. You had plenty of chances to tell me about this weeks ago, and you didn't."

"You're right. I'm sorry. It won't happen again. What's the second condition?"

"We give Rosario one of the rooms on the other side of the house, so she can't hear me when you're making me howl like a monkey at night."

I snicker. When I get Sarah going, anyone within a mile radius of our house could hear her screams of ecstasy. But since pointing that out wouldn't help my greater cause—namely, making sure my wife remains as happy and stress-free as possible—happy wife, happy life, right?—I reply with, "Deal. Rosario can take any room you want. Once she's here, you'll run the show."

"*I'm* their mother. Nobody makes important decision regarding their care without my permission. Including you."

"Absolutely."

"Why are you so dead set on having Rosario here?"

"Because our life is fucking awesome. And I'm going

to do everything in power to make sure we keep it that way."

"Honey, life can't be fucking awesome all the time," Sarah says. "Sometimes, the struggle is what makes life even more fun. It's hardship that makes you appreciate the awesome stuff, even more."

I pull her toward me and into my lap, and she immediately straddles me on her knees, slides her arms around my neck, and kisses me deeply.

"My love," I whisper into Sarah's lips. "I've already had more than my share of hardship in this lifetime. I've got no use for it anymore."

Sarah's shoulders soften. "That's fair. Don't worry, Jonas. Our life as Faraday, party of four, is going to be fucking awesome."

"I'm going to make sure of it."

She leans down and kisses me. And soon, the tip of my erect cock is pressing urgently against her warm entrance.

"Speaking of me making you howl like a monkey . . ." I whisper, a wicked grin unfurling across my face. "Is my newly minted MILF ready to howl like a monkey again?"

In reply, Sarah slides herself down onto my cock. "I'm a MILF, am I?"

"Actually, at the moment, you're a MIF. A Mom I'm Fucking—right fucking *now*." With that, I grip Sarah's hips and guide her pelvis in movement, back and forth. Back and forth. Until soon, she's riding me with fervor, and hurtling both of us to heaven, yet again.

"This is the last time I'm fucking you in our babies' room," Sarah chokes out, before throwing her head back and riding my cock like her very life depends on it.

24
SARAH

J onas and I are standing in the entryway of our house, having just arrived home from the hospital. We're each holding a baby in our arms. A baby we made by sticking our private parts together. And since we left the hospital, we haven't stopped marveling about the fact that the medical professionals at the hospital let us take these humans home with us. Forever. Without requiring us to get some sort of license or otherwise prove ourselves worthy.

"Home sweet home," Jonas murmurs.

"Yup." We've both remained frozen in place in our entryway, except for the fact that Jonas put the diaper bag down at his feet. I ask, "Why are we standing here?"

"I was waiting to see what you were going to do," Jonas says, "so I could copy you."

I giggle. "Why don't we sit down and stare at them while we wait for them to wake up? And when they do, we'll feed them?"

"Sounds like a plan to me."

We start walking toward the couch.

"What time do we need to return them to the rental place?" Jonas asks.

"Midnight."

"Good. Still plenty of time to stare at them in awe."

"Plenty of time."

We've both been joking like this since leaving the hospital. Neither of us can believe there's more paperwork involved in renting a car for a weekend than taking home a human forever.

We get settled on the couch. One baby per lap. And then, as planned, proceed to stare at our daughters' angelic, sleeping faces for several minutes without speaking. When we finally speak, we say the same sort of things we've been saying since they were born. We marvel at their faces. Their fingers. Their lips. We try to decide which features we've personally contributed. And through it all, we're calm and happy. Peaceful and filled with love.

"I told you we'd be able to handle this without help," I say.

Jonas snickers. "Sarah, they're both asleep, and we've been home for ten minutes."

"I'm telling you, Jonas. We've got this. You and me, with a little assist, now and again, from my mother. I've never been more certain of anything in my life."

———

"What the fuckity fuck?" I shout. "Why won't they stop crying?"

It's the middle of the night. And for the past two hours, a baby has been wailing in this house. Mostly, it's been Luna. Other times, it's Sol, after she's been awakened by Luna. And still other times, like right now, it's been both babies crying together, in stereo.

"Shh, baby," I say to Luna, frantically trying to pull down the flap on my nursing nightgown, but she's practically lurching out of my hands with her distress. "Oh my God, baby. You're acting like a lunatic. Luna the Lunatic." I fumble with my maternity bra, trying to get the poor girl what she wants, but apparently my fingers don't work at maximum capacity when there are small humans shrieking like banshees in my ears.

"When did Sunny eat last?" Jonas says, patting Marisol's back as he walks laps in the nursery "Is she hungry again, you think?"

"I just fed her a half-hour ago. Maybe she has gas?"

"I don't think so," Jonas says. "But I'll try rubbing her belly and burping her again."

"Maybe check her diaper again, too?"

Luna's cries are gaining steam, making me feel like my brain is short-circuiting. I finally manage to free my breast for her, but before she can get down to business, milk spurts out of my nipple and shoots across the room in a long, white stream.

"Circus tricks," Jonas says, laughing. "Wow, you're really digging this squirting-in-the-nursery thing, huh, baby?"

"Not funny," I say, even though I know, somewhere deep down, I'd find that joke hilarious if I weren't so fucking sleep deprived.

"She's starving, but she won't take my nipple," I say, as Luna turns her head and shrieks at the top of her lungs. "Why won't she take it?" I offer my breast to Luna, but, again, she's too distressed to suck on it. "Come on, *mamacita. Please.*"

"Maybe she needs a diaper change?" Jonas suggests. He's standing at the diaper changing station, opening Sol's diaper.

"It's worth a try," I say.

"Whoa!" he blurts. "I think I know why Sunny's been bawling. Holy shit. Literally."

My mom appears in the doorway, bleary-eyed. "What can I do, *queridos*?" The poor woman is sleeping standing up. For the past four days, she's been a saint. Helping us, day and night. But I can't keep running my mother ragged like this. The woman needs to finally get some sleep.

"Go back to bed, Mama," I say. "You can help tomorrow night, while Jonas gets some sleep, so he can finally get some work done."

"And what about you?" my mother asks.

I shrug. "I'm the one with the boobs."

As we all know, Luna has been rejecting bottles, even though she took them well enough at the hospital. Which means, at least for now, I'm her only source of food.

"I don't need to get any work done, baby," Jonas says. "I've cleared my calendar. I'll stay up every night, if needed, until Rosario comes on Monday."

I look at my mother to find her smirking at me. I've already told her about the nanny situation, and my objections to Jonas hiring one. In fact, I went on and on to my mother about my prediction that, upon Rosario's arrival on Monday, she'd have nothing to do. That, in fact, she'd be sitting around twiddling her thumbs because we'd be a well-oiled machine by then. My mother replied kindly to my comments. She told me to keep an open mind. She reminded me I'd have a month to decide, and not to worry about it now, even before Rosario's arrival. But looking at my mother's face now, I can tell she's inclined to agree with Jonas on the topic.

"Hey, Gloria," Jonas says, speaking loudly above both babies' wails. "Can you grab me a footie sleeper? Marisol exploded like a grenade. I think she passed half her body weight in poop."

"You've got it," my mother says, springing into action.

The babies' wails are synched up perfectly now—and in stereo. And, still, Luna won't take my breast.

"Should I heat up a bottle?" Mom offers.

"Yeah, that'd be good," I say. "Sunshine will be hungry soon, so we'll give her my breast while you or Jonas feeds Lunas."

"Why don't you finish diaper duty, Gloria?" Jonas says. "And I'll go get that bottle."

"Don't do it, Mom. He's giving you the shit end of the stick."

"And butt and thighs and private parts," Jonas readily acknowledges with a grimace.

Mom laughs. "That's fine with me. Whatever you need, I'll do it."

"Thanks, Gloria. This is a bad one."

When Mom takes over at the changing table, Jonas practically sprints out of the room like a prisoner of war set free, yelling, "I'm free!"

"Coward!" I shout at his back.

"Sorry not sorry!" he calls back from the hallway.

"That man is normally fearless," I say.

Mom chuckles. "If you saw this poop explosion, you wouldn't blame him for being terrified."

Luna's cries have become a bit less frantic, so I offer my boob again, and this time, she miraculously latches on and begins sucking voraciously.

"Oh, thank God," I mutter, melting into my chair and throwing my head back. "She's finally eating."

"*Pobrecita*," Mom says. "The poor baby tired herself out." She turns to Marisol on the changing table. "Now, isn't that better, *mamacita*? Yes, it is."

All of a sudden, Sol stops crying, like her sister before her. And just like that, the room is silent and calm.

Mom finishes putting clean pajamas on Sol and takes the glider across from mine with her.

"See?" Mom says. "Everyone's happy now. Nothing lasts forever."

"*Juepucha culo*," I mutter, using my mother's favorite curse, which she, in turn, got from *her* mother. "Am I a sea turtle who gave birth to eighty babies? It's hard to believe there are only two of them."

Mom chuckles. "Things will get easier."

Tears well in my eyes. "I sure hope so. I feel like I'm hanging on by a thread."

"Aw, sweetie. That's perfectly natural. You're not only adjusting to this brand-new life, you're also sleep deprived and your body is hard at work, producing milk. You're exhausted, in so many ways."

"But when won't I be exhausted?" I ask. "That's the thing. I can't press pause on any of this and say, 'It's okay, I'll catch up tomorrow, after a good night's sleep.'"

"Yes, you can. I'll stay until Rosario gets here. I'll tell the conference organizers my daughter needs—"

"No, Mama. Don't do that. Too many people are depending on you."

"But you're depending on me. And you're the only person who matters to me."

"No, no. I know how much this keynote address means to you. I was only venting to my mommy. I'm not asking you to fix anything. You've already done so much."

Marisol in Mom's arms makes a little sound that normally means she's hungry, so Mom slides her pinky into her grandbaby's mouth, which quiets her down. "Maybe you should see if Rosario can come a few days early," Mom says. "It seems like you could use an extra pair of hands."

I roll my eyes. "The last thing I need right now is to hear Jonas saying 'I told you so.'"

"Well, he *did* tell you so."

"Yes, I know."

"But I doubt he'd say that to you. He'd never kick someone when they're down."

"Jonas doesn't know I'm down," I whisper, before wiping the tears falling down my cheeks. "At least, not the full extent of it." My falling tears pick up speed. "I don't know what's wrong with me. I can't stop crying. I love them so much, but I feel like I'm drowning."

"Oh, sweetheart. This is totally normal. Tell your doctor. And tell your husband. You've got nothing to hide or be ashamed of. You'll get through this."

I sniffle. "Okay. Thank you."

Jonas enters the room, a bottle in hand, still looking a bit frazzled from the chaos from earlier. When he sees the serenity Mom and I are now basking in, his mouth hangs open in surprise.

"Looks like I should leave the room more often," he says.

"Is it *you*?" I tease. "Are *you* the drama?"

"Apparently so."

With a cute little wink that makes my heart skip a beat, Jonas hands my mother one of the bottles in his hands and she immediately offers it to Marisol, who takes it greedily.

Jonas stands over me, looking down at Luna. She's now fast asleep against my breast with her rosebud lips hanging open.

"Good job, Mommy," he says.

I look up at him, with tears spilling out of my eyes and his face morphs into a portrait of concern.

"I'm overwhelmed, Jonas," I whisper. "I don't know what I'm doing. I thought I would, but I don't."

Jonas gently takes my face in his palms and wipes my tears with his thumbs. "You're a natural, Sarah. Mother Earth, incarnate. Look at Luna right now. She's in heaven. As happy as a human being can be, because she's got *you.*"

I look down at sleeping Luna against my breast and then at Sol in my mother's arms. "I love them so much. I hope you know that."

"Of course, I do," Jonas says. He kisses my forehead. "And so do they."

I take a deep breath and look up at my husband. "Do you think you could ask Rosario if she's available to start a day or two early? I don't want to inconvenience her. Only if it wouldn't be a bother."

To my relief, Jonas doesn't look like he's about to say "I told you so." Indeed, he doesn't look the slightest bit smug or self-satisfied. On the contrary, his face is awash in nothing but love and devotion. "Actually, she's already mentioned several times she can start earlier, if we need her. All I have to do is say the word, and she'll be here with open arms and a loving heart."

I choke back a sob. "I'd really like that."

"Aw, my precious baby." Jonas pulls up a chair right

next to mine. He takes my hands in his and smiles. "Don't worry, love. We're in this together, okay? We're going to get the hang of this soon, and get you whatever help you need, whatever that is. And sooner than you'd ever believe, the only tears you'll be shedding will be tears of joy."

25
JONAS

Sarah shrieks with laughter and grabs her phone. "Do that again for a video!"

At my wife's command, I dip my body down into another push-up above Marisol on her back, and once again kiss her button nose beneath me—which, yet again, elicits hilarious peals of laughter from her, right on cue.

The twins are eight months old now. We came into the nursery earlier to snap our usual monthly photo of them with their gigantic stuffed Teddy bear—the photo we take on the same day each month to mark the girls' latest size and development—and then stayed after our photo shoot was finished to play and goof around with them.

"Put Luna on her back next to Sunny now," I say, hovering in plank position above Marisol. "I want to hear their laughter in stereo."

Sarah snorts. "Good luck with that."

It's an inside joke. As we've come to learn these past six months since the babies have been home from the

NICU, our beloved Luna isn't nearly as easy to impress as her sister. Luna *does* laugh, thankfully. Or else I'm sure our amusement about Luna's scowls and looks of disgust would have morphed into acute worry by now. It's just that getting Luna to let loose with even the slightest chuckle typically takes a Herculean effort, a tour de force of baby-friendly comedy, compared to the slightest hiccup or silly expression it required to send happy-go-lucky Marisol shrieking with raucous guffaws.

Sarah scoops our beloved Tough Nut to Crack off her blanket on the floor and positions her underneath me, next to Marisol. At which point, I immediately dip into another push-up, this time administering kisses on two little noses. To my utter shock, *both* babies react to my silliness with screams of laughter, all at once, which, of course, makes Sarah and me laugh along with them.

"Did you get it?" I ask.

"I got it!" Sarah confirms, holding her phone up with glee.

"Keep recording," I say. "I'm going to blow their little minds with this next thing."

I dip down again and give Sunshine a noisy raspberry on her bare belly, and, glory be, by the sound of her squeals, it's the funniest fucking thing that's ever happened in her short life. But when I dip down again and do the same thing to Luna's bare belly, our resident stalwart pulls a face of silent disgust that's so hilarious, I can't help collapsing onto the floor next to the babies and laughing uncontrollably.

Sarah flops down next to me on the floor, leans her forehead onto my shoulder, and howls along with me. Which, of course, makes Sol laugh even more, while Luna stares at the rest of us in fascination.

"I got all of it," Sarah says. "Oh my gosh. This is going to be my favorite video for the rest of my life."

I wipe my eyes. "Something tells me you'll have lots more favorites, as the years go on. If Luna already thinks my jokes are stupid and embarrassing at eight months old, what's she going to think of me as a teenager?"

"She's going to think you're the best daddy in the history of the world," Sarah says with a kiss to my bare shoulder. "Who tells the stupidest, most embarrassing jokes, ever."

When I've composed myself from laughing, I pick up Luna and sit her on my lap. "Are you always going to think my jokes are lame, Lunatic? Or will you give your poor daddy a break, now and again?"

"Oh, Daddy," Sarah says in her bored socialite voice. It's the one we always use for Luna. A silly voice better suited for an eighty-year-old dripping in diamonds and furs. "Of course, your jokes will always be lame to me. I'm too cool for school, dahling."

"Challenge accepted," I say to Luna in my lap. "Here's a good one. Knock, knock?"

Again, Sarah uses her Luna voice. "Dear God. Who's bothering me now?"

I chuckle. "A-hole."

Sarah giggles but resumes her Luna voice. "A-hole who, for the love of all things holy?"

"A *whole* bunch of poopie in your diaper!"

Sarah bursts out laughing, which makes silly Marisol follow suit. But Luna is singularly unimpressed.

I address our little Sunshine. "Thank you, Sol. At least one of you thinks I'm hilarious."

Sarah picks up Marisol, the one we're sure is a brand-new soul on her first trip to Earth, and speaks in the voice we always use for her. A bright, happy chipmunk voice that suits her perfectly. "You funny, Daddy! Keep those hilarious jokes coming!"

"Don't encourage him," I say, taking over Luna's salty voice for Sarah.

"Aw, come on, Lu," Sarah replies in Sunshine's cheery voice. "Give him a chance."

I sigh and roll my eyes on behalf of Luna. "The man doesn't even have functional nipples. He's worthless to me."

Sarah laughs heartily, which, of course, makes cheerful Marisol laugh, too. Which then, miracle of miracles, makes Luna break down and start giggling, too.

"Oh, gosh, I could do this all day," Sarah says on an exhale. "I don't think I've ever laughed as hard as I do when we're playing with the girls."

She sits Marisol onto the floor, so I do the same with Luna, and we pull out a set of wooden blocks for them to play with.

"It's fun that they're so different," Sarah says, as we watch them playing with the blocks.

"It definitely keeps things interesting," I reply. "We've got one who wears her heart on her sleeve and gives her love away like confetti on New Year's Eve, and one who guards her heart and makes you work for every ounce of love she decides to give."

"Exactly. Isn't it amazing they popped out that way?"

"It is. It'll be interesting to see their personalities flourish, as they get older. Will they stay this way?"

"Oh, I'm sure they will." Sarah hands Luna a block. "I wonder which of them will get her heart broken first? The one who gives her love away or the one who guards it fiercely?"

"Why would you say that?" I ask." Even thinking about either of them getting their heart broken makes me want to throttle whoever does the breaking."

"Oh, Jonas. Both of our daughters will get their hearts broken. It's unavoidable and necessary, in order to grow and figure out who you are and what you want."

"Absolutely not. Not my babies."

"Yes. I'm sorry to say."

"Nope. Because they'll never be allowed to date."

"Is that so?"

"Yep. Not until they're adults who can spot an asshole a mile away."

Sarah rolls her eyes. "With that approach, you'll only guarantee they'll sneak out their windows in the middle of the night as teenagers. Well, Luna will, anyway. And she'll probably drag Sol along with her."

"I'll put bars on the windows and doors. Problem solved."

"Wow. You're a genius," Sarah says sarcastically.

"I've got to do something. Look at them. They're already knockouts."

We gaze at our daughters playing with their blocks, and an overwhelming sense of joy and completeness envelops me. I slip my fingertip underneath Sarah's chin, turn her face to mine, and kiss her passionately.

"Wow," she says against my lips. "What was that for?"

"I love seeing you so happy. I love the sound of your laughter, mixed with theirs. It turns me on."

Sarah blushes. "I love the sound of my laughter, too. Especially when it's mixed with theirs and *yours*."

"Are you happy?" I ask.

"I've never been happier."

"Same here." I kiss her again, and my cock springs to life. "What do you think about us finally taking that weekend away?" I whisper. I've made the same suggestion before, several times, and Sarah's always said she's not ready yet. But it seems like something's shifted recently. Not only with Sarah, but with the girls, too. They clearly adore Rosario, and they've both settled into great routines now. So, why not get away and finally try out that box of goodies I gave to Sarah as a dangling carrot before the girls were born?

Sarah smiles and says the words I've been dying to hear: "Let's do it."

26

JONAS

I check my watch. "Come on, love. The car to the airport is here. Anything we forgot, we'll buy it when we get there."

"I just need a few more minutes," Sarah says. She's walking out of our bedroom now, heading to who-knows-where in the house. She says, "We don't need to be exactly on time for our flight, do we?"

She's right. We don't. I've reserved Uncle William's private jet for our weekend getaway to San Diego, which means our scheduled departure time is merely a suggestion. In fact, that's one of the best things about flying private. But not *needing* to be on time for a private flight doesn't mean I don't *want* to kick off our first weekend away, as soon as humanly possible.

I've reserved a five-thousand-square-foot private villa for us in San Diego, atop the beachside cliffs in swanky Del Mar, at the top-rated luxury resort in all of California, complete with a private butler. And, of course, I've got Sarah's bondage sheet and box of toys packed up and ready for its first bit of action, along with a whole bunch of lingerie I bought for Sarah to wear during our short trip. This weekend, I'm going to fuck my wife like she's never been fucked before. I'm going to scramble her brain and confuse her muscles and break her long-established habits. Shock and awe, baby! By the time I'm done with her, Sarah's going to be squirting like a fucking pro, without me needing to touch her magic trip cord with anything but the tip of my cock. She's going to discover new depths and power of her sexuality. And it's going to take our sexual explorations and mutual pleasure to towering new heights.

"The babies are still sleeping," I say, grabbing her suitcase and following her out of the bedroom. We said goodbye to them before putting them down, and Rosario's been living with us and taking care of them for over six months now, so I can't fathom what else she needs to do before heading out the front door with me.

"Yes, I know," Sarah says. She holds up the intercom connected to the nursery. "I just want to make sure we have all necessary supplies."

"We'll be gone two and a half days." Oh, God, I can't wait to fuck my wife till she sees God. When she does, she's going to say, "Oh, hi, Jonas."

One of the babies fusses through the monitor in Sarah's hand, and she freezes, listening intently. If I had to guess, I'd say it was Marisol rolling over in her crib.

"Just go and have fun," Gloria says. She and Rosario have converged on us in the living room. "We'll make sure the girls stay on schedule and have a wonderful time this weekend."

"Okay, thank you," Sarah says. But a half-second later, Marisol's agonized wail blares through the monitor. Panic seizes Sarah's face. "That was *Sunny*," she gasps.

And I can't say I blame her for freaking out. *Marisol never shrieks like that.*

All four of us rush toward the nursery. And when we get there, Sol is sitting up in her crib, red-faced and crying, hot tears streaming down her cheeks, while Luna sleeps in the next crib, blissfully ignoring her sister. The minute Marisol sees Sarah, she reaches up to her mommy with both arms, her little body jerking with violent sobs. Sarah clutches Sunny and kisses her forehead. And promptly freaks out. "Oh my God, Jonas." She looks at me, her eyes wide and full of fear. "She's burning up."

27
JONAS

This isn't the way I expected to be spending tonight with Sarah.

But given the anxiety-producing events of today, I wouldn't want to be anywhere else but right here, with my wife and daughters, counting my lucky stars they're all safe and sound. After spending three hours with Marisol in urgent care, followed by coming home and bathing her in a cool bath, followed by bouncing her for two hours while she sobbed uncontrollably, we're now sitting with our normally cheerful baby in the nursery in the wee hours of the morning, rocking her gently, lit only by a dim lamp in the corner.

Gloria went home hours ago, and Rosario finally went to bed just before midnight.

Poor Marisol's fever is still raging, though she's finally quieted down, and wild horses couldn't drag either of us away from her side.

Sarah's clutching Marisol to her chest while I've got Luna pressed against mine, simply because I enjoy holding my sleeping baby.

"Same as before?" I ask, as Sarah swipes Marisol's forehead with a thermometer.

"Same. But, hey, at least it's not going up."

"That's a good sign," I agree. "Let's take Luna's, too. Just in case."

She hands me the thermometer and I swipe it across Luna's forehead.

"Normal."

Sarah sighs with relief. "Let's hope it stays that way."

I kiss the top of Luna's head. "Should we put Sol in a cool bath again?"

"No. If the fever doesn't go down in a half-hour, we will. She's finally quiet now—let's let her rest."

"When can we give her Tylenol again?"

"Another hour."

We rock in silence for a few minutes, both of us lost in our thoughts.

"It broke my heart to see Marisol crying like that tonight," Sarah says. "She never cries like that."

"I know," I say. "I'd rather cut off my right arm than see her cry like that again."

Sarah juts her lower lip. "At least, cut off your *left* arm. You really need your right arm."

"I'd cut off whatever it takes not to see my baby cry like that again."

"Oh, that's a fun game of Would You Rather. Would you rather cut off your penis or see your baby cry like that again?"

I grimace. "Why would you go right there?"

"You said you'd cut off *whatever* it takes."

"I'm not gonna answer that question."

"You said it, not me."

We rock in silence again for another long moment.

"How about this one?" Sarah says. "Would you rather be born with no penis or have one and have it cut off to avoid seeing your daughter cry like that again?"

"What's with you and cutting off penises?

"Just one penis."

"I'm not going to answer any 'would you rather' question that involves cutting off my dick."

"So you'd rather be born without one?"

I pause. Sarah loves this stupid game. If I don't answer her, she'll keep going until I do. "Yes. At least then, I wouldn't know what I was missing. I'd be the shackled man in Plato's cave. Blissfully ignorant. There's something to be said for blissful ignorance."

"I like that answer."

"I like any answer that doesn't involve cutting off my dick."

Sarah giggles. "Would you rather be born with no penis or five of them?"

"Five," I answer without hesitation. "That's an easy one. I could use a latex glove as a condom and go all night long. After one dick has shot its wad, I'd simply replace it with the next."

"That sounds oddly erotic." She chuckles. "Would you rather crap your pants in public once a year for the rest of your life or crap yourself in private every single day?"

I laugh. "Where do you get this stuff?"

"Deep thoughts, dude. I can't stop having them."

I shake my head. "Once a year in public, I guess."

"Me, too. What's your reasoning?"

"If I knew that was my affliction, I'd fly to some distant, foreign country, crap my pants in public, and then fly home. Not that big a deal."

She laughs for a good long minute. "Unless people get

it on video and post it. These days, nobody is safe from global embarrassment."

"True."

"You're so good at strategizing, though. I never would have thought of doing that. Can I come with you and crap my pants in some exotic locale with you?"

"Of course. The family that craps together in public, stays together."

Sarah squeals with laughter. "Seriously, honey, you should call Hallmark. That's a Valentine's Day card if I've ever heard one." She rocks Sol for a moment. "Okay, another one."

"No."

"One more. Would you rather have a time machine that only goes back in time or a time machine that only goes forward in time?"

"That's easy. Forward. Always forward."

Sarah tilts her head. "You wouldn't want to go back to Athens and hang out with Plato and talk about the meaning of life? Or maybe go back in time and get to spend a day with your mother?"

My heart skips a beat at the thought. "That's tempting, I must admit. But I think I'd want to visit Sunny and Lu as old ladies, more than anything else. I'd want to ask them about their life. Tell them how much I love them, one more time."

She's clearly moved by that answer. "I love you so much, Jonas."

"I love you, too. What about you? Are you going to the past or the future in your time machine?"

"I'm going to the future. Fuck the past."

"Amen."

"Oh, I've got a good one."

"No."

"One more? Please?"

"Fine."

"Would you rather never go down on me again, or never fuck me again?"

I shake my head. "I refuse to answer that one based on the religious freedoms granted to me by the First Amendment."

She laughs. "Okay. I'm done."

"Look what you've done to me," I say. I lift the sleeping baby in my arms to reveal a gigantic bulge behind my pants. "Having a massive boner while holding my infant daughter isn't my favorite thing, Mrs. Faraday."

"All I did was let your imagination run wild for a hot minute," she teases.

"And run wild it did."

Sunny makes a little whimpering noise against Sarah's chest.

"Take her temperature again," I say.

Sarah grabs the thermometer and swipes it across Sol's forehead. "It went down a full degree."

"Oh, thank God."

We rock our respective babies for a long moment.

"I've got a good one," I say. "Would you rather piss yourself every time you listen to music or every time you have an orgasm?"

Sarah flashes me a sardonic look. "Real subtle, Jonas."

"What?" I ask, feigning innocence.

"Could your question possibly be designed to create a *teaching moment*, oh, Lord-God-Master?"

"And here I thought I was so clever."

"You can't use your Jedi mind tricks on me."

"Tell me your answer, Cruz. Are you gonna piss yourself when you hear music or when you orgasm?"

"If I must answer, then when I hear music."

"Really? You'd prefer to piss yourself *any* time you hear music than in the privacy of our bedroom, when it's just you and me?"

"You think you're so smart. Don't think I don't understand what you're trying to 'teach' me here, Jonas."

I laugh. "I'm just saying there's nothing to be ashamed of in the privacy of our bedroom. No fluid gushing out of you that isn't perfectly natural."

"I've already pissed myself enough in this lifetime, thank you very much. I don't need to worry I'm doing it in a hypothetical situation, too."

I crinkle my forehead. "What do you mean?"

Sarah pauses. "I was a bed-wetter for a really long time."

"How did I not know this before now?"

She shrugs. "There was never any reason to mention it to you."

"For how long?"

"Until I was ten or eleven."

My gears are turning. Everything suddenly makes so much sense to me now. "In other words, until a year or two after you and your mom escaped your father?"

"Yeah. Whenever my father used to terrify me, I pissed myself. And after we left, I continued to do it whenever I had nightmares about him."

A light bulb has gone off in my head. Suddenly, so much about Sarah makes perfect sense to me. She's been hardwired her whole life to hold *in* rather than push out. That's what Thailand was all about, I suddenly realize— her desperate desire to get out of her own fucking way and let go completely. Because she can't let go by herself, she needs someone or something outside herself to take her there. No wonder she's been curious about bondage lately—she wants to be dominated in every sense, figuratively and literally, so she can get out of her own damned way.

"I think your history of bed-wetting when you were terrified is tied up with your history of sexual dysfunction."

Sarah looks skeptical. "In what way?"

"Well, right before you have an intense orgasm, it feels like you're gonna pee, right?"

"Yeah."

"And the more intense the orgasm, the more intense that sensation?"

"Usually, yes."

"Well, it's all the same muscles involved in peeing and having an orgasm. Did you know that?"

"No."

"Do you ever need to pee so badly, when you finally do, it feels almost like you're having a tiny little orgasm?"

She looks amused. "Yes, actually."

"So, I'm no expert, obviously, but my guess is, from a very young age, you learned to associate that gotta-pee feeling with being terrified and ashamed. Which means you became hardwired to pull *back* from that sensation. To want to avoid it at all costs. Rather than to lean into it, to push past it, as I'm always coaxing you to do."

Sarah's face is absolutely precious right now. "I actually think you're onto something here."

"Of course, I am. It's Occam's Razor, baby." I wink. "The simplest answer is usually the correct one."

Sarah rocks in her glider chair silently for a long

moment, looking absolutely blown away. Finally, she smiles at me and says, "Thank you for figuring that out." She winks. "You woman wizard you."

"At your service."

I bite my lip, so I won't say more and make Sarah feel self-conscious. But holy shit, this revelation has only made me even more determined to take my wife some-where romantic, along with that box of goodies I bought her before the babies were born, and help her push past any remaining sexual hang-ups, once and for all.

28

SARAH

Take two.

We did it.

We finally made it to San Diego for our first weekend away from the girls. Admittedly, I hemmed and hawed a bit before leaving the house this morning, but the minute we boarded the private jet, I felt pretty damned excited about our getaway. And now that we're in the cliffside villa Jonas arranged for us, I can honestly say there's no place I'd rather be.

I throw open the glass doors leading out to the patio and gape over the side of the cliff at the sapphire-blue ocean yawning before me. "Jonas, this is amazing!" I race back into the villa and throw my arms around him. "Thank you!"

"Shall I open the bottle for you, sir?" our butler asks, motioning to a bottle of champagne on ice.

"No, I've got it," Jonas replies.

As the butler leaves, I race into the bathroom and squeal when I see the gigantic Jacuzzi tub. "Jackpot, Jonas! The tub is more than big enough for two!"

I crawl into the empty tub and smile at Jonas when he appears in the doorway, looking extra hot in his clingy T-shirt.

I waggle my eyebrows. "Are you game to kick things off with an underwater breath-holding contest?"

Jonas leans his shoulder against the doorjamb. "Actually, I've already planned the festivities for tonight. Take off your clothes, and I'll run the water for you."

"You're not joining me?"

He shakes his head. "Get undressed, love. I'll explain the ground rules for the weekend."

I stand up and begin peeling off my clothes. "*Ground rules*?"

He smiles wickedly. "Ground rules."

I toss my dress over the side of the tub, followed by my undies and bra, and when I get settled again, Jonas turns on the water and begins adjusting for temperature. When he's confirmed I'm happy with the temperature, he tells me to stay put while he fetches me some champagne.

A moment later, he returns with three things. A goblet of champagne, which he hands to me. A bag with the name of a lingerie shop splashed across it, which he places on the bathroom counter next to the sink. And a black velvet box, which he places on the ledge of the tub.

"What's that?" I ask, referring to the black velvet box that's drawn my focus. It sure looks like a jewelry box of some sort. Is there jewelry in there?

"Sarah, look at me, please."

I'm tipsy after all the champagne I sipped during our short flight, so wrenching my eyes off the velvet box takes a couple seconds. But when I finally shift my gaze to

Jonas', the smoldering look in his eyes commands my undivided attention.

"Oh, wow. Someone's feeling horny," I purr.

His demeanor is all-business, unlike mine. He says, "Sarah, tell me the sole mission and purpose of the Jonas Faraday Club, please."

"It's kind of hard to concentrate with that pretty box sitting there," I admit. "Is that a jewelry box?"

"You'll find out soon enough. Answer my question first. What's the sole mission and purpose of the Jonas Faraday Club?"

I bite my lower lip. "The deliverance of sexual excellence—*sexcellence*—to its one and only member—Sarah Cruz Faraday—for the purpose of giving her unending sexual satisfaction that's so fucking awesome, it causes her to experience the culmination of human possibility."

He nods. "At this point, we've climbed every peak in the mountain range known as Sexcellence, with one glaring exception. And this weekend, we're going to climb that peak. Repeatedly."

I can't suppress my smirk. Oh, Jonas. He plans to turn me into a bona fide squirter this weekend, does he, without needing to press the button on my vending machine?"

"Over the past several months," Jonas continues, "we've taken a bit of a hiatus from attempting to climb this last peak, thanks to the two small humans we created. But our hiatus is now over. Our climbing expedition begins tonight."

"Hey, I'm willing to give it a whirl," I say. "But I hope you're not dead-set on me squirting this weekend, because it's not within my control if I—"

"Quiet, please. Tonight, you'll speak only when I've asked you a direct question."

"Excuse me?"

His blue eyes flicker with heat. "I'm in charge tonight, Sarah. I want you to surrender to me completely, the same way you did when we first started climbing that very first mountain peak together. Can you do that for me?"

I bite back another smile. "Yes."

Oh, man. This is going to be fun. It's been years since Jonas demanded full control in our sexual relationship, and I must admit, I'm excited to return to this dynamic again, if only for a hot and sexy weekend of fun.

"Good girl." He turns off the water filling the tub and returns his attention to me. "To arrive at any new destination, we must follow a new path, even if that means carving it ourselves with a machete. Do you understand?"

I nod. "Yes."

In reality, I have no fucking idea what Jonas is talking about. And I don't think that's because of all the champagne I've had today, but because Jonas is speaking in riddles and metaphors. But, whatever. It doesn't matter what he means, or what new destination he's taking me to, literally or figuratively, I'm his to command tonight. I trust Jonas completely, in all things. Especially when it comes to sex.

"Good girl," Jonas says. "As you know, your pleasure has always been paramount to me. Your orgasms my most prized trophies. But not tonight. Tonight, you're here to serve *my* pleasure, which is the only thing that matters."

I raise my eyebrows. That's a shocking statement, coming from Jonas. And frankly kind of titillating.

"Whatever you want, I'll do it," I say. "It'll be my pleasure to give you pleasure."

"No, I'll be *taking* it."

"*Oh.*" I bite my lip as outrageous arousal floods me.

"But first." Jonas grabs the velvet box off the ledge, but he doesn't give it to me. He says, "Repeat after me, please. Jonas, you're in charge."

I repeat the words and add with a wink, "*Propiedad de Jonas Faraday.*"

He shifts the velvet box to his other hand. "As we both know, I'm incapable of deriving pleasure from your pain. But I *do* intend to fuck you so hard, you won't be able to think a coherent thought while I'm doing it and won't be able to walk properly afterwards."

"Sounds good to me."

"Please, only speak when I've asked you a question."

My stomach ripples with excitement. "Sorry. I forgot."

His Adam's apple bobs. "If I'm causing you discomfort or anxiety or anything short of actual *pain*, then I don't give a fuck. All that matters is what I want. If you say 'no' or 'stop,' I'll ignore you. If you say the word 'mercy,' however, if you so much as whisper that magic word, then I'll immediately stop whatever I'm doing, no questions asked. That word will be your emergency brake."

Oh my fucking God. Did Jonas just give me a safe word? I never thought I'd see the day.

"Any questions?" he asks.

"Nope. I understand. I'm so excited."

"Good girl. Now, I bet you're wondering what's inside this box, eh?" With a wicked grin, he opens the velvet box, making me gasp. Inside, there's a stunning diamond bracelet that's so dazzling and sparkling, it practically sears my corneas.

"Jonas," I gasp. "It's breathtaking."

His blue eyes twinkle. "Happy Valentine's Bullshit, baby."

"Oh, Jonas. It's spectacular. Did you steal it from Queen Elizabeth? It looks like it belongs behind glass in a museum."

His cool, business-like demeanor from a moment ago is gone, replaced by visible glee. "I had it custom-made for you. Look closely at the arrangement of the diamonds."

My heart crashing wildly in my chest, I lean forward and study the dazzling rocks, and quikly realize they've been clustered to create the appearance of the sun, the moon, and a whole bunch of glittering stars.

"It's a tribute to our family," he whispers. "It's my way of thanking you for giving me the girls. For being my sky full of stars." He touches the platinum bracelet on my wrist. "I've been meaning to upgrade this one for a while now."

I touch my platinum bracelet, my eyes wide. "I can't keep this one?"

Jonas chuckles. "Of course, you can. Upgrading doesn't mean replacing, love." He indicates the diamond bracelet. "One day, I'm sure I'll upgrade this one, too."

"I can't imagine how that'd be possible," I mumble. "It's spectacular, Jonas."

"Isn't it?" He removes the glittering bauble from its box and carefully latches it onto my wrist. "It looks beautiful on you."

"Thank you. Wow. I love it." I pull on his arm, and he bends down toward the tub and kisses me. "Let this bracelet remind you daily that our love is bigger and more eternal than any galaxy."

"Such a poet," I whisper.

He nuzzles my nose. "Only with you." With a kiss to my forehead, he leans back. "Okay, it's time to get this show on the road now, my love. Time for you to play by the rules and leave everything to me. Yes?"

"Yes."

"Good girl." He rises. "Drink your champagne. Relax. Touch yourself while you're in there, if you like, as long as you don't make yourself come."

I pull a face that says, "There's little danger of that happening." As we both know, I've never gotten myself off with my fingers alone—only with a vibrator, which I only use when Jonas is out of town. But even then, it takes me three times longer than it does when Jonas does it for me with his fingers and tongue. I'm thinking all of this. But what I say is, "Yes, sir."

He motions to the bag with the lingerie store's name across it, which he left by the sink earlier. "When I tell you it's time to get out of the tub, I want you to = dry off, = put on what's in that bag, and join me in the bedroom. Do you understand?"

Butterflies are ravaging my belly. "Yes, sir."

"Good girl. I'm going to get a few things set up in the other room. I'll let you know when I'm ready for you."

29
JONAS

Holy fuck.

It took all my will power not to join Sarah in the bathtub. Her tits at the water line were so fucking hot, I could barely look at anything else. Somehow, though, by reminding myself about the big picture here, I forced myself to stand and walk out of the bathroom, my cock throbbing mercilessly. Tonight is about pushing Sarah to places she's never been before. Which means I need to shock and awe her in new ways, not slide into a bath with her, the way I've done countless times.

In the bedroom, I grab the bondage sheet from my suitcase and, after skimming the enclosed instructions, get to work fitting it onto the hotel bed. Once it's in place, I connect and tighten the security straps and then attach the four soft cuffs. Once everything is in place, I tug forcefully on the straps, making sure Sarah's limbs will be secure, no matter how strenuously she thrashes and pulls.

Next up, I grab the sex toys I've curated for this evening's festivities and place them on the nightstand, at the ready. If I'm being honest, none of this stuff turns me on, other than the blindfold. But that doesn't matter. Despite what I said to Sarah in the bathroom about tonight being about my pleasure, and nothing else, tonight is only about fulfilling Sarah's fantasies. And I know full well my wife has been aching to explore her kinky side.

I hear a splashing noise coming from the bathroom, followed by the sound of Sarah moaning softly, and my cock responds like a trumpeter swan hearing the call of its mate. Damn, that was a sexy sound. Thankfully, it wasn't The Sound. No, it was the sound she makes before the big one, which means she's not all that close to going off in that tub. But, still, if I leave her in there for too long, drinking champagne and staring at that bracelet, she might get there. And I can't risk that. Not when I know bringing her to the bitter edge, and ten away, rinse and repeat, will be critical to getting her off as hard and uncontrollably as I'm planning to do tonight.

"Sarah," I call out. "Stop what you're doing right now and get out of the tub. Dry off, put on the lingerie I left for you, and come into the bedroom."

"Yes, sir," she calls back. "Should I let the water out of the tub?"

"Yes."

I take off my clothes and sit on the edge of the bed, trembling with arousal, and a few minutes later, Sarah floats into the room, looking like Aphrodite herself. The white lace of her sheer teddy sets off her smooth olive skin beautifully. Its cut accentuates every voluptuous curve. And best of all, Sarah's dark nipples and "OAP" tattoo are visible underneath the teddy's sheer fabric.

I rise from the bed. "Stop walking."

She does.

"Turn around. I want to see your ass."

When she complies, my mouth literally waters at the sight of Sarah's backside. In the back, the teddy I chose for her turns into nothing but a network of strings, all converging into one thin, white line that disappears down her ass crack. Or should I say it disappears down *my* ass crack, since her cheek is clearly stamped as belonging to me?

My chest is heaving and my mouth watering. "Bend over," I murmur. "Grab your ankles."

Sarah bends over, as instructed, and I'm treated to the delectable sight of the underside of her pussy peeking out through the sheer fabric of her lingerie. My mouth waters even more. Shit. I want to do what I always do to her. Eat her. Fuck her. Send her to heaven, and therefore myself. I want to make her come and then plunge my cock into her and feel her body constricting and clenching around me.

But no.

My baby wants to try kink. So, that's what we'll do.

I press play on the song cued up on my laptop: "Uprising" by Muse. Because victory will be mine tonight. And with the song blaring, I stride toward Sarah, my hard cock leading the way.

I inhale and exhale slowly as I approach her, trying to remain calm. And when I reach her, I grip her hip with one hand and my hard cock with the other. She's still bent over, holding her ankles. Probably wondering what the fuck I'm waiting for. And that's the point—making her marinate in arousal and anticipation. What would I normally do right now? Kneel down and go to church on her from behind. I'd make her come and then fuck her.

And she knows it. Which means I need to do something different this time.

"Jonas?" she asks. "Do you want me to—"

"I didn't give you permission to speak," I say. "I'm getting off on making you wait, and that's all that matters." I grin. "For breaking the rules, you'll stay in this position even longer."

Sarah shifts her weight slightly but says nothing.

After a bit, I rub my hard cock against her pussy, teasing her. Making her groan. But when I've got her shaking with anticipation, I kneel down behind her, push her G-string aside, part her ass cheeks, and lick the rim of her anus, eliciting instantaneous moans from her. I lick her for not even a minute when, without warning, her asshole clenches under my tongue and begins convulsing with what seems like a powerful orgasm.

Fuck. That wasn't supposed to happen. I merely wanted to get her close to the edge, without pushing her over it. Obviously, she's on fire tonight in a way I've never seen her before.

I lead Sarah to the bed, guide her to her hands and knees, and instruct her to stay put. Once she's situated, I grab some lube and a dildo from the nightstand and return to her. I slide a lubed finger to her clit and massage her in circles for a bit, until Sarah lets out a long, guttural moan and begins shaking violently on her hands and knees. She makes the sound before The Sound, and I know she'd come for me if I slid my cock inside her now. But nope. Tonight, I'm an ass man.

I peel off her teddy. It's smoking hot on her, no doubt about it, but it's already served its purpose. Made her feel sexy and new. From here on out, though, I don't want anything impeding my access to any inch of Sarah's body.

When I've got her naked, I slide my lubed finger into Sarah's ass again, while massaging her clit with my other hand, and when she's losing her mind and begging me to fuck her, I replace my finger in her ass with the tip of the dildo.

"Whoa," she gasps out, the second she realizes something's different back there.

"Relax," I coo. "I won't hurt you. Take a deep breath, baby. Good. Another one." As Sarah exhales, I gently push the dildo in a bit farther. Not too far, of course. I'm not normally into anal sex, so we rarely experiment with it. And I'd never want to hurt her. But, yeah, I definitely push the tip far enough inside her to make her eyes water and her dirty girl come out to play.

As she exhales again, I flip the switch on the dildo to its lowest vibration setting, while reaching around to massage her clit with my other hand again, and I'm shocked by Sarah's effusive reaction. Holy fuck, she's losing her goddamned mind.

Shit.

If I keep going like this, she's going to come. And that's ultimately not going to serve my greater goal.

I pull the thing out of her, guide her onto her back, and kiss her. I devour her tits. Lick her pussy. Bite her neck. And when I feel like she's back to baseline again, I slide the dildo inside her ass again, set to low vibration, and then slowly slide my cock inside her pussy.

"Holy fuck," she grits out. "Oh my fucking God."

Clearly, the double penetration is doing amazing things for her. And I must admit the vibration emanating from the dildo next door is doing incredible things for my cock.

"Oh my God," Sarah grits out. "Jonas. Oh my God. I'm going to come."

"Not yet."

As she gasps and whimpers, I thrust in and out, increasing my speed and depth, reveling in the sensation of her tight wetness vibrating and constricting around my cock. Holy fuck, this is like nothing I've experienced before. This is *good*.

I reach down to the vibe, flip it to the next highest speed, and simultaneously increase the depth and speed of my thrusts—and Sarah and I both simultaneously lose our shit.

"Yes!" she screams, her entire body lurching and jolting. "Oh my God. You've got to stop! It's too much. Don't stop though. Oh, fuck. Wait. No. Yes!"

I don't stop, obviously. Because she hasn't used the magic word. In fact, I flip the vibe on high and fuck her even harder, splitting her in two with my cock while holding that dildo firmly in place in her ass.

As Sarah screams my name, I reach between us and find her clit, and when I touch her there, she convulses like I've thrown a hairdryer into her bath.

"Oh shit. *Fuck,*" she says.

It's the last thing she says before her body twists and wrenches so violently against my cock—so forcefully—I'm momentarily afraid for her. Oh my God. I can physically feel her innards twisting like a wet washcloth being wrung out over a tub. This isn't a normal orgasm. Not even a powerful one. This is more like an exorcism. Whatever it is, it's so fucking hot, I'm close to passing out from pleasure.

Which means, fuck my life, I truly have to stop, or I'll come and that will be that for a while. Of course, I can get

Sarah off after I've already come. I've done it countless times. But there's no denying she gets off harder when I'm still hard as a rock and holding on by a thread.

Through sheer force of will, I pull out and gently glide the dildo out of her ass, and Sarah crumples onto the mattress, a sweaty, nonverbal pile of olive skin, matted hair, and erect, dark nipples.

My hard-on is raging. My chest heaving. The Muse song has been over for a while now. The room is silent, except for the distant crashing of the waves and our heavy breathing.

Wordlessly, I part Sarah's legs and lick the wetness off her thighs. She didn't squirt, but she's wet as fuck. And for now, that's good enough.

I voraciously devour her pussy like I'm competing in a blueberry-pie-eating contest on the Fourth of July, and Sarah throws her head back and runs her fingers through my sweaty hair.

I should probably secure her limbs to the bondage sheet at this point. That's what Sarah wants. But fuck that. Before I do what she wants, I'm going to get my baby to squirt all over the marble floor.

I scoop her off the mattress and bring her to the floor. Breathing hard, I bring one of her legs up to her ear and plunge myself into her sweet, warm wetness and fuck the hell out of her until she's growling like a bear caught in a trap.

"Yes," she says between gritted teeth, sweat pouring down her face. "*Yes.*"

With her legs open like this, and the angle I'm using to fuck her, the tip of my cock should be slamming her G-spot.

"When you feel like you're going to come, relax and let it go," I say. "Push out, don't clench."

With a loud groan, she comes again, this time like a roaring freight train. But she hasn't reached the peak I'm going for. And I won't settle for anything less.

I'm a man possessed. I pull my aching cock out of her and slide my fingers deep inside her, straight to her G-spot. It's swollen. Like a water balloon. I dig my fingertips into the middle of the swollen patch, and there it is. Her magic trip cord. Holy fuck, it's three times as engorged as when I used it to make her squirt in the nursery. Not only that, it's physically throbbing under my fingertips. I slide it between my fingers, dying to pull it, and stop myself. I promised I wouldn't push the Ding Dong button on her vending machine again—and a promise is a promise. Fuck! I let go of the trip cord and stroke her G-spot while kissing her mouth passionately, and she writhes and gyrates like I'm electrocuting her.

All of a sudden, I hear a subtle whooshing sound from deep inside her body, and my cock jolts as surely as if she just licked it from ball to tip. Oh my God. I've heard that sound only once before. My fingers inside her are physically aching with the urge to pull that trip cord. To make it rain. But I stop myself. A promise is a promise, Jonas.

I return to working her G-spot, getting her ramped up, until she's on the bitter cusp of release.

I lick her salty breasts and *stroke* her trip-cord, ever so gently, rather than milking it. I tickle it. Coax it. Flick it. But I keep my promise and don't pull it.

"Oh my God. Oh my God," she says, her voice desperate. "What's happening to me? Oh my fuck!"

"Come on, baby," I whisper. "Push out. Let go."

I flick her trip-cord again. And then return to stroking

her G-spot. Back and forth I go, back and forth. Luring her to the edge of the towering waterfall and inviting her to jump off. Back and forth. To the edge of the waterfall and away. Until she's hotter than the hinges of hell—but, still, she's not letting go completely.

Well, fuck.

I've never worked her this long and hard before. Normally, I'd have pushed her forcefully off one cliff or another by now and started fucking her, rather than sitting here tickling her fucking Ding Dong button for thirty fucking minutes. But, goddammit, I can't let it go. I want this. I *need* this. And I won't leave here without it.

There's another delicious whooshing noise. This one louder than before. I stroke her G-spot. Kiss her lips. Whisper to her that I love her. That I love her more than any woman has been loved in the history of time.

"Let me help you," I whisper. "Let me push you over the edge, Sarah. Release me from my promise."

"Yes," she says between gritted teeth. "Yes."

Thank God. I clamp my middle and ring fingers together, tightening my grip around that thick band behind her swollen G-spot, push down, and then up and in. As I pull up with my fingers, I kiss her deeply . . . And she's hurtled into Nirvana.

As her body releases a glorious orgasm around my fingers, a gush of fluid releases from her pussy and all over me. The sheer volume of fluid is five times more than the time I did this to her in the nursery—maybe ten times more. And even better than that, she's coming so fucking hard along with her ejaculation, she's flopping on the floor like a fish on a riverbank. Clearly, it's the most intense, full-body orgasm she's ever had. It's a full-body *seizure*, complete with flailing limbs and rolling eyes. By far, the hottest thing I've ever witnessed, bar none.

As Sarah flops and shakes, I lean in and lap up some of the wetness on her thighs and pussy, stroking my cock as I do.

"Fuck me," she gasps out. She reaches for my cock and tries to guide me into her, tilting her pelvis up to me as she does. "Fuck me, Jonas."

It's time. Now that I've gotten what I wanted the most, I'm ready to give her what she's been craving.

My breathing ragged, I scoop Sarah's sweaty, spent body off the floor and throw her onto the bed with a loud grunt. I slip the cuffs onto her wrists and tighten them, and she thrashes and purrs excitedly.

"I'm gonna fuck you till you pass out."

"Yes," she breathes. She tugs forcefully on both wrists, and when the restraints don't budge, she squeals.

"I'm gonna . . ." I stop talking and freeze. All of a sudden, I'm blinded by a memory. The image of my mother tugging against rough ropes around her wrists.

"You're gonna do what?" Sarah asks excitedly. "Tell me."

I take a deep breath, trying to shoo the mental image away.

Fuck.

If I'd been bitten by a shark at age seven, would I freeze and falter as an adult at the sight of a goldfish? Of course, not. Well, this is a goldfish, Jonas. This is all fun and games. This isn't real.

"I'm gonna fuck you so hard . . .," I begin, but I can't finish the sentence.

Shit. What's wrong with me? I can't let something that happened twenty-five years ago when I was a goddamned child define or limit my sexuality as a grown-ass man. For fuck's sake, I can do this and enjoy it. Or, at the very least, do it for Sarah.

Swallowing hard, I grab Sarah's right ankle and secure a cuff around it. Good. That was easy enough. I grab Sarah's left ankle . . . And my stomach seizes.

I see the big man's hairy ass, clenching and releasing as he thrusts into my mother. She's pulling against her bindings, screaming and crying.

I close my eyes and shake it off.

Stop.

Shaking, I secure Sarah's left ankle, rendering her completely immobilized and spread-eagle on the bed. And the effect on Sarah is obvious. *She loves it.* In fact, she's practically purring with excitement and arousal.

But I can't move.

I see the big man with the hairy ass pull out a knife and tell my mother to stop screaming. I cower behind her dresses in her closet, quaking and trying not to make a sound. She thrashes against her bindings and begs for mercy. But mercy never comes.

"Jonas?"

The walls are closing in on me. Oh, fuck, is this a panic attack? I haven't had one of these since I was a teenager. What the fuck is happening to me?

Sarah says something, I think, but her words sound warped and far away.

"Jonas, untie me," Sarah commands. "Right now."

A deep red stream of blood gushes out from between my mother's legs and floods the white sheets. Blood on the sheets. Blood on the sheets. She's screaming in agony. She's begging for mercy. But mercy never comes.

"Jonas!" Sarah screams. "Untie me right now!"

I wobble in place, trying to catch my breath. I feel like I'm going to throw up, but I can't command my legs to run to the bathroom. I'm stuck. Rooted in cement. I blink hard and stare blankly at Sarah. She's got a horror-stricken expression on her face.

"Mercy, Jonas," she says, tears squirting down her cheeks. "Did you hear me, love? I said mercy!" Her chin trembles. "Mercy, mercy, mercy."

30
SARAH

Jonas looks as white as a sheet. Like he's seen a ghost.

"Mercy," I scream. "Untie me, Jonas. Mercy!"

He blinks rapidly, several times, and, finally, loosens my restraints. As I pull and yank at the loosened straps, he sits on the edge of the bed with his back facing me and his face in his hands.

Once I've freed myself, I scramble across the mattress and sit next to him. "What's wrong? What happened?"

When Jonas doesn't reply, I slide my arm around his broad shoulders and squeeze him. And when a full minute has passed without him saying a word, I stand, lower his hands, and pepper every millimeter of his shell-shocked face with gentle kisses.

When my lips reach his, Jonas returns my kiss and pulls me into him, wordlessly guiding me to straddle his lap and take his body into mine. As I begin riding him, I wrap my legs around his waist and my arms around his neck, exhaling with relief and pleasure as our bodies move in concert.

He grabs my ass passionately as I move on top of him, lighting a bonfire inside me, and I begin riding him even more furiously.

It takes only a few minutes of synchronous gyrations and desperate kisses before I'm slammed with an orgasm that has me grabbing at Jonas' hair. As my climax racks my body, Jonas comes inside me, his arms clutching me like he's a drowning man in stormy seas and I'm his flotation device.

When our bodies become still and quiet, I kiss every inch of his beautiful face tenderly, the most gorgeous face I've ever beheld, and run my hands through his sweaty hair.

"I'm sorry," he says. "I wanted to do it for you."

I touch his cheek and look into his blue eyes—the sad eyes that captivated me from the first moment I saw them. "We did something better," I say.

He shakes his head. "There's something wrong with me. I thought I could overcome it, through sheer force of will. I thought . . ." He looks down. "I'm sorry."

"My love, listen to me. We did something *better*. So much better." I glide my fingers over the sun and moon and stars covering his chest, my diamond bracelet glimmering in the dim light. "'Love is the name for our pursuit of wholeness, for our desire to be complete,'" I say, quoting his homeboy to him. "Jonas, don't you see? We're two halves of a whole. You do for me what I can't do for myself, and I do the same for you. Together, we climb and conquer every peak. Sometimes, you're leading the way. Sometimes, I am. Sometimes, we're shoulder to shoulder. But always, we're together. Always, we're a team." I take his face in my palms and look deeply into his blue eyes. "Tonight, you pressed the button for Ding

Dongs on my vending machine, because I don't know how to press it for myself. And I asked for *mercy* on your behalf, when you didn't know how to ask for it yourself." I stroke his cheek with my thumb. "*That's* the highest peak, my sweet Jonas. That's the kind of love that's the amazement of the gods." Tears well in my eyes. "That's the culmination of human possibility."

31
JONAS

The tune blaring through our backyard speakers is Bill Withers' "Lovely Day." Of all the songs on Sarah's playlist for the twins' second birthday party, I think this one is my favorite. It's the perfect soundtrack for a sunny celebration of our beloved Sun and Moon with our closest family and friends.

"No, not like dat, Uncle Jo Jo," Gracie chastises. Apparently, I've done something wrong while pouring imaginary tea. "With your pinky up. Lik dis. Like a pwincess." She shoves a plastic tiara at me. "And you have to wear a crown at da tea party. See? Like Daddy and Uncle Rum Cake."

"Yeah, Uncle Jo Jo, get with the program," Ryan Morgan—the aforementioned "Uncle Rum Cake"— teases. He's one of Kat's four brothers—the Morgan brother Josh and I have grown closest to, since we're in business with Ryan and his wife on a chain of successful bars.

I'm not thrilled to have gotten myself roped into yet another marathon tea party with my adorable but bossy niece. But I suppose it's my own damned fault. A few months ago, when I arrived at a birthday party for Ryan's little boy, all Gracie's uncles on Kat's side, including both actual and honorary uncles, were already participating enthusiastically in a tea party with Gracie, and fuck if I was going to be the only uncle who didn't join in. The Morgan brothers are always jockeying among themselves to become Gracie's favorite uncle—the "uncle she loves the most," they always call it. And for some reason, on that particular day, I uncharacteristically felt the urge to steal the title away from all of them.

The good news? I succeeded. I tea-partied the fuck out of that tea party and wound up being the last uncle standing. I even out-uncled Gracie's goofiest uncle, Keane. Which isn't an easy thing to do. The bad news? Gracie now wants me, above all others, to play tea party with her forevermore. Which isn't something I'm feeling all that enthusiastic to do.

"Can Jack join the tea party?" Kat says, appearing with Jack on her hip.

"Jack can take my chair," I say, popping up.

"No, Uncle Jo Jo!" Gracie says. "You can't go! Jewemiah didn't wake up yet!"

Damn. I told her I'd play until we heard Jeremiah in the baby monitor. Fuck.

"Jack can sit on my lap," Josh says, and Kat promptly hands him over. He looks at me. "You're not going anywhere, Uncle Jo Jo."

"Jack is too wittle to pway!" Gracie insists with a scowl. "Dis party is for big girls, daddies, and uncles."

"As a big kid, it's your job to teach the little kids how to play," Kat says. "In fact, let's invite all the little kids at the party to come to your tea party. You can show them all how to do it. You'll be their Obi Wan Kenobi."

Ryan says, "The same way I used to be for your mommy when she was your age. Still am."

Kat rolls her eyes. "More like my Darth Vader."

As Kat and Ryan laugh together, a muffled sound emits from the baby monitor on the table.

"Saved by the bell," I say, popping up again. "Have fun, everyone. I'm on daddy duty."

Josh razzes me as I stride away. He calls me a liar. Says he doubts Jeremiah is even awake. And he's not necessarily wrong. As a matter of fact, Jeremiah typically makes little babbling sounds when he wakes from a nap. In fact, I think it's fifty-fifty that muffled sound indicated only that he was turning over in his sleep. But fuck if I'm going to admit that and pass up an easy chance to get the hell out of Dodge.

On my way toward the house, I check on the twins across the lawn and discover they're happily chasing bubbles with our dog and several Morgan toddlers under the supervision of Henn, Hannah, and Kat's oldest brother, Colby, and his wife. I chat with that group briefly, until happy babbling comes across the baby monitor in my hand. After bidding the group farewell, I stride into the house and through the kitchen on my way to my son.

"Are you getting him?" Sarah asks as I pass through the kitchen. She's standing at the kitchen island with her mother, Rosario, and our family friend, Georgia, putting the finishing touches on the lunch spread.

"Yep." I hold up the baby monitor. "He's babbling."

"How are the girls?"

"Happily chasing bubbles with Buster and a gaggle of Morgan kids, with lots of adult supervision."

"Perfect."

I head down the hallway and into the nursery, where I find my cherubic son, holding his toes and babbling gleefully to himself. When he sees me standing at the railing of his crib, Jeremiah's big brown eyes saucer, and he begins kicking his legs with glee. It's one of my favorite things in the world—eliciting happy kicking from one of my babies, simply from showing up at their bedside.

"Hey, buddy," I say, picking Jeremiah up. I give him a soft kiss on his forehead. "Did you sleep well?"

Oh, how I love these quiet moments with our miracle baby, Jeremiah Joshua Faraday. The doctors said there was a one percent chance Sarah would ever get pregnant again. And yet, here he is, totally by accident. It's true I was a fucking basket case during Sarah's pregnancy. Oh, God. But now that he's here, and everyone is safe and sound, I can't imagine life without him.

I bring Jeremiah to the changing table and get to work on his soggy diaper. As I complete my task, I glance at the walls, my heart swelling at the sight of Sarah's recent additions: Jeremiah the bullfrog leaping through the starry sky. Jeremiah the little prince riding his pony alongside his family on their various steeds. Jeremiah the one-eyed mini-monster frolicking with his beastly family on a grassy hill. And on and on.

A new diaper secured, I scoop Jeremiah from the changing table, hold him against the new leaping bull-frog tattoo on my chest, and head toward the kitchen. When I get to my destination, I discover the party has now moved inside in anticipation of the meal. Gracie is holding court at a kiddie table in the corner, lording over Jack, Lu, Sol, and a handful of Morgan little ones.

The big dining table is filled with our closest loved ones—Josh and Kat, Henn and Hannah, Uncle William, and various Morgans, all of them engaged in an animated conversation.

And where's My Magnificent Sarah? She's laying out the food with Gloria and Rosario while shaking her ass to the latest song on the playlist. Looking like Mother Earth. My wildest dream. My sky full of stars.

As I'm watching Sarah, a new song begins. And the second it starts, Sarah finds me across the crowded room . . . and smiles. The song is 2Real's latest smash hit, "OAP" —the cleaned-up radio edit, in consideration of our youngest party guests. It samples liberally from the '90s rap hit, "OPP" by Naughty by Nature, and features rapid-fire lyrics from 2Real about coveting another man's woman. Namely, a brown-eyed Latina with a husky laugh who, much to 2Real's chagrin, is hopelessly devoted to some other asshole who practices "sexcellence." Hence, the name of the song. "OAP." *Other Asshole's Pussy.*

Sarah laughs as the song barrels into its chorus, and I can't help laughing along with her. We've been on an incredible ride together since that crazy night in Thailand. Learned a lot about ourselves and each other. Become parents, three times over. We've loved each other fully, without condition. Taken the good with the bad and only grown stronger. Like Sarah wisely said that night in San Diego, we've reached the highest peak. Together. But only because we've realized there's no peak at all. There's only now. There's only love. There's only the journey that matters, rather than any particular destination. Destinations are slippery motherfuckers, after all. They've got a tendency to shift under your feet. But the journey? The present moment? The love we share with the ones who matter the most? It's truly all we have and all we'll ever need.

"Jonas."

I turn toward the source of the voice. It's Uncle William, holding two snifters of Scotch.

"You got a minute before we eat? There's something I want to talk to you about, in private."

"Of course."

I follow my uncle to the living room, where we make ourselves comfortable on the couch, with Jeremiah on my uncle's lap.

"Congratulations on the success of Climb and Conquer," he says.

"Thank you. It's been one hell of a ride."

"You should be very proud. It's one thing to expand a business you've been handed through birthright, but another to start a new company from scratch and make it so successful." He looks down at Jeremiah and smiles. "He's your spitting image. Wow." He looks back up and smiles. "I won't beat around the bush. I miss working with you and Josh, and I'd like to come aboard Climb & Conquer and help you expand it."

He briefly explains his idea. He says he invested in a sports-apparel brand several years ago that's clearing a gross profit margin that's way above industry average. He says he thinks he could spearhead expanding the C&C brand to include sports apparel, by using his newfound connections and expertise.

Of course, I'm elated. Not only because that exact expansion strategy is something I've always planned on. But because, ever since leaving Faraday & Sons, I've always hoped my professional path would cross with my brilliant uncle's again one day.

"This sounds like a great idea," I say. "Let's pull Josh aside and tell him what we're thinking, and then put together a more formal meeting to crunch numbers next week."

We shake on it. And then hug. I know I said we'd crunch numbers next week, but there's no doubt in my mind what we're going to do—and that it's going to become yet another dream come true.

———

The birthday party is over. Everyone's gone home.

Rosario's in the kitchen, unloading the dishwasher.

Sarah's bathing the girls in their bathroom, while I'm putting Jeremiah to bed.

After feeding him a bottle, I burp him and then walk around the nursery for a while, singing to him softly. Luckily, none of my babies has ever cared that I can't carry a tune. They actually like it when I sing to them.

When he feels limp against my shoulder, I lay him down in his crib and rub his belly for a bit, until his eyelids flutter and close, and his little belly rises and falls.

I tiptoe out of Jeremiah's room and down the hall, eager to see what books my girls are reading in their toddler beds. But they're not there. Did Sarah say yes this time to reading to them in our bed? I bet she did, as one last birthday present.

I walk down the long hallway toward the primary bedroom, and, sure enough, as I approach the doorway, I hear Sarah's soft, lilting voice, speaking in Spanish.

I peek inside the room and discover Sarah snuggled

up in our bed with our two girls—one on each side. She's reading *The Hungry Caterpillar* to them, translating into Spanish as she goes. As she reads to her daughters, Sarah is calm and soothing. Loving and gentle. And the girls clearly worship her. They're staring at her with rapt attention, reveling in her every word, her every sound. The woman is magic, and they know it. She's not only *my* everything. She's theirs, too.

When Sarah gets to the part about the caterpillar turning into a butterfly—*"una mariposa"*—she looks up and notices me leaning against the doorjamb.

"Join us, Daddy," she says.

"Dada!" the girls scream, like they haven't seen me for days.

"Hello, my little birthday girls." I crawl onto the bed and cuddle my family, and we talk and giggle for a bit, until the girls, and Sarah, have all fallen fast asleep. As my three sleeping beauties slumber, I gaze at them. Marveling at how much the girls look like their mother. I carry the girls into their toddler beds. And then return to bed with Sarah. I hold her close to me and count my lucky stars that she's mine.

She's my sky full of stars, this woman.

My everything.

She's my limitless ocean.

My Mount Everest.

My peak.

She's the sun, the moon, and the stars. My reason to breathe.

When Sarah smiles at me, redemption is mine.

She's my religion. My church. My sacred valentine.

Oh, my little Mount Everest.

My reason to breathe.

The goddess, the muse.

Sarah *Fucking* Cruz.

I touch the tattoo on the top of my right forearm and breathe deeply, an overwhelming serenity filling every nook and cranny of my body and soul.

I've done it.

I've finally found the divine original form of me, thanks to Sarah and the life we've built together.

Our love is the joy of the good, the wonder of the wise, the amazement of the gods. The greatest love story ever told. *The culmination of human possibility.*

32
BONUS SCENE: PERU
JONAS

Josh and I high-five and hug each other exuberantly, and then hug and high-five Jorge, our guide, Scott, the reporter who's been chronicling our Peruvian climb for *Climbing Magazine*, plus two members of Jorge's crew. We take a whole bunch of photos in various combinations. And finally, after all that, the five of us quietly take in in the incredible views from our perch on top of the world. We're at the summit of *Huascarán,* the highest peak in Peru, and to say the view is awe-inspiring would be a gross understatement.

Josh pulls out a flask, takes a sip, and hands it to me. "There's no greater feeling in the world s."

"Well, I can think of *one* greater feeling." I take a sip and gaze at the views all around me.

"Oh God, Jonas," Josh says. "Please, don't talk about Sarah again. I love my wife, too, you know. Every bit as much as you love yours. But I want to be in the moment."

I press my lips together. I know Josh loves Kat with all his heart, absolutely, but there's no way in hell he loves her as much as I love Sarah, simply because *nobody* on this planet loves their partner the way I love Sarah. We're the greatest love story ever told. But, of course, I'd never say that to Josh. Especially not right now, or he might push me off the fucking mountain.

"Everest takes two months, you know," I say after a while.

"Yeah, I know."

"I think this is enough for me," I say.

"Yeah, for me, too." He takes a sip from his flask. "Honestly, I don't think I could be around you away from Sarah for two solid months. I'd wind up shoving you off the mountain."

I laugh. I know my brother so well.

"Plus," Josh continues, "I have no desire to be away from Kat and Gracie that long, either. And whoever else comes along." He takes another sip and hands me the flask. "I didn't think you'd give up your lifelong dream this easily," he says. "You've wanted to climb Everest since you were a little kid."

I shrug. "I've got a different dream now. Being with Sarah. Building a family with her one day. Did you know one climber dies for every ten that makes it to the top?"

"Yeah."

"When I was younger, I didn't think care about that."

"Neither did I." Josh shrugs. "I had nothing to live for back then, really. Everything's different now."

There's a long beat as we both continue taking in the incredible views all around us, until, suddenly, I clap my hands together.

"If we're not going to climb Everest, then the odds are good this will be the highest peak we'll ever climb."

"Probably."

"Which means there's something I need to do while I'm here."

"What?"

"A little something I've been wanting to do for a while. I'm gonna go over there on my own for a couple minutes."

"You're gonna take a piss and write your name in the snow?"

"I'm not ten. Just give me a minute."

Sympathy washes over Josh's face, and I know he's rightfully understanding my mysterious task has to do with our mother.

"Hey, leave the flask with me," Josh says.

I hand him the flask and signal to Jorge that I'm going to walk a short distance around a large crag. When I've made my way around the bend to a private patch of real estate, I look around, feeling like I'm totally alone on top of the world. True, I'm only on top of Peru, but that feels close enough. The first thing I do is unzip my pants and take a piss, marking a big "J" in the white snow. Of course. But that's not why I sought out a little solitude for a moment.

I take off my gloves and reach my bare hands up to the sky, as high as I can, imagining I'm reaching all the way up to the clouds. I close my eyes and try to envision my mother reaching down to me from her perch in heaven, touching my fingertips with hers.

"I love you," I say softly, the cold wind whistling in my ears and nipping at my fingertips. "I love you, Mom."

My heart catches in my throat.

Fuck, my hands are cold.

I shove my hands back into my gloves, shivering and shuddering.

I look up toward the heavens, but no ray of light cracks the clouds, no soft female voice whispers into my ear. It's just the mountain and me and a bank of clouds rolling in. And that's it. Well, wait. There's one other thing, too. *Yes.* A brand-new thing—a sudden and overwhelming thing: a powerful feeling of *completion.* All of a sudden, I feel the urgent need to get off this fucking mountain. I've got to get home to my wife. Holy shit. I've got to get home to Sarah and make a baby with her.

I know in the past I've told Sarah I'd wait however long to start trying for a baby. I know I said the timing was completely up to her. But, suddenly, I feel like I've got to get home and convince Sarah to start trying for a family right away. I've got to make her understand there's nothing to be scared of. I'll tell her the family we're gonna create together won't be anything like what either of us knew as children. Our kids won't live in fear or cower in closets. Our kids will know security and love.

Our kids will make us whole.

I practically stumble down a grouping of rocks and race back to Josh.

"Josh," I blurt. "I'm ready to go home."

"What?"

"I've got to get off this mountain. I've got to get back home."

"Oh. Okay." He pulls out his phone from his pocket and begins dialing.

"What are you doing?" He knows full well there's no cell service up here on the top of the world.

"I'm calling you a cab."

We both burst out laughing. "Holy fuck. I can't wait to get home."

"Same here."

I exhale. "There's something important I need to tell Sarah."

"Please, Jonas. Let's agree this is a Sarah-free zone."

I smile broadly and shake my head. "No, brother. You should know by now, when it comes to me, there's no such thing."

THE END

Have you read Josh Faraday and Kat Morgan's passionate, kinky, wild love story? Start their trilogy with *Infatuation*.

Already read Josh and Kat's wild ride? Then enter the world of The Morgans, perhaps starting with Colby Morgan's heart-melting love story in *HERO* or Ryan Morgan's fiery love story in CAPTAIN.

BOOKS BY LAUREN ROWE

Meet Me At Captain's Series of Standalone Romantic comedies

Who's Your Daddy?

When thirty-year-old patent attorney, Maximillian Vaughn, meets a sassy, charismatic older woman in a bar, he invites her back to his place for one night of no-strings fun. It's all Max can offer, given his busy career; but, luckily, it's all Marnie wants, too. But when Max's chemistry with Marnie is so combustible, it threatens to burn down his bedroom, he does the unthinkable the next morning: he asks Marnie out on a dinner date.

Mere minutes after saying yes, however, Marnie bolts like her hair is on fire with no explanation. What happened? Max doesn't know, but he's determined to find out and convince Marnie to pick up where they left off.

Textual Relations

When Grayson McKnight unknowingly gets a fake number from a woman in a bar, he winds up embroiled in a sexy text exchange with the actual owner of the number—a confident, sensual older woman who knows exactly who she is . . . and what she wants.

No strings attached.

But as sparks fly and real feelings develop, will Grayson get his way and tempt her to give him more than their original bargain?

My Neighbor's Secret

When Charlotte gets into her new dilapidated condo to start fixing it up for resale, she finds out the infuriating stranger who's thoroughly messed up her life is her new next-door neighbor.

Also, that he's got a big secret.

She confronts him and proposes they work together to get themselves out of their respective jams, even though they both admittedly can't stand each other. Yes, he's let it slip he thinks she's pretty. And, okay, she begrudgingly thinks he's kind of cute. But whatever. They hate each other and this is nothing but a business partnership. What could go wrong?

The Secret Note: A Spicy Standalone Novella with HEA

He's a hot Aussie. I'm a girl who isn't shy about getting what she wants. The problem? Ben is my little brother's best friend. An exchange student who's heading back Down Under any day now. But I can't help myself. He's too hot to resist.

The Morgan Brothers

Read these standalones in any order. Chronological reading order is below, but they are all complete stories. Note: you do not need to read any other books or series before jumping straight into reading about the Morgan boys.

Hero

The story of heroic firefighter, Colby Morgan. When catastrophe strikes Colby Morgan, will physical therapist Lydia save him . . . or will he save her?

Captain

The insta-love-to-enemies-to-lovers story of tattooed sex god, Ryan Morgan, and the woman he'd move heaven and earth to claim.

Ball Peen Hammer

A steamy, hilarious, friends-to-lovers romantic comedy about cocky-as-hell male stripper, Keane Morgan, and the sassy, smart young woman who brings him to his knees during a road trip.

Mister Bodyguard

The Morgans' beloved honorary brother, Zander Shaw, meets his match in the feisty pop star he's assigned to protect on tour.

ROCKSTAR

When the youngest Morgan brother, Dax Morgan, meets a mysterious woman who rocks his world, he must decide if pursuing her is worth risking it all. Be sure to check out four of Dax's original songs from ROCKSTAR, written and produced by Lauren, along with full music videos for the songs, on her website (www.laurenrowebooks.com) under the tab MUSIC FROM ROCKSTAR.

Dive into Lauren's universe of interconnected trilogies and duets, all books available individually and as a bundle, in any order.

A full suggested reading order can be found here!

The Josh & Kat Trilogy

It's a war of wills between stubborn and sexy Josh Faraday and Kat Morgan. A fight to the bed. Arrogant, wealthy playboy Josh is used to getting what he wants. And what he wants is Kat Morgan. The books are to be read in order:

Infatuation

Revelation

Consummation

The Club Trilogy

When wealthy playboy Jonas Faraday receives an anonymous note from Sarah Cruz, a law student working part-time processing online applications for an exclusive club, he becomes obsessed with hunting her down and giving her the satisfaction she claims has always eluded her. Thus begins a sweeping tale of obsession, passion, desperation, and ultimately, everlasting love and individual redemption. Find out why scores of readers all over the world, in multiple languages, call The Club Trilogy "my favorite trilogy ever" and "the greatest love story I've ever read." As Jonas Faraday says to Sarah Cruz: "There's never been a love like ours and there never will be again... Our love is so pure and true, we're the amazement of the gods."

The Club: Obsession

The Club: Reclamation

The Club: Redemption

The fourth book for Jonas and Sarah is a full-length epilogue with incredible heart-stopping twists and turns and feels. Read The Club: Culmination (A Full-Length Epilogue Novel) after finishing The Club Trilogy or, if you prefer, after reading The Josh and Kat Trilogy.

The Reed Rivers Trilogy

Reed Rivers has met his match in the most unlikely of women—aspiring journalist and spitfire, Georgina Ricci. She's much younger than the women Reed normally pursues, but he can't resist her fiery personality and drop-dead gorgeous looks. But in this game of cat and mouse, who's chasing whom? With each passing day of this wild ride, Reed's not so sure. The books of this trilogy are to be read in order:

Bad Liar

Beautiful Liar

Beloved Liar

The Hate Love Duet

An addicting, enemies-to-lovers romance with humor, heat, angst, and banter. Music artists Savage of Fugitive Summer and Laila Fitzgerald are stuck together on tour. And convinced they can't stand each other. What they don't know is that they're absolutely made for each other, whether they realize it or not. The books of this duet are to be read in order:

Falling Out of Hate with You

Falling Into Love with You

Interconnected Standalones within the same universe as above

Hacker in Love

When world-class hacker Peter "Henn" Hennessey meets Hannah Milliken, he moves heaven and earth, including doing some questionable things, to win his dream girl over. But when catastrophe strikes, will Henn lose Hannah forever, or is there still a chance for him to chase their happily ever after? *Hacker in Love* is a steamy, funny, heart-pounding, **standalone** contemporary romance with a whole lot of feels, laughs, spice, and swoons.

Smitten

When aspiring singer-songwriter, Alessandra, meets Fish, the funny, adorable bass player of 22 Goats, sparks fly between the awkward pair. Fish tells Alessandra he's a "Goat called Fish who's hung like a bull. But not really. I'm actually really average." And Alessandra tells Fish, "There's nothing like a girl's first love." Alessandra thinks she's talking about a song when she makes her comment to Fish—the first song she'd ever heard by 22 Goats, in fact. As she'll later find out, though, her "first love" was actually Fish. The Goat called Fish who, after that night, vowed to do anything to win her heart. SMITTEN is a true standalone romance.

Swoon

When Colin Beretta, the drummer of 22 Goats, is a groomsman at the wedding of his childhood best friend, Logan, he discovers Logan's kid sister, Amy, is all grown up. Colin tries to resist his attraction to Amy, but after a drunken kiss at the wedding reception, that's easier said than done. Swoon is a true standalone romance.

Misadventures Standalones (unrelated standalones not within the above universe):

- *Misadventures on the Night Shift* –A hotel night shift clerk encounters her teenage fantasy: rock star Lucas Ford. And combustion ensues.

- *Misadventures of a College Girl*—A spunky, virginal theater major meets a cocky football player at her first college party . . . and absolutely nothing goes according to plan for either of them.

- *Misadventures on the Rebound*—A spunky woman on the rebound meets a hot, mysterious stranger in a bar on her way to her five-year high school reunion in Las Vegas and what follows is a misadventure neither of them ever imagined.

Lauren's Dark Comedy/Psych Thriller Standalone

Countdown to Killing Kurtis

A young woman with big dreams and skeletons in her closet decides her porno-king husband must die in exactly a year. This is not a traditional romance, but it will most definitely keep you turning the pages and saying "WTF?" If you're looking for something a bit outside the box, with twists and turns, suspense, and dark humor, this is the book for you: a standalone psychological thriller/dark comedy with romantic elements.

ABOUT THE AUTHOR

Lauren Rowe writes open-door spicy romances that will make you laugh out loud, fan yourself, swoon, and occasionally cry, on the way to the characters' happily ever after. When you pick up a Lauren Rowe book, you know you'll always be highly entertained and invested in the characters, you'll laugh at the banter and lovable cast of characters like they're your real-life friends, and of course the heat will be elite! Be sure to explore all the incredible spoiler-free bonus materials, including original music from the books, music videos, magazine covers and interviews, plus exclusive bonus scenes, all featured on Lauren's website LaurenRoweBooks.com